Absence

A METAPHYSICAL COMEDY

Books by Raymond Tallis

The Clinical Neurology of Old Age (editor)

Brocklehurst's Textbook of Geriatric Medicine and Gerontology (co-editor)

Epilepsy in Elderly People

Between the Zones

Fathers and Sons

Not Saussure

In Defence of Realism

Theorrhoea and After

The Explicit Animal

The Pursuit of Mind (co-edited with Howard Robinson)

Psycho-Electronics

On the Edge of Certainty

Newton's Sleep

Enemies of Hope

The Raymond Tallis Reader

Raymond Tallis

Absence

A Metaphysical Comedy

The Toby Press

First paperback edition, 2006
First published in Great Britain 1999

The Toby Press *llc,* 2005

pob 8531, New Milford, ct 06776-8531, usa
& pob 2455, London wia 5wy, England
www.tobypress.com

isbn 592641 54 7, *paperback*

A cip catalogue record for this title is
available from the British Library

Typeset in Garamond by Jerusalem Typesetting

Printed and bound in the United States by
Thomson-Shore Inc., Michigan

For Terry with my love

Classic narration of the realist kind is
on the whole a conservative form, which
slides our anxiety at absence under
the comforting sign of presence.

—*Terry Eagleton*

La vie est vaste, étant ivre d'absence.

—*Paul Valéry*

Aperture

One September evening in the late 1970s, a type 50/50 diesel engine was hauling a short train through growing darkness. It seemed to have given up travelling and was simply approximating. The train had left Birmingham New Street station over two hours earlier and had still not reached what, for three of its passengers, was its destination. There had been innumerable stops, some labelled and apparently purposive, others unlabelled and without evident purpose.

Unknown to themselves, the three passengers, each in a separate underpopulated carriage, were soon to become important to one another as major characters in the story that is to follow. But to say this is to cheat, shamelessly exploiting the power of preterite narrative to turn time from a scalar to a vector quantity. Besides, I mention Sister Janet Parker BA, SRN (who is checking, with a slight frown, the proofs of her article on Faecal Incontinence) and Dr William Welldorm MB, BS, FRCHD (who is spotting trains) only in order to lay them aside in favour of Dr Nicholas Page.

Dr Page, a medical practitioner in his thirtieth year, has at last fallen asleep, after an action-packed journey. Some of the action, it has to be admitted, had consisted of his packing the contents of a succession of cans of Brewmaster into his shapely frame. Although he has drunk enough to earn a good going coma, he is only lightly or fitfully asleep, obtunded rather than zonked, and is even now muttering to himself. He is recalling, perhaps, a weepy parting at Euston Station from Felicity, his girlfriend (the saline had been hers, not his). Or maybe he is re-running the highlights of his long, rather one-sided, conversation with the guard who had at first wished to punch only his ticket. If we have elected to join Nick Page at this late stage in his journey it is in order to spare ourselves a good deal of embarrassment. His address to the guard—garnished with academic puns and erudite allusions—was but a short stretch of a monologue, directed at various persons, that had lasted almost without a break from Euston station to a few moments back. We may imagine ex-passengers all over the South and Midlands of England informing their loved ones that they have discovered a new allotrope of Hell:

"There was this chap on the train crapping on for hours…I mean he went on and bloody on and bloody on! Imagine getting stuck in a lift with him!"

Who is this youngish man? What is he doing on this train? And what is the matter with him? Well he is a man in trouble and, for the first time in his life, he is seriously troubled. Until recently, Nick, a St Jidgey's man, had looked like being a hospital consultant, a future specialist of international repute, a leader of his profession.

St Jidgey's, founded in AD 906 as an alms house to commemorate the exemplary life of its eponymous saint, is one of the great teaching institutions of British medicine. It is notorious for the arrogance of its alumni: "You can always tell a Jidgey's man because you can't tell him anything." Nick's undergraduate career at Jidgey's had been spectacularly successful, rivalled only by that of Robert Perkins—*vide* (much) *infra*—with whom he had shared most of the academic honours available to his year. He had proceeded to obtain, in open competition, a series of much sought after junior hospital appointments. He had acquitted himself with honour in these posts. His long hours of hard work, his diagnostic acumen, his ability to manage the most malignant of consultant bosses without losing either his temper or his sanity, his assured presentation of cases at Grand Rounds, his superb self-presentation at interviews, secured an apparently painless ascent up the ladder—if one can describe as painless an eighty or a hundred hour week during which one was bleeped at ten-minute intervals day and night. In the meantime he had obtained his higher medical examination—the Diploma of the Royal College of Hospital Doctors or DRCHD—in the shortest time permitted by the regulations and ordinances of the examining body and had published several scientific papers. Inspection of his awe-inspiring curriculum vitae would show that that he had scarcely put a foot wrong—or outside of the intensely competitive atmosphere of that ultimate in centres of excellence, St Jidgey's Hospital. An MD was the last barrier between him and a Senior Registrar post at St Jidgey's after which he was virtually guaranteed a Consultant appointment at a five star teaching hospital, possibly even St Jidgey's itself.

And so Nick had taken time off from clinical medicine to conduct research which, he expected, would generate more publications and a doctoral thesis worthy of the degree of MD, and which might, epiphenomenally, lead to discoveries that could benefit humanity. Only a week ago, he had been Research Fellow in the Department of Haematology in St Jidgey's. His research had been going well.

He had been investigating the phenomenon of senile purpura. "Purpura" is bruising and senile purpura occurs spontaneously in old age. On account of the folk tradition that the bruises are caused by the devil plucking at the aged, trying to draw them from life, they are sometimes called "the devil's pinches". Nick had not been able to substantiate the claim that they were death's love-bites, but he had made considerable progress in identifying the defect in the wall of the capillary blood vessels that accounted for the bruising. He had already presented his results to general approval at a couple of scientific meetings. The success of his research was a foregone conclusion as he had conducted it under the direction of Professor Fibrin whose work on platelets had made him an international name. Moreover, unlike most of his colleagues at St Jidgey's, whose presence was as welcome as dysentery in a jacuzzi, Fibrin was extremely genial and genuinely kind. Nick liked him and he liked Nick.

7

So why is Dr Page now an ex-Research Fellow, mining his way northwards through the darkness (for darkness has fallen while we have been introducing him) away from the capital to the provinces? Occasionally individuals living in London respond to the call of the wild and go north—sometimes in search of the roots they have read about in a book purchased in W.H.Smith's. But all Nick's roots are in the South. And, besides, he doesn't have roots beyond an extended family that gathers to argue at Christmas and a few photographs and certificates in a biscuit tin in the parental home. No, he is going north in order to work—at the North Brompton Royal Infirmary. This extraordinary fact warrants further examination so that its extraordinariness may be fully appreciated.

The general rule that anything that has a top must also have a bottom applies to the National Health Service. If St Jidgey's represents the top of the NHS, the North Brompton Royal Infirmary or NBRI represents the bottom. So why is a man who has successfully fought his way up the ladder about to take up a post in the NBRI, and a locum post at that? To feel the full urgency of this question, it is necessary to understand the magnitude of Nick Page's achievement so far.

The hospital hierarchy is a pyramid. Many become House Officers; few find Registrar Posts; and fewer still get to be Consultants, except in certain so-called shortage specialities where anyone who is interested may apply here and now. In teaching hospitals, especially, it is the rule that while many labour on the lower slopes few reach the peak. In order that the peak shall be narrower than the base, most must drop off or get stuck. The irritating habit that consultants have of living to the age of sixty-five only exacerbates the situation. Things are not quite so bad as they might be for ambitious white males. Women—who foolishly get pregnant or look as if they might do so—provide a good deal of the requisite natural wastage. This makes sense because we know that the world would function much more efficiently without babies and having one shows a clear lack of the kind of social commitment expected of a doctor. When women are able to surface professionally post-natally, they are usually to be found working in Family Planning Clinics where they can spend their time appropriately advising other women in the art of avoiding pregnancy even if they fail to avoid the embraces of men.

The other factor in favour of white males is that many of the posts on the lower slopes—especially in unpopular specialities in unfashionable hospitals—are filled by overseas doctors who, as things are ordered at present, have little hope of reaching the top. They typically act out the unfulfilment of their ambitions in hospitals such as the NBRI. Their wretched rooms in hospital accommodation are lined with descriptions of jobs for which they have no likelihood of being short-listed. The especially sad aspect of this sorry state of affairs is that it is the high-flyers who come from abroad to the United Kingdom. They arrive on these shores with curricula vitarum that read like a dream. But the dream, unlike Nick's, has had the wrong location: the undergraduate prizes have been won in Hyderabad or Athens; and the prestigious posts have involved attachment to physicians and surgeons whose reputation does not extend to the inner circles of the Royal Colleges. Arrival in the UK brings the dream to an end: the prizes cease to flow; and the posts they occupy are far from the centres of excellence or even from the nearest postgraduate centre. Since the intention of many of those who come from abroad is to study for and to pass the Diploma of the Royal College of Hospital Doctors, frustration is inevitable.

Nick's career to date had been remote from places like the NBRI. Although he had read much in the medical press of the woes of overseas doctors stranded in the less popular reaches of the NHS, he had seen little of it first hand. Coming to work in the NBRI amounted virtually to dismounting from his career. What possible reason could there be for such an extraordinary act of self-sabotage? Simply this: he had had to leave St Jidgey's because he could no longer bear to remain there. This near-tautology does not advance our understanding to a great degree. Further explanation is required.

Dr Page has until now travelled not only professionally but also socially in the fast lane. Which is not to say that he is a social climber, rather that one of his preferred ways of socialising is by climbing into people's beds. This preference is satisfied not because he is a good doctor, which in the field of sexual competition counts for nothing, but because he is extremely good-looking. It is probably worth mentioning his appearance at this stage because it is well known that those with good looks are forgiven much—bad behaviour, stupidity, even intelligence. He is just above medium height, is well built, has thick fair hair, fine regular features and blue eyes whose glances are such as to place a frost of sacred terror over the pericardia of many females.

"He lays them and then lays them aside." No, that is unfair. But it cannot be denied that most of his affairs have been short-lived and that it is he, not the relevant she, who has broken them off. He has an eye, but not an ear, for pretty women. His razor-sharp mind finds their minds as disappointing as the minds of the average male and most post-coital discourses dispiriting. And so, without wishing to do so, he has caused a good deal of suffering. This suffering has worried him but not excessively—certainly not sufficiently to cause him to discontinue the behaviour that brought it about.

And then, one day last spring, his easy-going attitude to the vicissitudes of love changed. He fell for someone who did not fall for him. Or not at first. Or not completely. Or perhaps not at all. Her name was Susie and she came to work as a technician in Professor Fibrin's laboratory.

Perhaps it was because she, too, had blue eyes, a shimmering amethyst blue, that she was unimpressed by his; perhaps because she, too, had fair hair, longer and more fine-hued than his, that she was unimpressed by his fair hair. Perhaps it was because she too had full lips, fuller than his so that they were creased in their attempt to fit into the available space, that she was as apparently unexcited by his generous mouth as by the other features of his face that she could outshine item by item. Moreover, she didn't like his manner; the assumptions, for example, implicit in his greeting her one day by kissing her cheek—though to this she had responded, if not in kind, at least without overt hostility. Anyway, one lunchtime when they found themselves alone in the laboratory with some platelets, he had kissed her on the lips. She had closed her eyes and opened her mouth. Now while she may plausibly have closed her eyes to rest them after a morning of looking down a microscope, the open mouth did suggest a certain amount of acquiescence in the procedure. The conclusions Nick drew from this were, however, shown to be false. The following day, he had extracted her from the laminar flow cabinet, where she was drying her just-painted fingernails, and had taken her out for a drink. She had refused to let him hold her hand and reacted to the mildest of kisses as a princess might respond to the lecherous advances of a methylated dosser.

I won't document their relationship (or non-relationship)—what he did and how she did or did not respond—but state simply that for several months he seemed alternately to be making progress and going backwards. By early summer, he was past the point at which he could have shrugged off the whole affair, offsetting failure against his many successes under the rubric of "You can't win 'em all." For reasons that he did not fully understand, her yeses and noes were more crucial to his happiness than anyone else's yeses and noes had ever been—and infinitely more important than the outcome of the study of capillary fragility that had brought them together. His anguish was heightened by her obtrusive weekends that underlined his exclusion from her life. She would arrive at work on Friday morning with a travelling bag and the kit appropriate to the weekend's diurnal activities—wet suit, surf board etc.—and be picked up direct from work on Friday evening by the latest Porsche-driving boyfriend. And she would come in late on Monday morning exhibiting to his jealous eyes all the diagnostic signs of fatigue derived from strenuous intimacy.

So she became his continuous preoccupation. He was unable to forget her even when he was in bed with a new girlfriend. Susie's vacillation between welcome and rejection, however unconscious, seemed designed to maximise his suffering. In his sick old age, when there was a revolution on and he was tired and angry, Pavlov designed a particularly ingenious experiment. He took a group of dog volunteers and conditioned them to associate an elliptical light with the most delicious food and to associate a circular light with an appalling electric shock. He then investigated what happened when the dogs were presented with a light that varied continuously between an ellipse and a circle. They all went mad—every single one of them.

It would be an exaggeration to say that Nick went mad. Those who are unused to suffering are prone to overestimate the place of their own on the scale of human woe (though Nick's suffering was sharpened by the knowledge that he was himself being treated as he had in the past treated many others). And it would be unfair to hold Susie entirely to blame for his mental state. For at the same time that he was embroiled in his affair with her, other things were happening in his life.

For a start, he was coming near to achieving the goals he had set himself since his early twenties. There is nothing like arriving for making you question the value of the journey. Do I really want to be a Consultant in a teaching hospital for the rest of my days? Have I lived enough before I settle down? Even—or perhaps especially—the mindless hedonism of Susie's life was a critique of his own more serious existence. And there was a third factor that may have explained why his madness or near-madness or simulated madness took the form that it did.

Recently, Nick had again started reading books that lay outside his speciality of medicine. His research post had given him the leisure to do this for the first time in ten years. More specifically, he began to read philosophy. Now everyone is familiar with the dangers that lie in books, if not from first hand experience. As many addicts of the *Beano* are aware, Don Quixote was driven mad through reading too many romances. His mistake—which suggests that he was mad even before fell among novels—was that he thought that what he read in books could be applied to his life. Now this is silly but it is a hazard run by impressionable readers.

Nick, anguished by a love affair, facing what Mr Conrad described in "The Shadow-Line", was just such an impressionable reader. In his anger and despair, he looked to the consolations of philosophy to lift him out of the pit. Whoever directed him to the works of the recent French philosophers—in particular the writings of M. Derrida and M. Lacan—has much to answer for. In the ingenious writings of the Parisian *maîtres à penser* he found not only a mirror in which to view the senselessness of his condition but also the hint of a cure that was worse than the disease to which it was directed…But this is to look too far ahead. Sufficient to say that he took seriously ideas that others merely got tenured posts for expounding; tried quixotically to live by, at least inwardly, the unthinkable notions that the professionals merely lived off.

That, at least, goes part way towards explaining why unhappy love became for him as much an oral, as a cardiac or genital affliction. He had never been particularly reticent, but now he began *talking* under the pressure of ideas and feelings, to the point where he seemed to be clinically manic. A listener exposed to the flow of his jokes had a clearer understanding, ever after, of the relation between jokes and the unconscious, between humour and coma. If, as Mr Samuel Beckett (late of this planet) claims, the mouth is the anus of the face, Nick's verbal diarrhoea was a one-man cholera epidemic.

He did not, of course, lack insight into his condition. And that was why, in the end, he had to leave the laboratory. For he could see that his lovelorn state was getting no better. As the summer wore on, its successive landmarks—sporting, cultural and floral—witnessed no attenuation of his melancholia. On the contrary, he spiralled deeper into a maelstrom of depression. The Open found him gloomier than the Cup Final, the last night of the Proms blacker than the first, withered willow-herb more tortured than laburnum.

One day, after he had received a decisive no, delivered orally and backed up by a note penned in Susie's remedial class scrawl, he saw an advertisement in the *British Medical Journal* for a locum Registrar at the North Brompton Royal Infirmary. After a long, and difficult, interview with an initially astonished and finally exasperated Professor Fibrin, he obtained permission to terminate his Research contract three months early (on the understanding that he would finish his MD thesis) and so escape the endlessly tantalising presence, the standing refusal, of Susie.

Mmm…One of the first things a medical student learns is that ingenious explanations rarely lead one to the correct diagnosis. And one of the first things a contemporary student of English literature is taught is that many attributes of fictional characters—obsessive love or guilt, madness etc.—are just so many stylistic devices to enable the author to bring together material—jokes, aperçus, observations—that would otherwise remain scattered and unpublishable. For these two reasons, we should be suspicious of the explanation I have offered of the condition in which we find our physician-hero. Besides, we have performed only the most cursory physical examination and have carried out no laboratory investigations. However, the train is slowing down, signalling that Dr Page has almost reached the end of the journey taking him from the top to the bottom of the NHS. We are running out of time. In a minute he will wake and at once start talking and we shall not get a word in edgeways. Suffice it to remark that he will find others, at the end of his journey to the bottom of the NHS, whose lives have been broken up even more thoroughly than his, whose troubles may to some eyes be such as to set unhappy love at nought. To those who are struggling for survival in their chosen professions the search for self-fulfilment or happiness seems a luxury.

Take Dr Senanayake, for example. His life is falling apart. But no, let us keep him in reserve until Dr Page finds him for us and instead turn our attention, in the few minutes that are left to us before Page's tongue licks a thousand lexicons awake, to another character in this story—the little town of North Brompton.

North Brompton is a settlement of some 60,000 bodies and, one assumes, an approximately equal number of souls. It occupies about 10,000 acres, covering the good earth with objects that are of great interest to its citizens. Situated at an awkward distance from several locations that have a place in the national or even international consciousness, it is well known only to itself. But it doesn't seem to resent or suffer from its obscurity. Nor is positively, or exotically obscure; indeed, it stands to the kinds of town that attract tourists as Tuesday morning stands to Saturday night.

If nothing out of the ordinary has happened in the town, this is not to suggest that History has by-passed North Brompton: change has happened here as elsewhere; North Brompton has never been known to attract visitors on account of its being charmingly preserved. It would be inaccurate to imagine that its streets are alive with messages transmitted through time from earlier epochs. When things become old in North Brompton, they are recognised for what they are (Worn Out and No Good) and are pulled down. An attempt was once made to place a preservation order on a segment of wall that looked as if it may have been left over from the distant past but in the end this failed, through uncertainty as to where the Roman remains ended and the council estate began.

It would be truer to say that History has never been *made* in North Brompton: the impact of its sons and daughters has been distinctly local and the town has never been seen by envious eyes as a prize to be seized: nobody has bothered to invade it, and though predators have passed through it, their eyes have been fixed on other prizes. Of course, North Brompton has been influenced by historical events and trends initiated elsewhere. In its way, it has kept up with advances that have emanated from the capital. Fashion, too, has been trailed after in North Brompton, though here the lag effect is more obvious: the last mini-skirt to be worn other than as fancy dress or as a quotation was to be seen in its recently completed late-Sixties-style Shopping Centre.

Even though Dr Page's description of North Brompton as "a metastasis of nowhere" seems a little harsh, the town does give the impression of a place between one elsewhere and another, somewhere people end up rather than seek out. The most likely reason for ending up in North Brompton is that one was born there and didn't think to go anywhere else. The geography is undramatic to the point of being featureless but not to a striking degree. The heap of rusting cars by a metal shredder is the nearest North Brompton produces to a rise…

Like every other town it has what is called "civic pride"; and, as elsewhere, this is available in the Town Guide. Much of this pride, one learns, is invested in the fact that for centuries the citizens have been engaged in the production of locks and keys, devices that give access only to that to which they have denied access. The hidden meanings its products reveal have been concealed by them and the net gain in sense, meaning and knowledge is consequently zero. The armorial bearings—which show a key to nothing—reveal how…

But already the train is slowing to a halt and Nick is waking up. He is feeling, as one does after a drunken doze on a train, as if meaning has drained from the face of the universe. This will not stop him talking of course. The end of meaning will merely provide the occasion for more words—dead messengers still running with the news from the Battle of Marathon.

Part One

...the lover's discourse is today *of an extreme solitude*...[It] exists only in outbursts of language, which occur at the whim of trivial, of aleatory circumstances...

—*Roland Barthes*

Chapter one

North Brompton...this is North Brompton," the station informed the train slowing into it.

"Well, North Brompton," Dr Nicholas Page replied, climbing unsteadily down from the train. "It's between the two of us."

"This is North Brompton," the station repeated for the hard of understanding as Nick, stupefied by the tedium of the journey, by many cans of Brewmaster and by a malaise whose constant object was Susie's absence, walked across to the ticket barrier.

"Passengers wanting North Brompton should alight here," the loudspeaker persisted. The train, as though afraid of being asked to stay, was already drawing out.

"That's putting it a bit strong isn't it?" Nick observed, as the official extracted his ticket from between his teeth.

"?"

"*Wanting* North Brompton."

"Learn arfer towk rate."

"Come on, get a move on," a voice behind him said.

"Inspector, could you advise me as to the quickest and least dangerous route to the North Brompton Royal Infirmary?"

The man shook his head. Notwithstanding the promise inherent in the smart BR cap, the skull vault warmed by it protected only ignorance from the fresh North Brompton evening air.

"You are holding up the traffic," the voice insisted. "If you let me through *I'll* tell you how to get to the Infirmary."

In keeping with the wartime spirit of the station, background illumination was poor. Nevertheless, Nick could see that "the traffic" was alluding to itself; for only one other passenger had alighted from the train. He saw a tall girl in jeans, made taller by boots.

She handed in her ticket and the two of them left the station together, causing the black cinders of the ill-lit and empty car park to crepitate quite loudly.

"Where did you spring from?" he asked her.

"Same place as you."

"Where did you get on?"

"Birmingham New Street."

"If only I had known! I might have been spared decades of solitary self-communion while we tunnelled through the darkness with the expedition of an impacted stool in a centenarian's colon."

"It *was* a bit sluggish, wasn't it?" she said.

"I thought they were inventing stations just to hold me back from my urgent business. I'd never even heard of Diddington before today but that bloody train managed to wring Diddington South, Diddington Central and Diddington North out of it. Not to speak of Diddington Marine and Diddington Rovers."

"Urgent business?" she asked, turning towards him. He could not tell, because of the dark, what expression her face wore.

"I have come to North Brompton to heal the sick."

"You're a doctor?"

"By default. My true metier is that of a fantastic. Which way here?"

"A fantastic what?" she persisted. The sodium light was now sufficient to confirm what he had suspected—that she wore a slight, sceptical smile. Not hostile, anyway. Or dumb.

"Noun not adjective."

"*A* fantastic! So why are you here?"

"The prospects for fantastics are ghastly at present. We're being laid off in droves."

"So I had heard. Medicine's your fallback position, then?"

"Precisely...You don't work at North Brompton Royal Infirmary by any chance do you?"

"I'm a sister on Ward 27B. Female orthopaedics."

"A devotee of the martial arts!"

"And you?"

"From 9 A.M. tomorrow morning, Monday 29ᵗʰ September, I shall be Locum Registrar, or Ye Assistant Mountebank, to Dr William Welldorm."

"Willy Welly's Registrar? He hasn't had one of those for a long time."

"What's he like?"

"Most of the younger nurses think he is a fool. One or two of the older ward sisters adore him. They think he's a gentleman, a true physician of the old school."

"No incompatibility there. He probably believes in the old standards. Like 100 per cent mortality from traditionally incurable diseases for which the cure in this vulgar modern age has now been found. Or is my imagination now outracing reality?"

"I think you ought to make up your own mind. How long are you here for?"

"It depends how long they will have me. I'm down for two months but I might serve a second term. I've reached a rather wobbly point in my career recently."

"It must have been have been one hell of a wobble to land you up here."

"It was. Is. Where are we going, by the way?"

"Well, I'm going to the NBRI and you seem to have tagged along."

He liked her voice. It added a faint tinge of meaning to a world drained of it.

"Isn't it super that we're going to the same place!"

"Not precisely the same place. I'm going to the Nurses' Home and you, I imagine, are going to the Doctors' Residence."

"I don't suppose the contents of the two are immiscible."

"At NBRI they are."

"A dismal state of affairs. But nothing is immutable."

"At NBRI it is. We're a bit precise about these things round here."

"Well, to summarise the story so far, you are a nurse and I am a doctor."

"That sounds fairly accurate if not necessarily comprehensive."

"Good. So you won't mind if I now relieve myself of some of the eighteen cans of Brewmaster I consumed while our little crawler angstromed through the late September night."

"Feel free. Urinary incontinence is one of my special interests."

Nick peed against a luckless, gone to seed, willow-herb. Attempts to think of something appropriate to say while he urinated made his aching head ache more. In the absolute quiet he sounded like a shire horse. "Nobody told me that our little crawler wouldn't have a corridor."

"Better now?"

He nodded.

"Which way?" he asked, as he gestured towards an acceptable standard of hygiene by rubbing his hands on a dock leaf.

She indicated a sodium-lit highway that looked as if it led from nowhere in particular to nowhere in general.

"That magic orange grove?"

"Yes," she said, shifting her bag to the other hand. It must be heavy. She has been away for the weekend, Nick thought.

"Tell me about yourself. I rather get the impression that you haven't always been a nurse."

"I studied English literature before I joined Florrie's army. We turn left here."

"Unpack your soul. Let us exchange curricula vitarum beneath the visitant moon…" He continued talking for a minute or two and then stopped, aware that she was enduring rather than listening. "Tell me…"

Nick learnt that his guide had been Head Girl, a Ranger, a

county standard discus thrower and a writer of prize essays. Then there had been the University of Wessex where she had written more essays and won more prizes. After she had graduated she had been unable to find any way of being interestingly and usefully employed. At about this time, she had been dropped by her long-standing boyfriend.

"He was a shit, actually. Instead of having, or as part of, my nervous breakdown, I decided to do something worthwhile. I became a nurse."

"A bit like joining the Foreign Legion."

"That's the standard cliché, isn't it? Anyway, it's better to feel used than feel useless. Even though it's murder on 27B ward at present."

"Shortage of staff and the endless wrestle against gravity?"

"Everyone's off sick, bad backs, days off in lieu, holidays etc. Also the word has got round that the hospital is going to close so NBRI can't attract any nurses to work. Everyone wants to work in the new District General Hospital down the road. We turn left here. Now it's your turn."

"Myself? Difficult to summarise. I've lived such an extraordinarily detailed life. I haven't missed a second out of the last thirty or so years. So it's a bit of a challenge to summarise it all in a few well-chosen words…"

They walked on in silence. He listened to their contrasting footsteps—hers booted, firmer, his timelessly brogued—incising the lamplit stillness. Her tight jeans delineated long, slightly thick, thighs and a fullish bum. She was wearing a deep blue zip-up jacket which suited her very well indeed. Her face was absolutely gorgeous. Even in the sodium light, he could appreciate its smooth peach-bloom complexion. One of those faces whose inexhaustible attraction derives at least in part from the fact that you cannot somehow focus on it and and you don't know whether this indeterminacy is a matter of sight or meaning, of physical surface or of spiritual significance. Unlike Susie—but like Felicity from whom he had parted at Euston six hours or a lifetime ago—she had brown eyes. He thought he could detect, in their fleeting glances, a very slight but fetching dysconjugation of gaze. She had longish, nicely curled hair: countercurrents on the waterfall.

"Is North Brompton usually this lively?" he asked as they passed an old man out walking his dog. As if in response, the dog stopped, arched its back and gave trembling birth to a length of thick calibre brown toothpaste. "Do they lay on this kind of street theatre—performing dogs and so on—every evening and in every street? Or is this just for me?"

"Laughter and dancing come as readily to these people as breathing."

"You haven't really explained why *you're* here. You're obviously not local."

"Personal reasons."

"So what do you mean by 'personal reasons'?"

"Personal reasons."

"That seems a reasonable paraphrase. But you're playing your cards very close to your chest."

"With a figure like mine, that's quite easy," she said, turning to him with a slight smile that warmed the topmost layers of the inner permafrost.

"I like girls with senses of humour. So rare. In fact one is grateful if a large crowd of girls has one sense of humour between them. It's all that brain-rotting giggling between the ages of two and seventeen..."

"If I thought it was worth it, I would object to that remark. But you seem almost intelligent enough to make me suspect that that was what you would hope I would do. So I won't."

Silence fell between them. He looked at her and saw that her gaze was directed straight ahead.

"What's your name by the way?"

"Janet Parker."

"*Janet*. Who in the name of God inflicted that on you?"

"My mother. It was *her* mother's name."

"So she passed it on like a congenital disease."

"We can't all be called Marie-Clare. It'd be too confusing."

"Janet is about two thirds the way down the connotation scale between Susie at the the top and Margery, Thelma and Slurry at the bottom. What shall I call you instead of Janet?"

"You won't have to call me anything because our journey's over. Welcome to The North Brompton Royal Infirmary."

"Almighty God, it looks like a workhouse."

"It was once. It's going to close soon and they're letting it fall to pieces. Actually there's only a bit of orthopaedic surgery, some dermatology, a couple of wards of general medicine and about twenty long stay geriatric wards left. And a GU Medicine clinic. By the way, you're the first UK doctor, apart from the consultants that is, they've had here for about ten years. Leaving aside Dr McAdam and he doesn't count. Oscar will be pleased. I'll introduce you to him. He keeps the keys to the residences."

"I didn't see your name in the job description."

"As what?"

"Courier. Or under 'Hostess'."

"Oscar" she called through the window of the lodge. "I've got a new doctor for you."

A middle-aged West Indian came out.

"Pleased to meet you doctor."

"This is Dr Page."

"A white man, eh Sister? Thank the Lord! Well done doctor!"

"Oscar is our resident racist," Janet explained.

"Well," Oscar began. And then continued.

Nick did not like what Oscar was saying and protested.

"You wait 'n see, doctor. You'll see how they's behavin' because you'll be livin' in amongst them. Room 10 doctor, James House. Up the stairs, make a left turn and 'long to the end o' the corridor…And make sure you don' be disturbing our good doctor McAdam. That right Sister?"

"Right, Oscar," Janet responded with a smile whose significance was clearer to Oscar than to Nick.

"See you aroun', doctor."

"See you around, Oscar."

"Wow," Nick said.

He felt suddenly yet more depressed and headachy. Some of things he had heard from Oscar could have tripped off Susie's tongue. It was part of Susie's 360° solid angle dimness to espouse every prejudice that was going. The opposite of whoever it was who said "Nothing human is alien to me", nearly everyone she encountered was alien to her; and to her nothing alien was human. Short men, so-called intellectuals, Asians, people with posh voices, people with common voices, men with beards: they were all targeted by the various negative trophisms by which she kept the world at a distance from which it was small enough to be encompassed by her narrow mind and restricted sympathies. By this means she was able to make herself thoroughly and exclusively at home in it. If Nick had hated racism before he had met Susie, he now hated it all the more: it was part of a cast of mind that prevented his own virtues being visible to her and so kept him out of her bed.

They continued along a dark drive between the main hospital building and a high, and to Nick meaningless, wall. Still, it hadn't been built to have a meaning. Like everything else it just had a job to do. Stimulated by the comparative darkness and by the memory of the smile she had given Oscar—one of those gorgeous warm smiles that enclose themselves in double brackets, revealing white teeth that outdazzled even Oscar's—Nick was almost gallant.

"I would have offerred to have carried your bag only it looks a bit heavy."

"Don't mention it. Actually I turn off here to the Nurses' Home." The drive opened into a great empty space. A single halogen lamp illuminated the deserted prospect. Across a wide lawn was a Regency-style mansion. "*That's* your home."

Again, he was astonished at the beauty of her face. It seemed to re-open for discussion the recently refuted hypothesis that life had a purpose. He talked, delaying the moment of their separation and his return to solitude and Susielessness. The delay was not welcome.

"Do you ever stop talking?"

She looked and sounded genuinely impatient. Her bag, which she had not set down during his monologue, did indeed look heavy.

"It's just that you are so description-beggaring. Your face—even by halogen light…"

"Do you ever stop talking?"

"At the point of death—and at certain climactic moments when exhalation is committed to less filigree modes. Perhaps you would like to be present at one of my silences…"

"Bye bye now," she said firmly.

"Bye bye *for now*, perhaps."

"Maybe. I shall watch your progress at NBRI with interest."

"You wouldn't like to be one of its dimensions, I suppose? Its underlying theme, for instance?"

"I have had a tiring journey. Goodnight…And don't disturb Dr McAdam."

"Who's Dr McAdam?"

But she had gone. The swing doors she had disappeared through opened and closed. The sentence "PLEASE KEEP CLOSED IN CASE OF FIRE" broke and formed, formed and broke until the doors shuddered to a halt.

After briefly reflecting on a further widening of the chasm that lay between his desires and reality, Nick set out across the lawn. James House looked magnificent in full moonlight. It was a massive square mansion comprising two storeys of tall sash-windowed neo-classical splendour which dated from, he thought, about 1850. He especially admired the chimneys, one of which was giving life support to a small sycamore tree. He sighed.

The front door was locked and the doorbell unresponsive. The lion's face knocker smirked at him and came off in his hand. At the back of the house he found a crumbling flight of steps up to a dingy door. It opened. He groped along an unlit passage, rounded a corner and arrived unexpectedly in a magnificent though gloomy hall where he was confronted with a full reflection of himself, body and baggage, in a huge oval mirror. Tripping over his bags, he pushed open a pannelled door and found himself in a spacious lounge. A television was chattering to some decrepit leather armchairs, a few low tables, an ornate ceiling and long plum-coloured curtains reaching down to the parquet floor. He was about to withdraw when he noticed a newspaper erect in an armchair: human—possibly medically qualified—life.

"Good evening…I'm newly arrived…Nick Page…Locum

Registrar." The newspaper remained erect. A pair of grey-trousered legs uncrossed and re-crossed. A formless sound emerged. "I just thought I'd introduce myself...Say hello..."

"Mmmggghhh."

And that was it. The television chattered on, brightly listing drugs, crime, rape and suicide as causes or effects of something.

Nick withdrew. Attracted by light, he proceeded along another, shorter passage to what proved to be the kitchen. His reconnaissance of the fluorescent-lit scene before him was impaired by a trace of perfume that hung on the air. It travelled straight from his sense endings to the heart, and there detonated into anguished memories. The perfume, called Absence ("Makes the heart grow fonder" the advert said), owed its appalling potency to the accident of its association with Susie. Their entire relationship—from the first seemingly reciprocated gaze across the flow cytometer to the last reluctantly conceded embrace in the Temperature and Humidity Controlled Room—seemed to have been bathed in it.

Deeply shaken, Nick exited. Switching off the kitchen light, he plunged himself into near total darkness. He banged his bags against his left shin, his right shin and James House in fairly strict rotation. Emerging from the darkness into the hall, he ascended the stairs. In another dark corridor he identified the smell of cooking, the faintly sulphuretted fragrance of chemical fixative and the more decisively sulphuretted hogo of a recently patronised lavatory. Entering Room 10, he saw at once that the bed was occupied not by Susie but, like the rest of the known universe, by her absence.

He put down his bags, arrested by crescendo angina. For a short while he struggled against temptation but in the end succumbed. From his wallet he extracted a photograph. One glance was sufficient to abolish extensor tone from his knees. He was obliged to sit down on the faded yellow counterpane on which was stitched "NORTH BROMPTON DHA" in faded red.

Susie was picking a flower from an exotic Mediterranean shrub. She was turned away from the camera but there was enough of her on show to provide a perfectly adequate explanation of why the immediate past had been so marked by cardiac dysfunction, why the present was so empty and why the future seemed but a senseless trudge from the contingent Here and Now to the equally contingent Local Authority Crematorium.

Her long fair hair had been bleached ash-blonde by package holiday sun; and the same sun had combined with a faulty camera setting to give her long and shapely legs (unpeeled in shorts), her round shoulders (unpeeled in a boob tube), her lovely bangled arms etc., an even more magnificent tan. What was most painful about the photograph—more even than her beauty and the inaccessibility of the marvellous Nick-free mediterranean time she was obviously having—was that it had been taken by someone whom, he suspected, had also taken her.

He and Susie had once had a lunchtime drink at The Ruptured Varix, a snug little pub at the back of St Jidgey's Hospital, and together pored over her photograph album. The poignancy of the occasion— in which his infatuated curiosity and her vanity had blissfully dove- tailed—had been sharpened by the fact that nearly every photograph had been taken by some boyfriend or other.

He opened a desk drawer and placed the photograph next to a couple of mementoes left behind by a previous occupant of the room: a Silastic catheter tied in a half-hitch and a representative's sample of Paraprofen, a new wonder drug that was filling current issues of the *British Medical Journal* with reports of its most interesting side- effects. He closed the drawer and, looking through his own reflection in the window reiterating his lack of significance, saw meaningless roofs and, beyond them, a meaningless sky with ill-looking sodium- tinted clouds. He drew the curtains, wiping out his image and that of the night. He adjusted the arthritic angle lamp, extinguished the centre-light, sat down at the desk and wrote.

Dearest Susie,

Thank you for your brief note of whenever telling me, finally, to sod off. I apologise for my delay in replying but there are levels of suffering above which action is impossible.

Now that the pain has subsided to a gnawing ache reminiscent of bony metastases, I am able to write, though there is little point in doing so.

Before I met you, my life was full; then I met you; next I lost you; and now my life is empty. You found me a happy, ambitious and successful man; you left me a walking talking corpse, a directionless wretch drifting towards the doss house. How did you turn the world I was so at home in into a place of exile so that even the velvet air of this soft autumn night is as bitter as soot? Was it done deliberately; or was it as unconscious as most of the other actions in your life? As mindless as the educationally subnormal guitar-playing twerp you seem to prefer to me? Which thought is worse: that you had plotted my destruction; or that you had crushed me as absently as one crushes a cockcroach beneath one's feet as one runs along a nocturnal corridor in obedience to one's cardiac arrest bleep?

I loved you for your serenely perfect enigmatic face. And yet I have proof that the Susie behind it is as chaotic, as shallow as it is possible to be while still remaining identifiably human. I could empty Roget (Sections 2.9–2.10) without doing full justice to your vacuity. From this it follows that, if your face has any meaning, it must point to a realm outside of your personality, your real life, your actual behaviour. It does not signify a life that could be shared. But it suggests a life beyond life; the life for which we all live; the life without which life is just Monday, Tuesday, Wednesday…Your face, in short (like your arse and your tits and your blue, blue eyes and your smooth fair skin) is just a standing bloody lie.

To see this and to say this does not relieve my pain by one milli-twinge. Only a smile or a letter or a kiss or a—could do that.

He could hear footsteps in the corridor. Someone went into the toilet. Whoever it was had a poor urinary stream, signifying a prostatic enlargement interfering with the fluency of the lower urinary tract. By contrast, the flushed toilet roared with all the brashness of an early Harrington, and continued in protracted after-gurgles and borborygmi of the appreciative pipes. The footsteps returned and there was considerable muttering and jangling before the right key was inserted into the right hole the right way round. The name of the Son of God was intoned in a voice remote from reverence. The appellation was augmented with a middle name Nick did not recall from his fleeting acquaintance with the Christian faith.

Shortly afterwards, Nick heard a most ghastly sound. It was not the aura of a temporal lobe epileptic fit nor a siren announcing a nuclear attack—though it could have understudied for either—but, apparently, a kind of music. Hideous pipes and execrable strings prepared the way for a voice, and then several voices in chorus, that set the soul on edge and lit up all his pain receptors one by one.

The i of Nick's immiseration was dotted.

He decided to write to Felicity. A cheerful note that might, retroactively cheer himself up.

> Dearest Effie,
>
> Well I have arrived at North Brompton which has so far proved to be all that one might have hoped of a metastasis of nowhere. Arrival has made the British Rail carriage in which I travelled here with the speed of a curarised barnacle seem like Paradise Lost.
>
> So you are two hundred and fifty miles away. If Time is a great healer, it's an equally effective wounder. As the sundial said of the hours: *Vu rant omnes, ultima necat.* "All of them wound, the last one kills." As for Space, it's a real bastard, isn't it, my dear? If it weren't for Space, we should not have to make ghastly train journeys that take us away from one another. Without spatiality, there'd be no need for a nationalised railway system, ticket collectors, ASLEF, British Rail coffee and all the rest. Can it be that consciousness is inherently perverse, itself creating the conditions of its own suffering? (What magic thinkers, what transcendental idealists, we lovers are!) Causation (since we are speaking of the Kantian forms of sensible intuition) is ambiguous, like Time: though it is responsible

31

for our present separation, without it we wouldn't have met in the first place. So—a toast to the causal net! (Actually, if you *really* want to turn me on, could you buy some of those causal net stockings to wear when we next meet?)

I suppose you are fed up with my little jokes. And I am sorry I was drunk at Euston. If it is any consolation to you, I was much drunker at New Street. I could not bear my own feelings as the train put the greater part of a once-great nation between my hands and your still-great breasts. Anyway I am as bad when I am sober—as you well know from those hours in the last eight weeks when we have shared the same slice of the Venn diagram.

I am suddenly thinking of the autumn-coloured lovebite my passion placed on the lower inner quadrant of your left breast. Its evolution will measure out my absence, your absence, our two absences, from which we shall make two lachrymose Octobers out of the month of my exile. A haematological clock to match out the leaf-tones of the dying year. Take good care of it. In particular, keep it and its environs to yourself.

Between myself and North Brompton, I raise up a cardboard landscape of rhetoric. Thus shall I ward off Absence and the Night. I shall, in brief, *talk* myself out of The Ice Age and the insufficiency of Being that so much absence condemns me to. And, as promised, I shall on the stroke of midnight turn my thoughts to you, knowing that, by prior arrangement, you are thinking of me. Our thoughts shall intersleeve and we shall be as one. Our *ghosts* shall copulate…Not quite the real thing I know.

Thinking about you with mononeuronal persistence.

Love

N.

He put down his biro, faintly pleased at having already discharged a mildly distasteful duty before, like the writing of overdue holiday postcards, it became an irritant to his conscience. The musical lamentation from down the corridor stopped. Nick, momentarily more cheerful, found the strength to unpack and undress. His pillow provided sufficient bedtime reading: he read "NORTH BROMPTON DISTRICT HEALTH AUTHORITY" printed in dried menses on the linen repeatedly until, overcome by beer, the fatigue of travel and a multifactorial despair, he fell asleep just before the stroke of midnight, his ghost the absent object of Felicity's thoughts.

Chapter two

And another thing, Doctor," Sadie said "are don't want no more trouble over the tilette rolls. Arm fed up are am. We 'ad fower last week. Are dunner what thay were doin' with 'um. But wun…"—she glanced round the kitchen—"but wun dirty bugger (if thay'll excuse the hexpression)…"

"I'd rather you spared me the details…"

"And thay're hedgycated. Of course the meals they ate 'as a splurgative effect. Makes thay go to ground. Say what I mean?"

"Well I do and I don't…"

"Arm sorry to worry thay on thay're first moanin' 'ere at the 'ospital but Mr Burchnall from District Supplies is a tartfisted owd twerp and he's been down 'ere jumping on marn back—if thay'll hexcuse the hexpression."

"I do understand."

"Thank you Dr Page."

Sadie nodded to herself: point made. She was about four feet six inches, as thin as a February chaffinch. Nick put her age in double figures; which ones he was not sure. Her stiff, bushy, nicotine-and-grey hair stood out wildly from her scalp, like steel wool struck by lightning. It surmounted a deeply lined face, planted with tufts of hair in a manner reminiscent of a rock garden. The index finger that she raised to emphasise important points and to italicise the authority that lay behind them was afflicted with arthritis. A Heberden's node had deranged the distal interphalangeal joint so that the finger tip, lying at an angle of about twenty degrees to the rest, rammed her points not-quite-home. None of this was of any interest. All that mattered was that she reeked of Absence—Susie's perfume.

"How's about some breakfast…er Sadie? All this talk of toilet rolls is making me peckish."

"What would you lark? Baitn'egg?"

"I've got a bit of a hangover so a cup of tea and a vomit will do me fine."

"Are thought thay looked rate grain. What abate some Baychem spiders?"

"No medication thank you. These things tend to be self-limiting—so as to make room for the next one. Which way is the breakfast room?"

Sadie pointed down the hallway. Her arthritis conferred an unintended ambiguity upon this sign. An instinctive democrat who always respected majority opinion, Nick resolved the disemy by settling for the door indicated by two proximal phalanges that formed the greater part of her crooked finger.

Breakfast was taken in a lofty room. Nick noted long sash windows, an exquisite frieze representing the fruits of the earth, and a view across a rainswept but well-kept lawn of the hideously ugly hospital itself. Three or four tables were laid. At one of them, in the corner, was an erect newspaper: *The Tablet.*

"Good morning," Nick said.

"U'um."

"Ghastly morning, isn't it?" Mucus shifted in the other's upper respiratory tract failed to establish either a clearly affirmative or a clearly negative response. "I'm new here," Nick continued, though he was already beginning to suspect that his attempts at conversation were being interpreted as harassment. The newspaper was at last lowered, revealing a large, belligerent-looking head. The bossed forehead and small sunken eyes reminded Nick of a cartoon in his fourth form history book depicting Darwin as one of his simian ancestors. The cheeks had an alcoholic and/or choleric ruddiness. The chin had been cut in two places. Yesterday's laceration was surrounded by an island of grey stubble; today's had just stopped bleeding at the point where blood was about to mix with spilt egg yolk. "A blotched Scot, with bloodstains", Nick summarised to himself. The grey-black hair had been carefully brylcombed. It was an experienced face; the face of a man who had seen everything—and forgotten most of it.

"Welcome," McAdam said querulously, not looking at him.

"Thank you. I'm Nick Page and you must be Dr McAdam."

"Mmmm."

To Nick's surprise, the newspaper was again erected. End, apparently, of conversation. Needled, Nick resumed the rôle of conversational *banderillero*.

"I wasn't telling you my name to show off my general knowledge, you know." But *The Tablet* remained as rigid as if it had been xeroxed on tablets of stone. "Perhaps I could take up some points arising out of our rich conversation last night…"

Sadie came in, bearing tea and unasked for toast and an egg.

"Are dunna lark to see my doctors go to th'ospital withart solid snappins inside 'em."

"That's very nice of you, Sadie, but I don't think I'm going to be able to manage all that. Tell me, is that Dr McAdam in the corner?"

"Are after introduce thay."

"No, that's all right, thank you. It was the confirmation of a diagnosis rather than an introduction I was after, thank you. We've already met, you see. Ish anyway."

The door opened to admit Dr Dhar. Tall, plump, light brown, with a sharp chin cushioned on its double, mild-mannered, self-effacing to the point of self-extinction, he had a voice that, Nick was to find, faded from quiet to inaudible during a sentence of average length.

"Pleased to meet you, Dr Page. We have been…Dhar is my…"

"Call me Nick. What shall I call you?"

"Everyone calls me Dhar. My name is too complic…"

"Actually you've just come in the middle of a fascinating conversation that Dr McAdam and I have been having about some of the famous old traditions of this famous old hospital."

Dhar looked uneasily towards the newspaper and the ghost of a smile passed over his face. He took his place at the breakfast table.

"Do you smoke?" he asked, offering Nick one.

"Only passively."

"Do you mind if I…?"

"Not at all. I'm a latent necrophiliac."

Dhar considered this, sipping his cigarette thoughtfully.

"Plainly you are of a philosophical…" he concluded. "Thank you, Sadie," he said accepting his cup of tea with exquisite courtesy.

"Tell me about yourself."

Dr Dhar's curriculum vitae proved painful, as well as difficult, listening. He had been at the North Brompton Royal Infirmary or NBRI as Senior House Officer or SHO to Dr Welldorm for eighteen months. The post had originally been intended for a six month appointment but in the absence of any other applicants at the end of Dhar's term of office, he had remained in it for a further year. Prior to that, he had worked as SHO or Junior House Officer in Hackney, Stirling, Warrington, Bromsgrove, St Mawr, Dorchester, Liverpool, Stockton, Skegness, The Isle of Thanet, Truro, Salford, The Isle of Thanet (again), Rockall, West Bromwich, The Isle of Dogs, Southampton, Piddlehinton Parva, Fistula-in-Ano, Lerwick, etc. for periods of time ranging from six months to four days. He had been in the UK for nine years and was now aged 37. His purpose in coming to UK had been to obtain the Diploma of the Royal College of Hospital Doctors, otherwise known as the DRCHD, which was the passport to success in his native country. His intention had been to return to India once he had passed the examination.

Many things had conspired to frustrate this aim: the lack of suitable posts or his exclusion from such posts; the total absence of training in the unsuitable posts he was offered though they were "recognised by the Royal College of Hospital Doctors as suitable for medical training"; isolation from Centres of Excellence where the higher discourses could be heard or overheard; the disruptive effect of repeated moves (27 locations in nine years); and, as a last straw, a change in the examination regulations. He was due shortly to have his sixth and, by the rules, his last go at the Final Part of the DRCHD. In a month's time he was planning to take four weeks' unpaid leave to attend a course in Scotland. The total cost of this would be approximately £1000 and further disruption of his family life. Perhaps it was fortunate that this was the final push since Mrs Dhar, who had, with the exception of posts lasting less than a week, followed her husband up and down the country, was losing patience. She was missing her family back in India, none of whom had seen their little daughter Bulbul, now aged three. As for Bulbul, the Dharling was according to Mrs Dhar missing not having a grandma very badly. Mrs Dhar had even talked of going back with their daughter to resume her career as a lawyer.

"So your life has been ruined by the need to get a qualification that, when you return to India, will be of no practical use?"

"No use in my work but of the *utmost* signif…If you have DRCHD on your plate, everyone will want to consult you."

"So you learn all about renal transplantation and the interpretation of cardiac catheterisation findings to return to practise medicine in a country where children are dying of diarrhoea."

Dr Dhar sipped at his cigarette.

"It's crazy," he conceded.

"The last phase of colonialism?"

Dhar nodded his head, cautiously. *The Tablet* was suddenly lowered and Dr McAdam, unpeeled, walked out.

In the standing position he proved to be not as big as the large head had led Nick to expect. Big Ears let down by little legs.

"'I always made an awkward bow'," Nick commented, footnoting his new colleague's departure. "Now, Dr Dhar, tell me about my duties."

"We haven't had a Medical Registrar for so long that you may find you don't have all that much…to…"

The post had been repeatedly advertised in the medical press but had not attracted medically qualified applicants. Essentially, Nick's role was to supervise Dr Dhar in looking after Dr Welldorm's patients in Ward 6A and to do Dr Welldorm's out-patient clinic which, prior to Nick's arrival had been Dr Dhar's responsibility. He and Dr Dhar were on call together one night in two but very little happened, general practitioners tending to refer their patients to the new DGH down the road.

"Sounds like a doddle."

"This place is due to close…as you probably…"

"It all sounds very promising. And what do you do in the evenings. Squire those who sport the XX chromosome?"

"We are not allowed to have any parties or…"

"Why?"

"Dr McAdam doesn't like…"

"Why don't you tell him to fuck off?" Nick asked. "Excuse the genital-demotic, but I adopt it only by way of emphasis."

Shocked, Dhar looked round the room to make sure they had not been overheard. "In our position, you have to be careful. He has a lot of influence…"

"With whom, for God's sake?"

"Dr Welldorm. Sister Kinmonth."

Dhar had become suddenly very interested in his toast and marmalade. Careless talk costs lives.

Leaving aside a few outhouses—one was filled with coke, another contained two wheel-less bicycles, the third a heap of derelict bedsteads and the fourth proved to be the mortuary—the NBRI was of an appallingly simple design. No major structural alteration had followed the decision to transform it from a workhouse into a hospital. Its sooty redbrick looked as if it had been stained by a thousand red winter suns setting on a millennium of bitterly cold industrial evenings. It was enormously long, its three storeys marked by small sash windows which, to judge by the density of spider's webs, had been jammed shut for decades. The stark exterior was relieved only by magenta guttering and rainwater pipes. A broad corridor, nearly one hundred yards long, went down the length of the main building. The wards were either side of this concourse, a series of transepts: the south transepts were 1A to 27A and the north transepts 1B to 27B. Most of them were now empty in preparation for the closure of the hospital.

Nick paused for a second, astonished by the length of the highway. He inhaled the smell of disinfectant, here unchallenged by Absence, and observed a scene before him which was Breughel-like in its compendiousness. Nurses, porters, an occupational therapist, a patient on a trolley, another walking with a urine bag in his hand, about a dozen cleaners in different coloured uniforms, a mouse-like ward clerk, a furtive administrator in a grey suit, and a smartly dressed drug rep. carrying an executive brief case, were quickly picked out by his practised eye. It was the Breughel connotation, perhaps, that made him think that the downward sloping concourse—the gradient was quite marked, the workhouse having been built on a slight gradient—would be an ideal setting for a drunken skateboard contest. His bleep went off.

"You can answer it in 6A," Dr Dhar suggested.

Nick located the phone in Sister's office.

"Dr Page at Extension 314," he said.

"Outside call for you, Doctor."

As he waited to be put through, he tried to outstare a solitary goldfish complacently loafing in green-stained water.

"Nick. It's me. Felicity. I just rang to say I love you and I'm missing you and I'm sorry I was such a pain yesterday…"

"Felicity! Great! You beat me to it. I was just going to ring you. Must be ESP."

"I couldn't wait till tonight. I just *had* to explain to you how I felt and…"

Where there should have been sadness, or guilt or compassion or pity, there was only a sense of having had an overdose of Felicity or at least of not having recovered his appetite for her. He was aware also of being eavesdropped on by the switchboard.

"Super. I'm so glad you rang."

But Felicity continued, explaining what this had meant and what that had meant and how she hadn't understood the other at the time but now did. Et cetera, et cetera.

"Is he going to be yammering on that phone all morning?"

"Dearest, I must let you go. Someone wants to use the phone," he said. "Anyway, I've written you a letter…Bye."

Sister Kinmonth, who had come in, asked her question and gone out again, re-entered. She glared at him long enough to complete the process of identification.

"Sister, I'd like to introduce…" Dhar began.

"I haven't got time for all that caper now, Mister. There's three bed baths to do and Mrs Johnson's gone wandering off again. I told you she needed sedating. We've got three nurses off sick and so it's down to me, the SEN and a handful of auxiliaries. So if you'll excuse me…By the way," she added, "there's a pile of accident forms for one of you to sign. Three patients fell out of bed over the weekend—including Mrs Aliotis who's dead."

Sister Kinmonth, Nick noted during this subliminally brief presentation, was tall with a dead pale, freckled face. She had short black hair, a rather flat chest and thick legs with ill-defined calves. He put her age at between thirty and fifty. She was clearly one of those evenly ill-tempered ward sisters who did not suffer fools, or their sub-division junior doctors, gladly. Life was a tearing hurry and medically qualified personnel were bolasses around her unshapely ankles. St Jidgey's had a few of those, though there was usually more subtlety in their rudeness.

"I've got some little jobs for you, Dr Dhar," said the ward clerk rummaging in the case-note trolley. Despite her white coat, she reminded Nick of a nun; perhaps it was her sallow face and rimless glasses. He had been aware of her listening to his phone call.

"Miss Steele, I'd like to introduce Dr Page…"

"Pleased to meet you, I'm sure," she said with firm dismissiveness. "Now there's a pile of discharge prescriptions for you to write and a Part One Cremation Form on Mrs Aliotis…"

"She has died, then?" Dhar enquired.

"I think it is unlikely that a cremation form would be required otherwise."

A self-satisfied smile, at once emphatic and empty, underlined the put-down.

"Very true," Dhar conceded. He seemed unable to take offence.

Perhaps his soul had been marinated so long in bitter experience he no longer noticed.

Nick was beginning to feel astonishment as well as anger at the manner in which doctors appeared to be treated in the NBRI. What he had witnessed corresponded to the dismal story of Dhar's CV as content to form. He had a sense of biding his time.

Sister Kinmonth returned. "One of you had better go and look at Mrs Ratoff. She looks bloody horrible to me."

"Care to take a turn with me, Dr Dhar?" asked Dr Page, preparing to make his first professional foray into 6A ward.

They hurried down the ward which was a ferment of bed-making, bed moving and bed bathing. Cowed patients awaited re-possession of their personal space. A nurse was drawing curtains round what proved to be Mrs Ratoff's bed.

"She looks bloody horrible to me as well," Nick concluded, after careful examination. "I'd say she was suffering from what the older physicians used to call death but which we now tend to designate by the gentler term of cardiac arrest."

"What are you going to do about it?"

"As she probably died about an hour before you came on duty, I fear that attempts at resuscitation would be unrewarding. I think she has more need of a theological than a medical opinion. Although she might wish to test the claims of alternative or complementary medicine. It would certainly be a much-needed coup for the homeopaths and aromatherapists if she responded."

"It *would* bloody happen when I'm up to my eyes in it," Sister Kinmonth said, doing her best as she left to slam the curtain.

They followed her out. "Very inconsiderate of the ex-lady but the Reaper takes very little account of sub-lunary timetables, Sister. I think Dr Dhar and I had better do a ward round before any other tax-payers shake off the Kantian forms of sensible intuition."

"*What!*"

"Space, time and causation."

"Did you say you are planning to do *a ward round*?"

"At your convenience, of course."

"I've told you. I'm up to my eyes in it."

"Has the concept of a ward round not penetrated this far north, Sister?"

"Don't try to be funny, Mister."

"Mister never merely *tries* to be funny. He always succeeds."

"Well you can't have a nurse."

"We'll manage on our own."

Dr Dhar and Nick went back to Sister's office. Miss Steele was putting the phone down, her thin lips made thinner by mutual pressure.

"Mrs Floyd, who was booked to come in, isn't. That was the GP's receptionist on the phone. She died over the weekend."

"Oh," said Dr Dhar, at a loss, as a sensitive person always is when he or she hears that a total stranger has died.

"She *would* do after I've done all the paperwork."

"I am getting the impression that the dead of North Brompton are a pretty thoughtless lot, Miss Steele. You could always offer the paperwork to the Local Authority to help them prime the crematorium so it'll be nice and warm for Mrs Aliotis."

"Which of you is going to do those discharge prescriptions?" Miss Steele said, not looking up from the note trolley where she was rummaging to no apparent purpose.

"Dr Dhar, would you mind…while I read through the case notes?"

"You're not having the notes yet. I haven't finished sticking in the path lab reports," Miss Steele protested.

"Are you Dr Welldorm in drag?"

"I beg your pardon?"

"I thought not. From which it follows that you are not my boss." She looked up, with an arrested I-beg-your-pardon on her face. "So stop telling me what I can and cannot do. You may have exercised unwarranted authority over doctors who, coming from abroad and being in a vulnerable position may be uncertain of the rules, but you're not going to order *me* around. On this perfectly ordinary Monday morning you will be surprised to learn that you are facing a crisis of legitimation. I *am* going to read through the case notes to find out about the patients under my care. In the meantime, Miss Steele, you might consider making Dr Dhar and myself a cup of coffee, after which we—that is, Dr Dhar and I—are going to do a ward round."

Miss Steele closed the lids over the case-note trolley and went out.

No coffee materialised.

Two hours later, they were back in Sister's office. In the interim, Dr Page and his colleague had repeatedly disrupted essential nursing procedures—bed-bathing, toiletting, brushing and sprucing—with nonessential medical ones such as talking to and examining the patients, arriving at or checking diagnoses, planning investigations and treatments, and altering drug régimes. Tidy beds had been untidied while patients had been got on to them for gratuitous examination; fully dressed patients had been undressed for the same flimsy reason; and observation charts positioned neatly at the end of beds had been displaced merely in order to utilise the information they contained. Not so much a ward round as a search-and-destroy operation.

Dr Dhar, warmed by unprecedented self-confidence, was sitting beneath the NO SMOKING notice, smoking, and drinking the coffee Nick had made for them both. In the course of the ward round, Dhar had summarised each of the patient's histories but, in the angry bustle of the ward, Nick had had difficulty in catching what he had said. Lip-reading was difficult because Dhar's lip-writing was tiny. What Nick could catch made excellent and impressive sense—to a degree that, when one considered how his contributions had doubtless usually been treated, was almost heart-breaking. Kinmonth burst in and Dhar at once extinguished his cigarette.

"Well, what's all this caper about?"

"If by that you mean the alterations Dr Dhar and I intend to make in the medical management of certain patients..."

"I haven't got time for all that nonsense..."

After a further minute or so of futile argument, Nick became exasperated.

"Sister, is this supposed to be a hospital or a soup kitchen or some ghastly experiment in communal living?" He was, seemingly, talking to himself as Kinmonth had sat down at her desk and was looking through the off-duty sheets. However, he persevered. "I would suggest that you take up pen and paper and note down the various changes I wish to make in the *medical* management of the patients. I have already made some changes on the treatment cards."

"I knew today was going to be a bloody disaster," said Kinmonth to Steele, who was nervously pretending to have resumed filing the path lab reports. Dr Dhar, rivetted to his chair and caressed by smoke from his stubbed but still smouldering cigarette, looked desperately uneasy.

"How *many* changes have you made?"

"There's something on most patients."

She closed her eyes.

"How *many* changes?"

"I said 'On most patients'."

"Jesus bloody Christ."

"They're all necessary, Sister. And the Bible does not record that the Son of God rejoices in a middle name."

"How do you know they're necessary?"

"I went to medical school and have spent a further six years in postgraduate training. Would you like a copy of my cv?"

"You're trying to be funny again, Mister."

"Conation, as I have told you before, is not my style. Incidentally, this is a medical not a surgical ward. From which it follows that I am 'Doctor', not 'Mister'."

"Let me have a look at those drug cards." She snatched the treatment book from him. "I wish someone'd teach you doctors to write. What's this? Well we haven't got *that* on the ward—whatever it is—and we haven't got *that*…"

"I presume this hospital runs to a pharmacy."

"They'll go mad."

"I can stand any amount of psychosis in the pharmacy if it's a question of the difference between treating the patients and poisoning them. Anyway, let's go through the changes." As he did so, Kinmonth exhibited increasing impatience. "And finally I have stopped Mrs Johnson's Depressine and put her on a diuretic for her high blood pressure. We now know that Depressine causes depression and as she is currently living inside a depressant, to wit this hospital, poisoning her with Depressine is rather gilding the lily. Anyway, it probably accounts for her strange behaviour…I think that's the lot, Sister. I am very pleased that we've found we can work together as a team. And now Dr Dhar and I will retire for lunch. Thank you…"

Nick was bleeped as they walked across to James House.

"Oscar here, Doctor. How are you enjoying life among…?"

Nick did not like what Oscar said next.

"I'm having a lovely time, thank you Oscar. But I presume you didn't ring me up to make racist remarks that set my teeth on edge. What can I do for you?"

"There be a parcel an' a letter for you, Doctor."

"Great. I'll come and collect them later."

Nick took his place at the dining table. There was an animated conversation in progress.

"So, I replied back to her. 'Staff Nurse Lenier,' I said, 'You mustn't talk to me like that. Please show a little respect. We are all working together for the good of the patients.' I think she understood. Ah! Here he comes, the dragonslayer."

The speaker, an extremely solid man, probably in his mid-thirties, stood up as Nick came in. He wore his white coat buttoned to the top and its collar turned up. He was South India dark and his thick black brylcreemed hair was swept back in a luxuriant quiff. His face seemed charged with well-being and good humour.

"Sananayake, Orthopaedics. Pleased to meet you."

"Nick Page."

"Young Dhar has been telling me how you have started breaking in Madam. I am already of the opinion that you have been sent to deliver us from Kali's evil spell." He exhaled noisily through airways devastated by cigarette smoke. This was laughter and, curiously, it was infectious. Infected, Nick found himself laughing.

"Well then, what are you doing in this hole?" Nick asked.

"Like every other poor bastard here, I am studying for a higher exam. I am giving myself one more year and then, if Dhar and I have not succeeded in achieving our aims, we shall carry out our suicide pact."

The smile that played across Sananayake's handsome face had to Nick a suggestive ambiguity.

"I suppose your present post was advertised as 'Suitable for Higher Surgical Training'?"

The question prompted wild laughter.

"Yes," he said at last, wiping the tears from his eyes "very suitable for higher surgical training." And he was again convulsed by laughter. Dr Dhar, meanwhile, was succumbing to a minor variant of the same symptom.

"But there's no training?" Nick said, doggedly maintaining his *faux-naïf* spirit of enquiry.

"Naturally there is not. Who speaks of training when survival is all?"

Training, it seemed, was virtually forbidden. There was no teaching of any sort at NBRI and study leave to attend courses held elsewhere was actively discouraged.

"So why are you working here?"

"Because, without a higher exam, I have nowhere else to go. And they took us on here because they couldn't get anyone else. We are stuck with them and they are stuck with us."

"And so," Nick said, "come 19-whatever and there are more UK-trained graduates than can find jobs, you'll find yourself out on your ear."

"Precisely."

San had already sent his wife and two children home. They hadn't been able to stand any more.

"Dr McAdam must be a great inspiration to you all," Nick said, provoking more laughter. "Where is he by the way? Has he been removed to another Exhibition of Living Sculpture?" Apparently, he was rarely seen between breakfast and the evening. "What does he do? What's his background?"

Sananayake explained. Dr McAdam had been a junior doctor at the NBRI since he had been houseman to Dr Welldorm's predecessor in the early 1950s. He had stayed on and had become, under at Welldorm's patronage, a permanent Medical Assistant at the hospital. It was a classic case of seniority achieved by calcification *in situ*. During these thirty years, his duties had shrunk to the point where they consisted of providing essentially custodial care to patients in one long stay ward. Any actual medical problems that arose on the ward were dealt with by the other junior doctors. He visited his ward daily at 10 A.M. and left it at about 10.30 A.M., after a cup of coffee with the aged Ward Sister who still hoped to marry him, his day's work finished. He also provided nominal cover one night a week and one weekend in five, when junior staff were at liberty to consult him over especially difficult medical problems. No one had exercised this liberty since the early Seventies, when his credibility had finally evaporated.

"How old is he? Has he been carbon dated?"

"We estimate mid-fifties," San said.

"And what does he do when he is not working?"

"He photographs flowers and develops the photographs himself…You will have noticed the smell in the corridor of James House. He complains frequently of the smell of our cooking. And he plays music…"

"Yes, I noticed that as well."

"We understand from one of the older ward sisters that he is a churchgoer. Judging by the state from which he returns from church sometimes, we suspect that he worships at the shrine of St John Walker…And tonight you must take some Scotch with us, Dr Page."

"Call me Nick."

"And you call me San. By the way, I forgot to tell you. Dr McAdam is Clinical Tutor—he helps us with our Higher Medical Studies."

"Wild, even hellish, laughter should greet that observation."

"And, unofficially, he makes himself responsible for our morals."

"How?"

"He forbids parties in James House."

"On what grounds?"

"The noise. There was a party in 1968 that kept him awake all night."

Oscar entered. "Your parcel, Doctor. And a letter"

"Thank you Oscar. You make me feel like a princess, delivering my mail to me personally."

"He never does that for us," San said after he had left. "Racist swine."

"What is it between you all and Oscar?"

"It goes back to the early 1960s when a Dr Patel was here. In those days there weren't any phones in the doctors' residence and the porter had to go round to a doctor's room if he was needed on the ward at night. Shortly after Oscar came, by mistake he roused Dr Patel, who was having his end away...Dr Patel was not pleased as the wooing had been long. There then followed a free and frank exchange of views in which racial origins, the inherited basis of intelligence and various other topics were discussed."

"I see."

"Anyway, Oscar has been a racist ever since. I did once suggest to him that he join the National Front and if he was refused membership he ought to complain to the Race Relations Board on grounds of racial discrimination."

"History seems to be a potent force in this hospital. To enter the NBRI is to hear the clamour of swords long crumbled to rust..."

San nodded, exhaling smoke.

"And what about *your* history, Nick?"

"Abreact me with Scotch tonight and I will tell you all. Or some, anyway."

Nick opened the parcel in his bedroom. The scent of Absence left by Sadie, who had been making his bed, prompted the absurd hope that it might be from Susie. It proved to be a Black Forest Gâteau "From the Girls in Haematology" at St Jidgey's:

> We're all missing you. We thought this would remind you of us, being the nearest colour we could get to purpura. Come back soon!

Love from…

They had all signed it—Popsie, Dot, Tina, Miranda…
Except, of course, Susie.

Chapter three

Nick was transporting a particularly vicious whisky-induced headache through the rain when his bleep went off, firing at the rapid crash call or emergency tone. The cerebrospinal fluid slopping round his brain made him disinclined even to walk; none the less he ran. He snatched up a phone in the nearest ward. After the usual eternity, during which he envisaged the anoxic brain of a citizen of North Brompton shutting down neurone by neurone, the switchboard answered.

"Dr Page here. Where's the cardiac arrest?"

"Nowhere. Dr Welldorm would like to see you in his room."

"Does he require urgent medical attention?"

"Bye."

Nick sat in the empty ward office with his head in his hands, waiting for his brain, his stomach and the outside world to come to some kind of accommodation. Anger occupied the spaces not already possessed by nausea, brainache or shortness of breath. When, after a few minutes, he ventured to stand up, he was pleased to discover that the ward had docked safely. He carried his malaise-ridden body to Dr Welldorm's room. As he knocked on the door, his bleep panicked again.

"*Come in*, I said."

"You were bleeping me. I'm Nick Page."

"Yes, I have been bleeping you for some while. Sit down, Dr Page. I have some correspondence to finish...Now where were we, Maureen?"

Nick did as he was told. Peering through the chinks in his hangover, he focused on the nearest approximation to an object of interest. Dr Welldorm's secretary read back her shorthand. His automatic evaluation of her material basis was highly theoretical as his anorexia for all forms of matter, or any activity that involved movement, was total. Welldorm resumed dictation.

"New paragraph. I shall arrange to see him again in my private rooms in a month...but if you are worried about him in the meantime...I shall be pleased to see him earlier...Yours etc...Next, a letter to Dr Conrad about Robert Smith...Dear John, Thank you for referring this pleasant young man whom I saw in my private rooms yesterday..."

Welldorm was of medium height and quite well-built. He had a boyish face and grey hair cut very short. There was a weary physicianly wisdom in his voice, which had doubtless at first been cultivated but which now seemed spontaneous. He leant back in his revolving chair, one hand on his magnificent mahogany desk, staring into a distant corner of the high-ceilinged room. Many of the papers piled on the desk looked as if they had been there for months, some perhaps for years, a few in the lower layers turning to peat.

The room was well supplied with bookshelves. Some of these were occupied by out-of-date textbooks and heaps of back—far back—copies of *The Lancet* and *The British Medical Journal* which, like the various medical curios distributed round the room, were more of antiquarian than of scientific interest. Materia medica, however, were outnumbered by items relating to what was clearly Welldorm's ruling passion. One long shelf was entirely occupied by various Acts of Parliament relating to the railways. The 1839 Act, leatherbound and with the title in gold letters, was especially handsome. There were several editions of Bradshaw and many much-thumbed timetables covering all regions. There were some newer volumes with brightly coloured dust jackets. Their titles, for the most part in Ulverscroft-sized print, could easily be read from where Nick was sitting: *Jane's Railway Year*, *In Memory of the Deltics*; *50/50 Class Diesels*. The emphasis, of course, was on steam: *The World of Steam*, *The Glory of Steam*, *The Age of Steam* and—even—*Steam Dreams* which, Nick thought, might be superheated wet ones. There was a newly opened issue of *The Railway Magazine* on Welldorm's desk next to a heap of *Lancet*s still in the sleeves in which they had been posted. Among the many studio portraits of steam engines was a large picture over the mantelpiece: The City of Truro completing an historic record-breaking run, and arriving in Paddington on time.

The smell of disinfectant was overlaid by a gorgeous musty aroma—dust, old furniture, accumulated time. Maureen, on the near side of the desk, uncrossed her stockinged legs and the sound, to Nick's hyperaesthetic senses like a match being struck, brought him back sharply to the here and now.

"That will be all, Maureen."

"Thank you, Dr Welldorm."

Her transition to the door confirmed the previously noted patability of her bottom. Nick's disapproval of his own thoughts was even more theoretical, by several orders of magnitude, than the appetite implicit in his assessment of Maureen. We desire that which which we see others desire, he thought wearily to himself.

"You have managed, Dr Page, to upset a remarkably large number of people in a remarkably short time," Welldorm began, directing his gaze at a bunch of grapes in the frieze.

"You mean Sister Kinmonth?"

"Sister Kinmonth was extremely—and in my opinion justifiably—outraged at the manner in which you barged into her ward on Monday morning, started ordering her and her staff about and decided that you were going to alter a long-established—and in my opinion effective—ward routine to suit your personal convenience."

"I only wanted to do a ward round."

"I am aware of that, Dr Page. But there are ways of going about things…"

"I didn't think it was an unreasonable…"

"I'm sure you didn't. You may think changes are needed in a place which someone like you, young and inexperienced and fresh from a teaching hospital, may regard as a backwater. But there are ways of implementing change. And you ought to remember that the NBRI was serving the people of North Brompton long before you were born and certainly before last Monday morning. If changes are needed, *evolution* not *revolution* is the way to bring them about…"

"I wanted only to do a ward round…" Nick repeated, this time choosing a word order that would ensure that "only" would have the correct scope, thereby removing the only possible impediment to understanding.

"You obviously didn't make that very clear to Sister."

"With respect, I think I did."

"So it all boils down to communication. That's what medicine's all about: communicating with people. That's something they don't bother to teach you at so-called centres of excellence."

"Sister Kinmonth and I were communicating perfectly clearly. I wanted to do a ward round before I moved on to my next job, she saw this as unwarranted medical interference in her management of the patients. She thought I was superfluous; whereas I am paid by North Brompton District Health Authority to think and behave otherwise."

"I'm not going to engage in an argument with you, Dr Page. Sister Kinmonth has been running 6A ward virtually single-handed against incredible odds. As you will have realised, this hospital has in recent years received a diminishing share of District funds and is shortly to close. This makes it extremely difficult to attract nursing staff. Junior medical staff on the other hand are two a penny. I would ask you to bear this in mind. Frankly, your time would be better spent supervising the activities of the house officers than interfering with the way the ward is run. I don't mind telling you, I'm not very happy with the standard of care set by our coloured brethren…Now I intend to commence my ward round at 11 A.M. precisely and I expect you to be there. I cannot—and will not—tolerate lateness."

At the door, Nick took a deep breath and fixed his gaze on The City of Truro. There was nothing more to be said. Welldorm was already attending to some papers in the geologically most recent layer on his desk. Nick seethed his way to the ward and, seething, waited with Dr Dhar for Welldorm to arrive. At precisely 11.47, Nick abandoned the wait and, taking with him a reluctant and unhappy-looking Dhar, went to lunch. Sadie, reeking more than ever of Absence, had just served soup when their bleeps emitted a crash call tone. A summons to Dr Welldorm's ward round.

"I was certainly not going to be kept waiting by you two any longer. You will find my instructions about the first two patients in their case-notes. I urge you to read and act upon them."

The ward round continued. Patients were greeted with a politeness that struck Nick as being enacted purely for demonstration purposes. Any response from the patient went unheard as Welldorm turned to Kinmonth to ask how "we" were doing. Dhar was occasionally required to supply details of the history or physical examination or the result of a laboratory test. Nick, who was longing to sit down, was largely ignored. They came to Mrs Johnson.

"How are we doing, Sister?"

"Much better since Dr Page stopped those tablets," Mrs Johnson, quite uninvited, chipped in. She winked at Nick. Freed of the side-effects of the tablets, she was almost euphoric.

"Which tablets, Sister?"

"Depressine, Dr Welldorm."

Welldorm remained quite still, looking towards the foot of Mrs Johnson's bed, while inwardly he veered to confront a new kind of fact: somebody altering the medication he had prescribed.

"Why did you stop them, Page?" he asked without looking up.

"Depressine is a depressant, Dr Welldorm. Mrs Johnson was becoming depressed and confused."

"You have evidence for this claim? Or are you relying on revelation?"

"It is well-described in the literature."

"Reading the latest scientific papers in the latest high-powered journal is one thing, Dr Page, and the practice of good clinical medicine is quite another. A wise physician relies on his own experience and not on *The Journal of Half-Baked Ideas*. No amount of clever-clever science, Dr Page, can replace the clinical experience of a physician with a bit of nous. Those of us who have been around long enough to have seen a few pseudo-scientific fashions come and go do not immediately start prescribing the latest wonder drug to be advertised in two pages of glorious technicolour in *The Lancet*. A wise physician sticks to the drugs he knows from experience…"

"A physician makes the same mistake a thousand times and boasts of his experience," Nick thought to himself. Welldorm, who had his eyes closed to aid memory, was reciting:

"'Be not the first by whom the new are tried
    Nor yet the last to lay the old aside…'

That's a wise saying and you would do well to remember it."

"But *somebody* has to be the first to try the new and somebody else has to be the last to give up the old. Unless a nation-wide dead heat is pre-arranged."

"He's got you there, Dr Welldorm," Mrs Johnson, bubbling over with returned joy, put in.

"It will be better for you if I pretend I haven't heard that fatuous and impertinent remark, Page. Mrs Johnson will resume Depressine 0.5 mgms b.d. as from the next drug round, Sister."

"Thank you, Dr Welldorm," Kinmonth said, her face animated by a slight, almost girlish, smirk. She was leaning on the monkey pole suspended over the bed, rocking from side to side. Nick's head throbbed in phase with her slight movements.

"And now, with your permission, Dr Page, we shall continue the ward round as Sister and I are both rather busy people."

They eventually reached the last patient, a Mr Ansell who was suffering from an exacerbation of his long-standing severe chronic bronchitis. Welldorm took his hand and, talking past the navy-blue face behind the oygen mask, asked airily: "Well, Dr Page, what have science and the centres of arrogance got to offer here? What new advances have I been missing out on? You're going to offer us a cure for Mr er...er..."

"Mr Ansell," Kinmonth supplied.

"Well there have been no recent breakthroughs in the management of this condition..." Nick conceded.

"Of course not. What this chap needs is a new pair of lungs, isn't it? That right Dhar? And, like so many of the illnesses we encounter in so-called civilised society, it is self-inflicted. Here the cause is smoking, a habit like many others that begins as a pleasure we do not need and ends up as a necessity that gives us no pleasure. The answer, of course, lies in prevention...And self-control." He laid down the patient's hand, having neither taken the pulse nor offered comfort; the action was a mere physicianly gesture that contributed neither science nor humanity to the management of the patient.

"Posturing prick," Nick thought, as he looked away from Welldorm's self-satisfied boyish face to the bloated blue face of the man behind the mask. For Mr Ansell, the air the rest of them were breathing without even noticing it had to be wooed, begged for, with every panted breath. As far as his cardio-respiratory system was concerned, North Brompton might have been the Alps and he at the top of them. Nick looked up to see Welldorm's pleasure at his own aphorism drain from his face.

"What's this, Sister?" He picked up what, even to an untrained eye, looked like a packet of Player's. The trusty, bearded face of the sailor, ironically encircled by a life-belt, guaranteed the quality of the carcinogens within. Kinmonth reached across the bed to receive them from Welldorm.

"I'm going to give these back to your wife, Mister," she said to Mr Ansell, as she expropriated them. There was no response. Above a certain level of arterial carbon dioxide, Nick thought, one loses all desire to defend one's rights.

The company of healers walked away from Mr Ansell's bed

while Kinmonth subjected him to a savage rearrangement of pillows. He continued his lonely journey into anoxic coma, dragging in the air through the capillary tubes he had for airways.

In the ward office, Welldorm debriefed them, after he had fed the goldfish from a packet that Kinmonth handed to him.

"Right, gentlemen. Next week I expect to find you here when I begin my round and not to have to raise you from the ends of the earth. Thank you, Sister."

Doctors Page and Dhar made to return to their interrupted soup.

"Before you go," Kinmonth said, "which of you is going to write up the medication that Dr Welldorm ordered?"

"You won't catch me putting my name to what *that* doctor ordered. I have my reputation to think of. Whether Dr Dhar…"

That evening, Nick recounted his impressions to an appreciative audience in the lounge of James House. There were present Doctors Dhar, Sananayake, Chung, Poulantzos and Rai. Dr Chung was a very young-looking lad from Hong Kong, looking precisely as Nick might have expected him to look. His conversation was confined to a few banal remarks. However, he was pleasant, and he seemed keen and conscientious. Most importantly, he appreciated Nick's jokes.

His fellow Senior House Officer on the geriatric wards was Dr Socrates Poulantzas, a Greek who had come to the United Kingdom in order to extend his experience of neurosurgery in British centres of excellence. His special interest was microneurosurgery of the spine. He had been even less lucky than Mr Sananayake, having secured during the course of an eighteen-month stay in the United Kingdom only two weeks of surgical experience. Several promised supernumerary training posts had failed to materialise. He was usually ill-shaven, angry, and voluble about his troubles. He attributed most of his misfortunes to an extension of British policy in The Near East which, he said, consisted of following the rule 'Divide and Conquer'. Nick had already caught a glimpse of his pale and very overweight wife. She had been arguing with him in the main corridor of the hospital. With tinted, horn-rimmed glasses, a young child swinging from each hand and a third howling in a pram, she looked desperately unhappy. They lived in a caravan in the hospital grounds. This was called 'married accommodation'. A similar caravan had recently caught fire and burnt to the ground in approximately fourteen seconds. Nick saw that he was going to enjoy Poulantzas' exemplary bitterness.

Dr Rai was a short, kyphoscoliotic South Asian who worked on the dermatology wards and helped out in the GU Medicine clinic. He walked with a peculiar rolling gait and, like Dhar, spoke rather indistinctly. In his case, however, it was to conceal his ignorance. Uniquely among the junior staff he appeared to have no thirst for knowledge or drive to self-improvement and was not studying for a higher medical examination. He was in no hurry to do anything—to answer his bleep or to return to his dissatisfied wife and unsatisfactory life back home where, as he later explained to Nick, "it would be much more difficult to drink and smoke".

"Or he is too bloody arrogant or he is a bloody criminal," Poulantzas said, when Nick had completed his account of his dealings with Welldorm.

"I think your disjunctions are wonderful, Socrates…"

"Call me Socks."

"…but there are other possibilities. It may be that he feels threatened by knowledge. There is the factor of honest-to-goodness ignorance. After all, you don't learn much about the side-effects of drugs from *Jane's Railway Year*…Now where there is ignorance, there is, as Lucretius said, also fear. Perhaps we could try instilling the Coroner into his coronaries…By the way, what were the instructions he wrote in the notes of the two patients he saw while we were guzzling soup?"

"I'm afraid I couldn't read…And Sister Kinmonth was too…to explain them for me…" Dhar said.

"I'm not surprised you couldn't read them. I've been trying to decode something he wrote in the case notes of a patient I saw in outpatients this afternoon," Nick said. "Welldorm's 'handwriting' looks like the polygraphic recording of a Parkinsonian tremor. More Rorschasch ink-blot than script…Well you'd better ring him tomorrow and find out what he wants or he'll accuse me of plotting against him."

There was unexpected laughter.

"Nick," San said, with a gorgeous, resigned, whole body smile, "you don't *know* this place. Nobody gets hold of Welldorm after Wednesday lunchtime."

"Or he is seeing his bloody private patients or he is watching his dam' bloody trains," Socks explained.

Welldorm, it appeared, had an extensive private practice based in North London. He commuted there every Wednesday on the 2 P.M. out of North Brompton, with several railway timetables on his knee, and there he remained until Friday. The weekend he usually spent travelling on InterCity Savers between hot nodes in the British Rail network. Lines of communication were restored only on Sunday night with his return to his batchelor flat in the NBRI. As a sop to his conscience, he would ring the hospital when it occurred to him to do so, to see if there were any "problems". He always summoned his junior staff on the crash tone of the bleep, the urgency of the situation being that the phone call was costing him money. There were few acute problems that could be usefully discussed with someone 150 miles away. Over the years, the local general practitioners had come to appreciate the kind of consultant cover that was available at the NBRI and had responded by sending only non-acute or apparently irremediable cases there. Acute medicine went to the big District General Hospital down the road.

"Good," said Nick. "Another weapon."

His bleep went off.

"Outside call for you, Dr Page."

"It's me. Felicity."

"Hi."

"I just rang to say that I am missing you horribly…And I love you."

"That's very nice…I'm missing you, too…Look I've written you a letter," Nick said, remembering that he had forgotten to post it.

"You *have*? That's lovely. Now I've got something to look forward to."

"Yes."

"I love you," she reiterated. This time, it was slightly more emphatic; an insistent self-citation. Nick became aware of the nauseous headache Sadie's soup had re-activated.

"Thay should tell 'em to lave thay alone when thay're eating thay're males. Ast 'aving a pace of pie?" Sadie shouted from the kitchen.

Nick raised his thumb to indicate that he would like some pie, that he would be returning to the table shortly and that he didn't want to be disturbed for the immediate present. An expressive thumb.

"I love you, too…Felicity, dear, I've got to go…"

"You *do* think about me, don't you?"

"All the time. I've only got to go now because someone has had a cardiac arrest and they're getting impatient. Thank you for ringing. Take care."

He downed the receiver. San, who was waiting to answer his bleep, winked at him.

"More of your women?"

"*More*? Who are the rest?"

"Sister Parker on 27B asked me to keep an eye on you. I'd better answer this bleep."

"*Did* she? That's most interesting. Because there does seem to be a shortage of biddable XX in this hole."

"You can say that again," San concurred, as he waited for the switchboard to reply. "Of course, they won't look at *me* twice. Married and an alien—you can't get much lower than that."

Nick put his hand on San's shoulder.

"San, do me a favour. Send my greetings to Sister Parker. I might even wander up to see her sometime. Better still, you ask me to see one of your patients when she's on duty."

"No problem, Chief." He answered his call. "Sananayake here… I'll be along shortly. More Scotch tonight?"

"We have sensed that you are a troubled soul and we would like to help you…"

"Very perceptive of you, San."

Three hours and about six Scotches later, Nick went to bed. He slept heavily but briefly. He woke. He tossed. He turned. Briefly slept again. And woke. And got out of bed. He staggered to his desk, in the grip of a terrible malaise in which body and mind were indivisibly implicated. He remembered San's pointing out that many had lived without love but few without salt, water and a steady job.

Dearest Aporia,

Your absence denies me that plenitude of being so essential for sleep. If you no longer love yourself, because you are not loved by the one person whom you wish, above all others, to love you, then sleep—the happy capacity to mate with oneself—is no longer possible.

I am a hollow. Nothing nothings itself and operates under the name Nicholas Page. My existence is merely adjectival, my actions only adverbs of inoperancy. And yet, this nowhere where I live is a kind of inverse centre of the world; for wherever I am, there too is the capital of your absence. That absence which unpicks the text of reality, unhinging it from reference meaning and truth, reducing presence to the mere trace of a trace...etc., etc.

Chapter four

Nick hesitated outside the closed door of Sister's office on the Orthopaedic ward. It was handing over time and Sister Parker was going through the Care Plan with the newly arrived shift, updating them on the progress of their charges. She was also, by the sound of it, taking the opportunity to deliver a short secular sermon on the management of urinary incontinence.

"You see, it's not enough, Nurse Jones, just to report that your patient has been incontinent and to change her and so on. Florrie's Army isn't just a mop-and-bucket brigade. You've got to step back and think *why* she is incontinent. Everything has a reason. Does she, for example, have difficulty getting out to the toilet? After all, she has got severe arthritis, hasn't she?...Come in!"

Nick regretted having knocked, preferring at this moment to overhear, rather than interrupt, her. Her very pleasant voice, in which a dark Saturday night music could be heard through the good Wednesday morning sense, belonged, like the proposition "Everything has a reason", to a universe of meaning from which he had been expelled.

"And by the time the lady has managed to get her arthritic fingers round those buttons and zip fasteners and pulled her knickers down from her pendulous boobs to her knobbly knees, she's probably already wet. So you can see how incontinence isn't just a matter of a dicky bladder but also...Come in...Come *in*!...of the ward environment and people's attitudes—*your* attitudes...Come in, for Heaven's sake!"

Reluctantly, Nick entered. Sister Parker was seated at her desk, a pile of Care Plans in front of her. Next to her was a black-haired staff nurse in a lighter blue uniform, a large bank nurse in white and three nursing auxiliaries in a light beige check.

"I didn't want to interrupt a most persuasive presentation."

"We had finished. Thank you," she said, indicating to the nurses that they could go. "And don't forget, we could do with some more pyjama bottoms. Now, Dr Page, what can I do for you?"

"Mr Sananayake asked me to see a lady of his who had been operated on for a fractured neck of femur and has now developed a rather alarming tendency to bruising."

"Staff Nurse Lenier, could you please take Dr Page to see Mrs Knight. I hope you'll excuse me but I've got to sort out the off-duty rota. Perhaps we can discuss her management after you have seen her."

Nick followed Staff Nurse Lenier out of the office and into the ward. The scene was of the kind that had captured the popular imagination, with some of the patients on traction, their bandaged, injured limbs being retrained by weights hung on ropes. What did not correspond to the popular idea of an orthopaedic ward was that many of the beds were filled not with young men but elderly ladies. Even so, in contrast to 6A ward, all was *ordre et calme* even if *luxe* and *volupté* were not too evident.

They arrived at Mrs Knight's bed. She was not on traction, having been admitted for a pelvic fracture following a fall. She was to be mobilised as soon as she could tolerate weight bearing. Unhappily, mobilisation and weight bearing were not going quite according to plan. An enormous octogenarian, she had an unfortunate tendency to mobilise under the influence of gravity and consequently to weight bear on her fundament rather than her feet. There were massive bruises on her arms and legs and she had two black eyes that met one another on the bridge of her nose. She looked at him with drowsy puzzlement.

"She's a bit confused," Staff Nurse Lenier explained as she drew the curtains round the bed. "We put up cot sides to stop her falling out of bed but she somehow manages to climb over them."

"And so accomplishes the same fall but from a greater height, with more interesting orthopaedic consequences. No wonder Mr Sananayake is kept so busy. Mrs Knight, how are you? I'm Dr Page. Mr Sananayake asked me to see you."

"She's a bit deaf. You'll have to shout."

"Do you have a hearing aid?"

"Yes she does but she refuses to wear it. Last night she put it in the glass of water for her false teeth."

"Mrs Knight," Lenier said, taking the old lady's hand, "Dr Page has come to see you about the bruising."

"Dr Page, did thay say? 'E's been dead for years."

"This is a different Dr Page," Nick said, quite unruffled by the charge of being dead.

"Ask Tommy if er's downstairs 'e could make a cup of tea… Where 'er been all nate?"

"Who's Tommy?"

"Mr Knight. He died about twenty years ago," Lenier whispered.

"Mrs Knight, how long have you been bruising?"

"Are 'aven't touched a drop for years."

"Try the other ear."

"How long have you had these bruises on your arms and legs?"

"Never 'ad a bruise in marn lafe."

"Do you know where you are at the moment, Mrs Knight?"

"Arm not bloody daft yer know."

Examination proved as difficult as history taking. Mrs Knight, not entirely convinced that she was in hospital or that Nick was a doctor, did not want to have her body explored by someone who was not, after all, the late Mr Knight. Her grip on Nick's wrist proved surprisingly powerful.

"Gerrof marn belly. Tinner tharn, so layveet aloon."

Nick took the hint and, after a necessarily incomplete examination of the abdomen, was not entirely unhappy to omit inspection of, for example, the groin.

"Thay're quite a nace crowd, 'ere," Mrs Knight declared to the rest of the ward as doctor and nurse departed.

Sister Parker had completed drawing up the off-duty rota.

"Well, Doctor?"

"History and examination were unavoidably incomplete. Nevertheless, I feel confident that her bruising is unlikely to be due to a disturbance of her reticulo-endothelial system. She doesn't appear to have enlarged glands or a big spleen or liver. I should think that the most likely cause of her discolouration is acute gravitational poisoning."

"Meaning?"

"Newton's disease."

"Meaning?"

"That she is covered with bruises because she fell out of bed."

"But it is pretty extensive bruising."

"Then she is a pretty extensive lady. Also, as you get older you bruise more easily. The capillaries are more fragile. I was researching into this at St Jidgey's but alas…However, I should be grateful if you would ask for Mr Sananayake to arrange the following investigations to rule out any clotting defect…"

"If I get you some coffee, would you fill in the blood forms?"

"Done."

"So what is the diagnosis?" Staff Nurse Lenier asked.

"*Diagnosis!* You know not what you ask! Senile purpura most likely, if the laboratory results are normal."

"Senile purpura?"

It seemed unlikely that Staff Nurse was interested in the diagnosis and more likely that the conversation had other purposes. She was moderately, but not overwhelmingly, attractive. Nick appreciated her jet black hair, dark skin colouring and her long smooth neck. He noted, at the base of her neck, a love-bite which he estimated to be about three to four days old.

"Senile purpura. Otherwise known as the Devil's pinches. There is a folk tradition that they are caused by the Devil trying to pluck the aged from the planet, luring them to the eternal flames beyond space, time and causation. I wasn't able to confirm this in the research I was doing at St Jidgey's but I still like to think of them as death's love-bites. They are, in a sense, the opposite of *juvenile* purpura, of which I see a splendid example at this very moment. As regards the latter, I suspect it was not Thanatos but Eros that made this little exit from the varied tints and stinks that make up the senseless, clanking mechanism of ordinary, intolerably dull daily life…Like Mr Lawrence's apples, we bruise—as well as booze—ourselves our exits from the world."

"One sugar or two?"

"Sister Parker! Two please."

"If you'd like to get the toiletting going, Judy. And ask Nurse Jones if she would give Mrs Williams a suppository."

Lenier complied.

"Exit Staff Nurse."

"I thought she was in grave moral danger, Dr Page."

"Remarkable how your beauty is quite unquenched even by that unbecoming Sister's uniform. The dark brown of your slightly dys-conjugate gaze reminds me of instant coffee. Or the 0.00005 denier tan of an exemplary St Tropez thigh."

"That's enough sexual harassment in the workplace. What about Mrs Knight?"

"In my opinion, her confusional state is much more important than her bruising and of much greater medical interest. Now you might be inclined to argue that her deranged mental function is due merely to her great age, that it represents the return of entropy, the inescapable re-assertion of the Second Law of Thermodynamics, the ineluctable autumn that comes to all living things, the inevitable collapse of the civic order that must accompany the equally inevitable return of natural chaos…That it signifies…"

"I'm on an early and want to get the ward sorted out before I leave. I was due to go half an hour ago."

"On the other hand, you could put away your tragic sense and look for remediable causes, of which there is no shortage in this lady. She is dehydrated. You are trying to correct this but you will not make much progress until her unnecessary diuretics are stopped. I have crossed them off. She is desperately constipated which must be in part due to dehydration and this, as you well know, will be making her incontinence, in part due to her diuretics, worse. I suspect that she has a urinary tract infection because I could smell it from the end of the bed—but here I am teaching my grandmother to suck eggs. The antibiotic which I have prescribed will also treat the chest infection that she seems to have at the same time and which must also be contributing to her confusional state. I shall look forward to revisiting her world when it is rehydrated, resalinated, detoxified and adequately oxygenated. I should not be surprised to find the cognitive, moral, social and civic orders there restored."

"I'm impressed."

"I sing as well—and perform card tricks."

"So when are we going to see you again?"

"Back of the hospital at 4.30?"

"I mean on the ward."

"I mean off the ward."

"Sorry, Dr Page. I'm not in your catchment area."

"But I offer a regional, rather than a district, service."

"I'm out of your region."

"But my catchment area is co-terminous with desirable womanhood."

"The boundaries have just been re-drawn to exclude me."

"Encountering your face, desire might know itself for the first time."

"I can think of circumstances where that kind of crap might go down well. But your patronising and rather dated style is wasted on me."

"Sigh. What about Staff Nurse Lenier, has she got anyone to bite her pretty neck tonight?"

"I don't know. You'll have to ask herself yourself."

"On second thoughts. Anyway, there's my bleep…"

"Thank you for calling, doctor."

The reason for his being bleeped rather took him by surprise: a medical emergency. A man had been brought into the Accident and Emergency department in deep coma. Only a few hours before he had been eating a hearty breakfast and complaining to his wife that his bacon was under-cooked. The same wife was now accompanying his snorting body to the hospital and providing the medical history that the patient was not able to deliver himself. On the basis of this history and a brief examination of the patient Nick was able to reassure Mrs Payne that the cause of her husband's current condition was not under-cooked bacon. He drew up a management plan and attempted to contact his junior colleague. The switchboard put him through to Dr Dhar's residence where the latter had seized the opportunity to swot up the indications for measuring pulmonary wedge pressure in cardiac failure.

"Dr Dhar?"

"——"

"Am I through to Dr Dhar's flat?"

"This is Dr Dhar's flat."

"Could I speak to him, please?"

"I will get him."

While Nick waited for Mrs Dhar to fetch her husband he could hear the Dharling howling, her little rage apparently limitless.

"Dhar," Dhar said.

"Dhar, old chap. An extraordinary thing has happened. A GP in his innocence and/or ignorance has sent us in an *acutely ill* patient. Think of it: an acute medical emergency in the North Brompton Royal Infirmary! I want to tell you about him. James Payne is a man of forty-five who, according to his wife, complained this morning of a severe headache of such sudden onset that he thought he had been struck by someone. Shortly afterwards he became unconscious. I've just seen him in Accident and Emergency. He's profoundly comatose and, apart from some doubtful left-sided signs, the only other neurological abnormality is that he has a rigid neck. Diagnosis, Dr Dhar?"

"Sorry?"

"Can you hear me?"

There was a pause while Dhar, almost inaudibly, requested his wife to ask Bulbul to be a little quieter. The child responded by howling even louder.

"Sorry?"

"Can you hear me?"

"Plainly."

"Well, this man, who, as you were about to tell me, has sustained a *subarachnoid haemorrhage*, needs various investigations and I'd be grateful if you would fix them up…"

"I'm sorry?"

"Meet me in A&E and we'll talk there."

The fluid Dhar obtained at lumbar puncture confirmed Nick's diagnosis.

"We'd better talk to the Neurosurgical Centre."

"Oh God," Dhar said, with a look of total dismay. "They always give us a bad time."

"Of course they do. That is the role of The Centre of Excellence: to shit on the The Periphery of Disaster, discourage it from referring patients and bawl it out when it refers them too late. I'll do the phoning. I'll enjoy it."

The neurosurgical senior registrar at The Russell Brain Institute of Neurological Sciences answered his bleep promptly.

"Perkins…" Doctors in a hurry don't waste time reciting their titles where the bare patronymic will suffice. "Perkins. You wanted to speak to me." Nick, startled, at once recognised the name and voice: Robert Perkins, his old rival from St Jidgey's. A mischievous idea crossed Nick's mind. He assumed an overseas accent.

"This is the North Brompton Royal Infirmary."

"Name, Doctor?"

"Dr Ghosh. I am Locum Registrar to Dr Welldorm and to cut a long story short, we have just admitted a splendid forty-five year old chap with a subarachnoid haemorrhage and we should be grateful if…"

"What is your evidence for this assertion, doctor?"

"The history is classical, the physical signs are in keeping and the cerebrospinal fluid is uniformly blood-stained."

"What else?"

"Is that not enough, good sir?"

"No it is not. What other evidence do you have for your assertion?"

Nick had had enough of being bullied. He changed his accent.

"Well, I went to Night School and once read some books lent to me by the St John's Ambulance."

"What on earth are you talking about?"

"Leave off the third degree, Robert. This man I'm telling you about has had a fucking subarachnoid haemorrhage and I'm trying to make it easy for you. He's too ill to move at present but if he surfaces a bit, I should be grateful if you could take him over so that you can finish him off with an angiogram and the usual neurosurgical gambits…"

"Who is that speaking?"

"It's your old adversary Nick Page. Remember me?"

"Nick? Nick Page?"

"The same."

"Why didn't you say so?"

"I thought it'd be interesting to see how A Centre of Arrogance looks from the tilt shot of the periphery it is supposed to serve."

"What the hell are *you* doing in a hole like the NBRI? I mean it's all sunkissed brethren there isn't it? I have had some ghastly conversations with our commonwealth colleagues."

"I'm sure they found them ghastly as well," Nick said, surprised by the intensity of his anger. Oscar's remarks were tolerable because deconstructed at source; Perkins' were not.

"Well, fill me in, Nick. I thought you were still at Jidgey's."

"I was Fibrin's research registrar and his blue-eyed boy. But I jacked it in."

"Why, for God's sake?"

"I lost my appetite for the universe."

"So you're there with the Foreign Legion?"

"That's the usual cliché, isn't it."

"There's my bleep."

"And there's mine," Nick said, not to be outdone.

"I'll make a note of your man's name and you ring me back when you think he's ready for transfer. Look, we must meet. There's a nice bar here at The Russell Brain."

"We must," Nick said, thinking, "we mustn't". "Thanks for your help. Cheers". He put down the receiver and then picked it up again. "Dr Page here."

"Outside call for you, doctor."

"Nick, it's me, Felicity."

"Hello!"

"I had to ring. I've just got your letter. It's lovely. But I'm still missing you horribly. I've *got* to see you. I can't stand not seeing you."

"No point coming this weekend. I'm going to be run off my feet and you'd just be hanging about and getting depressed and we'd end up having a row like we did when you stayed that weekend at St Jidgey's."

"When can we meet, then?"

"Angel, I've got a man in A&E in coma," Nick said, slightly disorientated at discovering that his excuse coincided with the truth. "I've got to go. I've already written to you again," he said, referring to a letter he intended to write that afternoon.

"This is horrible, Nick. Will you ring me back later?"

"I'll try."

"Love you."

"Love you, too, dearest. Bye."

"Thank you for seeing my Mrs Knight, Chief. You made a big impression on 27B." San exhaled smoke and laughter.

"On Sister Parker?"

"Quite definitely, yes. She'd have you seeing all our patients if she had her way. She balled me out about those diuretics. I didn't mind, as she's a good nurse. Not like the mega-bitch Dhar has to put up with on 6A."

"Is she attached to anyone at present?"

"Never lets on to me. Why don't you ask her? An unmarried

Caucasian might find out a bit more than I have after a year of constant questioning." San leaned back in his armchair and raised his legs on to a pouffe. "We have been discussing your sorrows, Nick and puzzling out how we can help you."

"You had a case conference?"

"We did. To be quite honest, some of us did not think your situation as grave as you have portrayed it. One of us"—and San assumed Dhar's voice—"even went so far as to say that, plainly speaking, some of us are wishing we had your problems."

"Rather than your own."

"Precisely. But then those who lives are ruined, whose hopes are blasted, who have known exile, rejection and humiliation as our daily bread, find it difficult to grant the functional disorders of the heart the kind of serious attention they deserve."

"What you are telling me is: 'Don't get too churned up just because meaning has drained from the face of matter'? Or have I misread you?"

"Cigarette?" San said, extinguishing his own. Nick shook his head and waited while San lit another. "It is easy, of course, to put another's sorrows in perspective."

"One man's death is another man's anecdote," Nick said, a little peeved.

"Precisely. So we feel that the solution to your troubles is not to deny them but to put them behind you. And the best way to do that is to discover new troubles similar in kind but of a lesser intensity. A homoeopathic remedy."

"More women?"

"Another woman, anyway."

"I shall think about it, doctor." The sitting room door opened. "Evening, Dr Dhar. Dr Chung."

"By the way," San said. "There was a representative from a pharmaceutical firm looking for you this afternoon, Nick."

"Don't tell me. He was trying to push a non-steroidal anti-inflammatory drug?"

"Naturally."

"Let me guess which one. Paraprofen?"

"Right again," San said, relaxing even further back in his chair and treating Nick to his gorgeous whole body smile.

"Poor sod. The most expensive launch ever. They spent nearly a million quid trying to persuade doctors to use it. Now everyone's talking about its side effects. We nearly killed an old woman with it in my last job. Actually, I've found it quite good for hangovers. What does he want to do for us? Fly us to Spain?"

"Show us a 'non-promotional' film on joint disease and take us out to The Crashing Boar for dinner."

"Bugger that. No. I'm going to follow your advice, San. Find another woman. For that we need to have a mess party, eh."

"A party?" Dr Dhar asked, incredulously.

"A party?" Mr Sananayake echoed from far back in his arm-chair.

"A party?" Dr Chung re-echoed.

"Yes! *A fucking party*. Don't you think it's about time that Venus and Dionysus visited this Saturnal spot and saved our souls from thrombosing with boredom and despair?"

San thought it was about time. Chung was not too sure. Dhar exhaled smoke and uncertainty.

"Passed, nem. con. So let's get together the bright lights and the dark darks, the women and the booze, the breast and the bottle, the convex and the concave, our desires and their objects and have a little party, courtesy of—who was it?"

"Wayne Pharmaceuticals."

"Why not give that rep. a call tomorrow and try to fix something up?"

Dearest Aporia,

It never stops raining in this town. And of course it's Verlaining in my heart as well. What a pair are we, the town with the wet streets and the man with the soggy heart. The organ in question still beats at a steady 80 per minute. It doesn't appreciate that it has metaphorical status as well as physiological duties and simply fails to notice that it is broken.

You have brought to desolate culmination my long and

terrible love affair with matter called 'consciousness'. I now have incontrovertible proof that the world is governed by accident rather than design. I sit here, the frozen hypocentre of your ghastly world-destroying "No!", conducting a cost benefit analysis of life and finding that I cannot balance the books.

It is midnight. I hear the squat tower of Our Lady of the Assumption, architecturally outshone by the council estate surrounding it, tolling midnight, announcing that its Sisyphean fingers have reached the top of the hour-hill and are about to embark on another futile circuit. I draw back the damask curtain and unveil a portrait of an unhappy man looking into the depths of a wet-roofed insomniac night, unrelieved even by comparably hydrated dreams. I look through this hollow face to the senseless dark and your absence...

The phone conversation with bloody Perkins had unsettled him. The absolute misery of living on a Susie-less planet he had almost learnt to cope with; but additional relative glooms, arising from less absolute causes of misery, had pitched him back into the howling emptiness at his own centre. Perkins had made him fully aware how he had abandoned the brightly-lit places of the world. He had turned his back on the centres of excellence and success for good—indeed metaphysical—reasons. But that action also had an external surface that could be described in one word: failure. Robert's knowledge of his present whereabouts had reduced his internal drama to that external surface. And he had never been a failure before.

Felicity's phone call had unsettled him further. He had no need to guess at the misery his cold unavailability must be causing her. His own lack of feeling towards Felicity gave him an inside view of Susie's indifference to him. And then there had been Sister Janet Parker's coolness. Perhaps she was not as available as he had assumed since their first meeting.

Writing to Felicity bored him. He had tried to concoct various non-wounding reasons why they "could not go on any longer". There was only one reason: he fancied her insofar as she aroused him sexually and in-between-times found her dull, annoying or pitiful. He abandoned the letter in favour of writing to Janet. This, too, proved harder than expected. She was so obviously "aware", he became pentied. In the end, he settled for a brief note.

Dear Sister Parker,
It was a great pleasure to renew your acquaintance. I look forward to futher collaboration on behalf of the health of taxpayers in the catchment area of the NBRI.

I am reliably informed that a bubble-gum machine has been recently installed in the centre of North Brompton. It is open twenty four hours a days, thus supporting North Brompton's claim to be a CIS-Atlantic Las Vegas. I should be more than pleased if you were able to set aside some time to take a turn with me to visit this latest wonder of our numinous age.

I await your reply.
Yrs. ever
(Dr) Nicholas Page MB ChB DRCHD (UK)

PS. For ease of reply I enclose a pre-paid card. Please tick where appropriate.

YES

NO

MAYBE

PISS OFF

"Fine, so that's the history, Dr Dhar. And what were the positive, that is to say abnormal, findings on examination?"

"Well, he was not anaemic…"

"*Positive* findings…"

"Well, he was not jaundiced, there were no abnormalities in the…"

"Just the *positive* findings, Dr Dhar. Of course, it is laudable to note the absence of certain features because such absences are generated by your activity of observation rather than being furnished by the object before you. And, moreover, the cultivation of the absent is a peculiarly human characteristic. For animals, absence is a feature-less nothing: it is not. Whereas for us humans, it is an infinite filigree surface sculpted by language under the influence of our desires—or by our desires under the influence of language—you will, I imagine, be aware of the quarrel between M. Lacan and M. Derrida—and embodied in the sigh-stained hot air we exhale in our public or private discourses. Man, the promising animal, the DRCHD-taking animal, is also the absence-making animal. *Nevertheless*, we must control our love of absence for the sake of an expedient attention to what is present. For we must remember that absence is the medium of longing and love and unhappiness, in short the hench-person of death. So, Dr Dhar, unless you wish to become the DRCHD-failing animal, you must learn to give the positive findings, the abnormalities that are present, rather than those that are not, when they are asked for…"

"If you two are going to gab on for hours, I'm leaving you to it…"

Sister Kinmonth went.

"There are times, of course, when absence has its positive features."

The positive findings were that Mr Simpkin was paralysed down the right hand side of his body and had a severe speech deficit. Comprehension was, so far as could be judged, intact; speech production, however, was confined to repeatedly saying "But…But… But…"

"So what do you propose to do for Mr Simpkin?"

"Dr Welldorm would say that all we can do is 'wait until the sap rises'."

"Kindly step to one side, Dr Dhar." Dhar, startled, complied. "Good. Now we are out of earshot. How old is this man?"

"Sixty-eight."

"So he has been paying contributions to his national health insurance for about half a century. And all we offer him when he falls ill—for the first time in his life if the history you have given me is correct—is inactivity guided by a misleading metaphor. I don't think that's giving him value for money…" Nick outlined a detailed management plan. "…And finally we need to seek the advice of a speech therapist. And the sooner we get these things going the better. If we wait for the sap to rise, it won't: we need to pump it up ourselves. So let's begin by chatting to him and explaining to him why half his body has defected to the outside world and he finds himself in a peculiar place that combines the attributes of a bedroom and a street..."

"Dr Page, could you come and look at this please?"

It was Staff Nurse Lenier, on loan to 6A ward.

"May Dr Dhar come as well, or is this a private viewing?"

They followed Staff Nurse Lenier into the sluice. She picked up a shiny bedpan labelled Mrs Charnley. They stared down into the pan and saw their own images peeping back up at them between three exceptionally large, very pale stools.

"Sister Kinmonth's long-lost and more attractive siblings perhaps?" Nick's reflected image smiling at Lenier's received a slight answering rictus. Thus presented to him, her face seemed momentarily very attractive.

The ensuing discussion established that Mrs Charnley, whom Nick had not yet met but by now felt quite sure would be charming, probably had intestinal malabsorption.

"Dr Dhar, could you kindly excuse us a moment while I have a quick word with Staff Nurse Lenier?"

He seeped away.

"I see that the macule at the base of your peerless neck has begun to fade and has not been renewed. Has the passion that made it, and allowed it to be made, also faded? Am I in with a chance?"

"Kinmonth asked me to do the TPRs," she replied.

"Evasive. But then there can be little time for silken dalliance on a busy medical ward."

The last patient was Mr Ansell, who was continuing to die of the effects of cigarette smoke. Nick offered what comfort he could.

"'Arve solved the problem of the tilette rolls, Dr Page and arm very sorry to say that I think it's Dr McAdam 'oo 'as 'ad 'em. Since he has been haway, 'arve not been 'aving henny trouble in that lane at all." She extracted Nick's dinner, partly oxidised, partly raw, from the oven. "Marned you, arm still not very pleased." She took off her oven gloves and wiped her hands down her nylon overalled hips and wagged her index finger. "Some dirty bugger—if thay'll hexcuse the hexpression—has been wrating grafties on the tilette dower. It looked lark personal remarks, though it were Grake to may."

"Confess, Chief," said Mr Sananayake, coming into the kitchen and putting his arm round Sadie's shoulders.

"How clever of Sadie to spot it was in Greek," Nick said. "I thought it might cheer up Dr Poulantzas while he defaecated."

"Are dunner lark it, Dr Page. Dr McAdam's ingrowin' 'airy enuff withart provocating."

"I'll wipe it off after lunch. But on one condition."

"Woss 'at, doctor?"

"That you change your perfume. Absence stirs up too many memories. I promise that I'll buy you something that I think you—and more to the point Mr Sananayake—will like even better."

"Well that's extemely generous of thay, doctor. Now here's your males."

They addressed themselves to Sadie's *cordon noir*. A few mouthfuls were sufficient. In order to minimise the offence to the cook, they scraped the contents of their plates into a sharps box San had lifted from the ward. San lit a cigarette.

"What was all that about perfume, Chief?"

"Absence reminds me of Susie. The clash of connotation and denotation was killing me. One has to keep love and death in separate compartments of consciousness. Whatever Freud says, it's my personal experience that Eros and Thanatos make rather ghastly bedfellows."

"I see. By the way Nick, the chap from Wayne Pharmaceuticals is coming here this afternoon. He wasn't too keen on the idea of a party."

"Why not?"

"Well, he did try to fix one up a few years ago and McAdam complained to Welldorm who managed to get Wayne products banned from the pharmacy for a while."

"Rather counter-productive from the rep's point of view. That bastard McAdam is attracted to the possibility of happiness like a heat-seeking missile to the hull of an enemy ship…Unfortunately I can't see the rep this afternoon, I'm going out. Do you think you could speak to him on my behalf?"

"What do you want me to say to him?"

"Try and persuade him to cough up. Tell him that we don't want any noise—just a bit of quiet music, plenty of booze and a floor quilted with lovely women to fall on to when we can no longer stand."

"And a few boxes of Paraprofen for our hangovers?"

Chapter five

"A t least it's not raining," Janet said, as she met up with him by the porter's lodge, the conventional ten minutes late.

"Three successive minutes without precipitation. Soon someone's going to declare a drought. But your beautifully tailored anorak prepares you for any weather...And I like your jeans. *Very* snug."

"They make my bottom too fat and my thighs look thick."

As they walked away from the hospital, he argued that there was nothing wrong with a touch of gluteomegaly.

"It proclaims that here is someone who is really here. Solid, irreducible presence..."

"And 'totally relevant to our age' I suppose."

"Yes and no. Their resonance is antique. Doric columns of warm reality, centrally heated pillars of plasm...And of course they contribute to that altitude that I so love in women. How tall are you?"

"About five foot nine and a half."

"As for your face—what can I say? That inexpressible peach-bloom, those dark brown eyes, and that ever so slight strabismus, as if you were still far-gone in last night's pleasures and haven't yet focused on the world of words and clothes and work and streets and skies and all those superfluous things outside of the raptures of con-cupiscence…"

"Mind that dog-dirt."

"Now, what about me? Am I the kind of chap a girl would look at twice?"

"Or a dysconjugate gaze would look at four times…"

"What do *I* remind *you* of…?"

"Nothing whatsoever…You mentioned a bubble gum machine."

"Later, Discobolos. Like North Brompton herself, it's best seen in total darkness. May I take your hand?"

"Why?"

"Because without a galvanic current of happiness flowing from your body to mine I shall lack the will to go on."

"I find that an insufficient reason for yielding to what is quite blatantly an advance of a sexual nature. Do you ever stop sexually harassing women—or talking?"

"Only at the point of death and at the moment of ejacula-tion."

"You've said that before."

"A self is a field in which certain actions or events have a very high probability of recurrence."

This seemed to bring the opening formalities to an end. They walked side by side in silence, shrinking a little from the gusting wind, their eyes narrowed against the occasional dust swirl. It was colder than it needed to be for late October: cold enough to be utterly mis-erable but not sufficiently cold to be in the slightest bit exciting or picturesque. Nick was about to remark that he regretted the general rule forbidding thermal underwear on assignations of a romantic nature when they arrived at their first destination.

North Brompton Central Library, where they intended to con-sult the Town Guide, was a Victorian building with "AN AWAKENED NATION WILL HAVE A THIRST FOR KNOWLEDGE" chiselled over the entrance arch. The parquet floor turned their entry into an assault on the furniture-polished silence.

"We have a thirst for knowledge," Nick announced to the balding, horn-rimmed librarian, who responded in a booming voice after the short pause necessary for cortical processing.

"You may use certain of the facilities of the library without formal membership. That is to say, you are at liberty to consult, but not to borrow, printed material. If you wish to remove printed material, then you must join the library. The principle condition of your joining the library is that you should produce evidence of your identity and proof that you are resident or working in North Brompton."

"None of my predicates, attributes or possessions amounts to a uniquely referring or rigid designator guaranteeing co-reference of the term 'Nick Page' and the indexical 'I' when this person now speaking utters it. Does that create an insuperable problem?"

"Your driving licence would suffice."

Nick sorted through the contents of his wallet.

"I have tracer cards from Genito-Urinary medicine clinics of five continents. But if you had any idea of my inner emptiness you would not mock me with talk of my 'identity'."

"I think we'll just have a look round, thank you," Janet said.

They wandered at random, savouring the scent of polished wood and ageing books. Nick paused before a tramp sleeping soundly in front of Jeffcoate's *Principles of Gynaecology*, opened at the chapter on Intersex.

"Here we are: the awakened nation swigging knowledge."

"If you carry on like this, I'm going out…" Janet said, taking down *North Brompton Metropolitan Borough: Official Brochure* from the shelf.

The Preface informed them that North Brompton had a population of 60,000 and that it covered an area of nearly 10,256 acres. Sections of the guide had such enticing headings as "Saxon to Superstore" and "Fort to New Town". Nick read out a description of the town's armorial bearings that gave a useful insight into the spirit of the place and its people.

"Per saltire vert and OR foun fer de Moline counter changed in fees point a fountain. CREST—issuing out of a Saxon crown per pale OR and vert a demi."

Janet told him to be quiet as the tramp was stirring out of his dream of fair androgynes.

North Brompton, they learned, had until recently been a prosperous light and middle engineering town, its main product locks and keys famous all over the world. Even now illicit desires in five continents were separated from their objects by stout Noes manufactured in this town.

"Here's something we mustn't miss," Nick said, eagerly turning the page. "A Modern Shopping Precinct! I bet you can buy all sorts of local craft articles there, like packets of cornflakes and pairs of socks and 4 inch screws. Touristy rubbish, I suppose, but it might be fun trying to beat down the prices."

They lingered over a photograph of Dewdrop Road. Its houses might once have been described as "typical workers' cottages" but were now part of a "Housing Action Area". A picture of North Brompton Library portrayed the very room they were sitting in. It showed several citizens in the upright position selecting improving material from an educational display. There were no slumbering tramps dreaming of the mysteries of Intersex. Also under "Amenities" there was a double page spread devoted to the new District General Hospital with full frontal views of the Russell Brain Institute of Neurological Sciences.

"I'm surprised they haven't got a mugshot of the Russell Brain's own superbrain, neurosurgical senior registrar, Robert H. Perkins, removing a genuine, homegrown North Brompton meningioma..."

"You know Robert Perkins, do you?" Janet asked, on this occasion looking at him.

"We were medical students together...Why, do *you* know him?"

"A bit...Well, I've heard of him."

"He was an arrogant, overweening, mononeuronally ambitious shit. I spoke to him on the phone the other day about a patient and I discovered that he hasn't changed a bit."

"'North Brompton has another hospital—the Royal Infirmary—which has served its people for many years and is shortly due to be closed,'" Janet read out. "So much for the poor old NBRI."

The closing pages of the brochure were devoted to proving

that North Brompton was well supplied with transport. There was a full page colour photograph of the intersection of the M64 with the M59 taken at night, showing on one side a thick streak of yellow headlights that had whizzed one way past North Brompton and one the other a thick streak of red tail lights that had whizzed past it the other way.

"They obviously felt that people needed reassurance that they could get out of the place when, after twenty or twenty-five minutes, they had exhausted its charms...Curious that there's no reference here to the proposed twinning arrangements with New York...Or was it with a Paris cemetery?"

"No reference either to your bubble gum machine. I hope you weren't making it up."

"You are responding so exactly to the spirit of the occasion that I should like to rack up sexual harassment three points on the Virago scale and kiss your hand."

"I think we ought to get out before we're thrown out."

Nick thanked their host for the opportunity to down a few at the Pierian Spring. He added that the quest for knowledge had no real end-point and was driven by a quenchless thirst.

The weather that greeted them when they came out of the library was spiteful rather than merely miserable. They walked down the High Street past shops whose names were familiar enough to excite no comment; indeed, they were so unexciting they actually threatened the very continuation of consciousness. Nick felt a portable abyss or two opening up. When Janet paused for no apparent reason by a woolshop, meaning itself seemed in danger of coming to an end in a smart but unfashionable twin-set worn by a headless dummy. Urgent action was necessary. He guided her to the central refuge between the two halves of a zebra crossing near the geographical, cultural and intellectual centre of the town.

"Sit down here," he commanded, wiping the top of a bollard with his scarf. "Now, look at those. They never mentioned them in the brochure." He pointed to the cloud-hung sky. "Cumulus are my favourite variety. What about you?"

"My favourite, too," Janet said, raising her voice above the traffic that made the now-wet street hiss at them. "Boulders carved from mist."

"That sounds too polished for bollard talk to me. That's rehearsed." She made a little moue which, although a citation, looked especially attractive in the cherry-red of the newly lit sodium lamps. "Just look at that fine specimen above Kwik Save yonder. Like one of those gorgeous, uninsurably overweight Rubens nudes." He closed his eyes and recited:

"Her ample boobs (a satyr's Christmas gift)
From myths derive their bra-less underlift;
And though she over-fills her full-lipped face
Her mighty bum's redeemed by classic grace..."

"So you really *do* like women with big bottoms, then?" Janet enquired, shifting hers a little on the bollard.

"*Some* women, *some* big bottoms. The girl who smashed my happiness had a medium-sized bottom, I think. But, of course, desire, as opposed to appetite, does not resolve its object into material components. Now what I particularly like about cumulus is the way it is both vague and edged."

"A chiselled mist?"

"That's very good! We ought to pool our metaphors."

"Two minds with but a single text," Janet said, dismounting from the bollard and wiping the moisture off her jeans.

"Our four eyes become one gaze, our two I's one we, our two wees one wet patch."

"If only, it were possible...." she said, rather absently.

"Specify the ghastly facts that make your conditional apparently counterfactual."

"What about this tour of North Brompton? I thought you were going to make me see this town 'as if for the first time'."

"She said with characteristic elusiveness, thus furnishing this unhaunted midshire town with a carnal symbol of the discarnate lost insight that haunted him."

"I'm frozen."

"I distinctly heard your ovaries crack. It is now opening time. Well past. Let's go to The Spider Naevus."

"I'd rather we didn't."

"All right, I know somewhere we can go and not be seen."

"How perceptive of you."

"Life serves up the same rather simple plots without embarrassment, year in and year out."

A series of navigation errors ensured that their journey took in a Housing Action Area and a Modern Shopping Precinct. Seeing them in real life after reading about them in the brochure was, Nick said, like experiencing a dream come true.

"An especially intriguing feature of the shopping precinct is the way in which it transforms a mild October breeze into a revved up zephyr of extraordinary malignity so that chip papers, crisp packets and dust that might otherwise lie rather listlessly on the floor become quite animated."

Janet realised the extent of her guide's unreliability only when they passed a Victorian building with "AN AWAKENED NATION WILL HAVE A THIRST FOR KNOWLEDGE" chiselled over its entrance arch.

"Where are we trying to get to?"

"Kevin's Wine Bar."

"Yuk."

"No like?"

"It's a ghastly pseud place. But I'm not going to argue with you because it's cold and wet outside."

"Beautiful effect the rain has on the town, don't you think? See how the sodium light on the wet tarmac looks like spilt marmalade."

"Your remarks are beginning to wear me down. You're worse than attention-seeking: you're *concentration*-seeking. We turn left just past this church. You realise that we're just at the back of the NBRI."

"Of course! Our Lady of the (Groundless) Assumption."

"Your colleague Dr McAdam goes to mass here."

"I suspected he might be a sucker for a nice introitus. I'm told they do a very good Body and Blood of Christ there, though you've got to arrive early if you want the best cut."

"We cross over here. I used to believe in God myself."

"He probably used to believe in you. I wonder how you became disillusioned with each other?"

"Here we are. Kevin's Wine Bar."

Nick saw at once that it was a place that he, too, could quickly get to loathe. The menu chalked on a blackboard, the meaningless fish-net scrotum hanging from a nail and containing two glass balls, the display of chickweed salad and other vegan tripe on the counter, posters advertising agitprop plays, a large notice board—where the concerned, the committed, the engaged, the embattled, the oppressed, the gay and the glum advertised their wares or their woes—all dovetailed in Nick's gorge and made it rise. He waited for some considerable time while a voluminous female in a personalised marquee concluded a phone call. He read various notices inviting him to A NATURAL DANCE WORKSHOP, A MEDITATION (WITHIN YOU, WITHOUT YOU) WEEKEND, and to A PROCTERITE MOVEMENT COURSE. Massage, reflexological therapies, yoga, flower remedies for common health problems (like cardiac arrest) and a variety of diets were also on offer. Ye mountebank, bearing the promise of Health, Happiness and Hampstead in ten year old wrappings, was alive and well even in North Brompton.

The notice board awoke memories Nick would have preferred to have forgotten. They reached back to his teens and early twenties: to the early Seventies and joss sticks and pot and radical talk; to ghastly individuals whose self-importance so outweighed their wit and intelligence, never mind their actual value to the world at large, that they were simply unable to notice how boring they were or were quite unashamed about it; and to earnest available girls who were transformed by the event of ejaculation from their exciting bodies to their dull minds and dim selves.

The woman was still on the phone.

"She's brought it on herself...Yes...It's awful...But you mustn't let yourself get all knotted up over it...She's alienated everyone who's tried to help her...Yes. I've tried like all the others...Someone should tell her...It just perpetuates ill-feeling."

Here was a Caring Human Being, rounded in spirit as well

as in body and haberdashery, who recognised no alienating division between work and her personal life. Nick's heart sank.

"Excuse me," Nick said. "Do you mind if I nip into the kitchen and make myself something to eat. I'm famished."

"Adrienne, I'll have to go. There's somebody wants something. I'll ring you back in a few minutes."

"I feel jolly bad about wrecking your conversation."

She took his order in that no-nonsense manner that makes nonsense very attractive. He ordered two pizzas, two bowls of fresh fruit salad and cream and a large carafe of red wine. The aim was to get it all over at once, as he didn't wish to interrupt another phone call. You can provoke people so far and then they snap and he didn't wish to be around when the patronne lost her guy-rope. He took his carafe of table wine to the table Janet had selected. An uncomfortable white-painted wooden chair received his descending bottom. The table rocked on its unequal legs. A few dead roses in an empty wine bottle completed the bistroid air of informality. He poured out two tumblers full of rot gut and, wincing at the first dysphoric mouthful, challenged Janet to explain why she disliked such a charming place.

"It's pseud, isn't it? The sticks trying to be Hampstead and failing."

"My dear Janet, the sticks is everywhere. Even Hampstead isn't a tor on consciousness giving it a definitive overview of itself."

"Well, it's provincial, then."

"What's wrong with the provinces? Here, in the white spaces on the map, birth is as miraculous as in that senseless agglutination of overgrown villages that calls itself London. Orgasm is as all-engrossing here as it is one hundred and fifty miles away. Suffering is as extreme, death as absolute. Fire is as hot; and here, just as in Hampstead, all the fire engines are called DENNIS…"

"You're quoting from the Town Guide."

"Yes, from the section entitled 'Two Contrasting Intellectual Traditions', where it also compares North Brompton with Paris, very much to the advantage of the former."

"Two pizzas," the patronne announced.

"Granted, the nearest thing this town has to a restaurant

requires you to bring your own ambience and even then they charge you corkage on it. Nevertheless," Nick said, pointing with a speared fragment of pizza (it had the consistency of an Arizona cowpat at the end of the dry season), "you couldn't say that any place where people—as in Our Lady of the (Groundless) Assumption—eat their own gods is *dull.* So don't knock the provinces. We are all equidistant from eternity and the centre of reality…Now, since you've almost finished your pizza and I've scarcely begun mine, why don't you tell me a bit more about yourself."

She talked about her nursing career, mainly, Nick suspected, to avoid talking about matters of greater interest. Her immediately prior post had been that of Incontinence Advisor to the North West London District Health Authority.

"You ought to write your memoirs: *All Creatures Wet and Dry.* Why did you give it up?"

"Personal reasons."

"Very uninformative. Though, I have to admit, even non-referential discourse can excite when it issues from someone candle-lit, smiling and structurally sound who looks as beautiful as you do at this moment. I could almost eat your peachy face instead of this ideologically sound pizza free of monosodium glutamate and anything that could be mistaken for flavour…You have carefully omitted to say anything about the rôle played in your life by those who tout the XY chromosome pair."

"It's your turn to talk now, while I eat my pudding."

"If you insist. For a start, you ought to know that I come from a very old family. We are connected to primal slime by an unbroken line of primogeniture. The Pages were one of the first forms of life to change over from RNA to DNA. So much for my ancestry. As for my life, anything I might say about it would be a crude paraphrase—like the *Blue Peter* version of *Of Grammatology*—and would do little justice to the felt life or to the rich foliage of my accumulated memories…"

"I find it difficult to imagine you having parents," Janet said, licking the cream off her spoon. The relish with which her tongue performed its task lit a small fire in the north-west corner of his void.

"Imagining the actual is always the most exacting of the tasks that a citizen's consciousness sets itself. Coffee?"

"I'll get the coffee. I've had enough street theatre for one day."

Nick studied her as she waited to be served and the patronne finished her resumed phone call. A tall, pretty girl with long thighs and a comfortable bottom. She was not Susie; and, as not-Susie, she was part of The Absence of Susie. The occasion, attenuated by that absence, suddenly lost its roundedness, its fullness.

"The plot thins," he thought to himself as Janet returned.

"This place *is* bloody pseud. That woman behind the counter is *so* affected…as well as being rude. And incompetent. She can't even pour coffee without filling the saucer as well."

"Affected? The use of such a term presupposes a rather naïve conception of the origin and nature of behaviour. The 'authentic' self, far from being the authentic origin of our behaviour, is itself a tropological construct…Perhaps this becomes apparent only to those who have lost that comfort and who know that the talking self is but a hollow hollering."

Janet busied herself sopping up the coffee spilt in the saucers, using a recycled paper leaflet bearing a few recycled ideas.

"I mean the woman behind the counter there probably is a caring person—but she has to act it as well, to signal it to herself. Like the rest of us, she has to dramatise what she is in order to bring her life nearer to generality and hence to the ideality and sharp-edgedness of articulated thought. Just a few minutes ago, *you* were trying to round off your situation by calling North Brompton 'provincial' and so identifying yourself as being 'holed up in exile', a situation that has a long literary tradition behind it. We want, my dear Janet, oh so desperately, to be words. As for the self we are trying to be (which, as Fichte said, is an act not a fact), it is but the shadow cast by the language in which we conceive of it. What am I but the text I weave over the world in which I am cast?"

"You have gone awfully serious and awfully unoriginal all of a sudden. I suddenly feel as if I am back at university, listening to an undergraduate who, like you, assumes I haven't read the sources you are pinching your ideas from. Funny how men use other people's ideas to chat up women with."

"The table wine has gone to my head and replaced my natural gaiety of soul by an inferior plastic humour."

"So where are you heading, Dr Page? What's the game plan?" she said, leaning forward a little, consenting to the interdigitation of his digits and hers. "I didn't sugar the coffee, by the way."

"Like every other male, I wish to be enormously successful, greatly admired and slept with by the absolute best of copulanda."

"So what's gone wrong?"

"I am a howling lost soul, unhinged by a worthless woman. Also I have a touch of indigestion from a progressive but ill-cooked pizza."

"So you have been laid low by a worthless woman and have thrown up your magnificent career. Is that it?"

"Stunning Haematology technician throws over the author of such papers as *The Epidemiology and Mechanism of Senile Purpura* for an oligophrenic twerp who drives highly tuned cars by day and highly untuned guitars at night. Or a brainless Beach Boy who couldn't tell the difference between a strangulated hernia and hairy cell leukaemia. Both of them loaded of course but thick as scyballa."

"Have *you* never made anyone unhappy?"

"I think it's about time we started talking about you."

"A sensitive point?"

"The folk theory about the scar tissue that forms in broken hearts is that it has hypersensitive nerve endings."

"Scar tissue can be insensitive, too."

"Tell me how useful you found the moral code you learnt from Brown Owl when it came to dealing with the social consequences of the fact that your eternal soul had been packaged for its journey through space-time in such a delicious body."

"Pass."

"All right, try this one: are you happy?"

"Yes, most of the time."

"Christ. There's only one thing more boring than a male and that's a contented female."

"You don't really like women do you?"

"Susie has taken away the idea of the future and left me imprisoned in an eternal present moment."

"The boundress! And there hasn't been anyone else since?"

"There have been others, of course. But they are or were only spars of wood to cling on to after the shipwreck."

"Is that how *they* see their place in your life?"

"A case of any portal in a storm. More table wine: it has been fermented from some of the most polished tables. Let us cup on till the world spin."

She occluded her glass with a long-fingered, elegant hand. The smooth dorsum was still lightly tanned from the summer.

"I really ought to be going fairly soon."

"But it's only 9.30," he said, genuinely dismayed and dismayed at his genuine dismay.

"I'm on an early tomorrow and that means being up at six."

"On that feeble note of excuse, let us take our leave of this diverticulum and launch our vivid unoccasioned selves upon a startled and more deeply unoccasioned North Brompton."

"I must pop to the ladies. How much is my share?"

"You pay next time."

"You're assuming there *is* going to be a next time?"

"I should say that was implicit in my statement, yes."

She looked down at the table in a way that maximised the potential that the peach-bloom of her cheeks had for causing suffering. Nick knew he was going to hear something that would underline the basic philosophical truth that to be placed is to be exiled.

"I've got news for you mate…I'm almost engaged."

"So *that's* why you were holding back on the XY front. 'Almost' engaged. He's bought the ring and you've said yes-ish."

"It's not quite as clear cut as that. We've been going out a good while."

"A bloody medic, I suppose."

"Yes. You know him. You were at St Jidgey's together."

"Don't say any more. I wish you well…"

She looked up at him, her mouth parted in a slight smile that left her white teeth just off stage. As, later on, he thought back over this moment, he imagined that there was at least as much embarrassment as triumph in the polysemous expression on her face.

"Don't you want to know who it is?"

"I can guess. But I'd better warn you: if you marry Perkins, you won't marry a neurosurgeon, you'll marry neurosurgery. You'll be fitted round the edges of his eighteen-hour working day. Every time one of you is going to have an orgasm his bleep will go off and he won't ignore it."

"I get the feeling that you're not the sort of person who would be very graceful in defeat."

As they left Kevin's, they were met by a light but wetting rain. The wind had dropped: meteorological spite had given way to wingeing. He linked his arm with hers and they wandered past a series of terms—Marks & Spencers, Woolworths, Dixons, Tesco—that added up to no statement whatsoever. The High Street, North Brompton was an ideal correlative of his inner void. Angered, he remembered the cardboard landscape of rhetoric.

"You look no less beautiful for being attached to Robert Perkins. But then beauty, being essentially structural, can survive almost any behavioural aberration apart from not sticking to a diet." She wasn't responding—indeed appeared to be distracted by the items in the meaningless fluorescent-lit windows they were passing. He gave up. "Since you think the night is no longer young, I suppose we ought to head back to base camp by the shortest route…"

She turned to look at him.

"The night isn't *too* old," she said, softly.

"It bloody is. What you told me in Kevin's has aged it horribly."

She took his hand into her warm, long-fingered one.

"*Really* so old?"

"Your touch has suddenly rejuvenated it."

"I could manage one quickish drink," she said.

The Cock and Bottle was not a good choice, even for one squiring a Continence Advisor. The beer owed what little flavour it had to the washing up liquid left on the glasses and conversation was a shouting match against the so-called background music. Janet's revelation about Robert seemed to solve her in a rather disappointing way. In a quiet moment while the juke box reloaded its magazine, she yawned a three-note yawn.

"A missing fragment of Palestrina?"

"Actually, I really am tired. I was on an early this morning as well."

"Why do people want to sleep so much? After the first ninety minutes, it's mere repetition, as the EEG demonstrates."

As they walked back hand in hand he began to desire her continuing company more intensely. It had stopped raining and there was a clear, starry sky.

"I suppose I ought to talk to you about the firmament," Nick began.

But they were already entering the main gates of the NBRI.

"Good evenin' doctor, good evenin', Sister."

"Oscar! Don't jump out like that. I thought it was the darkness talking."

"Guilty conscience, eh doctor? Switchboard been looking for you earlier. No less than two young ladies tryin' to speak with you on the telephone."

"Thank you. Good night, Oscar."

"Good night, doctor. Good night, Sister."

"Thus begins the rumour that will turn our evening together into a night together. Having an affair in this place would be like walking around with your underpants outside your trousers. You let go of my hand pretty smartish, didn't you? As if Oscar's voice were the current and my just-widowed paw the terminal."

"Too bloody right," Janet said.

They came to a potential parting of their ways.

"Coffee?" he asked.

"It has been a nice evening."

"Your choice of the perfect tense implies that it is perfected in the sense of being finished."

"Yes, though we never got to see that bubble-gum machine. I wonder if it really exists."

"We're going to have a mess party soon. I do hope you'll…"

She came close to him, brushed her lips against his and, before he could encircle her with his arms, vanished through the swing doors into the Nurses' Home.

He stared at the doors for a while, watching the sentence "PLEASE KEEP CLOSED IN CASE OF FIRE" split at the caesura, its two halves move away from one another, hold aloof, race towards union, connect, break, connect, break, connect; and break until the doors shivered to a halt and the sentence, trembling, quiesced to completeness, leaving him outside of them, in the kingdom of words, negation and absence.

Part Two

Think on me,
That am with Phoebus' amorous pinches
black,
And wrinkled deep in time.

Chapter six

On the London train, he drank and thought. And thought and drank again. What would he say to Felicity? He summoned up her face—full lips, dark eyes, neat nose—and saw the wounded expression that would greet him at the station. She was probably thinking about him now, annoyed that he had got the later train. So he was thinking about her who was thinking about him who was thinking about her. The idea of this infinite regression of mutual reflections passing back and forth between their consciousnesses, refracted through five cans of Brewmaster, made him feel giddy. And depressed. Behind his depression was not so much pity for Felicity as despair over his own exclusion from Susie. What a mess. He thought and drank. And drank and thought. And drank.

He took out her letter. It had arrived yesterday but, recognising her scrawl on the front, he had postponed reading it. She was bound to ask him what he thought about its contents, so he needed to do his homework. On the other hand, he didn't want to have to skim through it twice. Felicity's letters would have benefited from a 250-word abstract on page one.

The contents were rather as he had expected: her side of one of their telephone calls dashed down verbatim. He skipped large tracts.

> Florence Nightingale Nurses' Home
> St Jidgey's Hospital
> LONDON WSW 24
> Wednesday
>
> Dearest Nick,
>   ...You see (and I may as well be honest) I've got a horrible feeling that I don't matter to you as much as you matter to me and that while you're getting on with your life, I'm just enduring mine, waiting for you. I know I shouldn't say this, because it'll only put you off.
>   [*Pages and pages*]
>   ...It was ghastly saying goodbye at Euston. I wish you hadn't been drunk. I don't want to nag you but I wanted to feel close to you and you kept cracking jokes and larking about. I suppose you wanted to cheer me up but it did make me wonder whether it was only me who needed cheering up and you felt cheerful enough already.
>   [*Pages and pages*]
>   I often go to the station just to sit there and have a cup of tea because it was the last place where we saw each other. It seems to bring me closer to you, though the Sunday afternoon after we had parted was absolutely ghastly.

The letter continued for dozens more pages. Felicity's biro scrawl got wilder and wilder. He took a long draught of Brewmaster. And thought. He offered the end-product of his meditation to the girl sitting opposite him, mainly because she was attractive but also because she was reading an article in the *Nursing Times* on the management of incontinence.

"Compared with the pain of loss, compared with the hope and misery and joy of anticipation, compared with the despair of yet again being fobbed off by the elusiveness of the other, possession is a kind of blurred daze, isn't it? As Marcel Proust demonstrated at such appalling length, the actual present—the now of fulfilment—is fatally flawed. Don't you agree?"

Nurse Anon's only response was to shrug her shoulders and to snuggle deeper into her article on 'A Rational Approach to Urinary Incontinence' which, Nick was interested to notice, had been written by a certain Sister Janet Parker SRN, BA, until lately, South East Convener of the Association of Incontinence Advisers. It was one of a series of six, the last two of which were to be devoted to an equally rational approach to Faecal Incontinence. Janet seemed to be carving a nice little niche for herself in the sphincters.

Nick sighed. His other letter proved to be the *St Jidgey's Gazette*. There was to be an appeal for a memorial to the recently deceased Lord Stool. Nick had been his houseman and his spirits had been almost extinguished by the man's exasperating irrationality and rudeness. It was a pleasant surprise to discover that he had died: one tends to assume that the really ghastly things in life are irremediable and go on for ever. He discovered on the next page that they do: the expired physician's successor was the poisonous Roger Machin, appointed at the very early age of thirty-two.

The *Gazette* contained a brief biography of Machin, summarising his career at St Jidgey's and elsewhere, his prizes, his research interests, his extensive publications and his hobbies. His personality, his private life and his real interests, all well known to Nick, were not referred to. Nick had once, unknown to himself, 'collaborated' with Machin on a piece of research related to clotting disorders.

The original idea had been Nick's; Nick had drawn up the research protocol and had secured Ethical Committee approval; Nick had obtained the blood specimens, analysed them and drawn the conclusions from the results; and Nick had written the paper. Machin had once briefly discussed the project with him and had looked at the finished paper. He had changed one sentence (for the worse) and, while Nick was away on holiday, had sent it off to *Clot*, an international journal devoted to the study of blood coagulation. When the paper appeared and was subsequently quoted, it was attributed to Machin et al and not to Page et al. Nick, enraged, had approached the "principal author". Machin, affecting astonishment at Nick's protestations, had accused him of paper-grubbing and pleaded alphabetical order.

Nick soothed his resurgent rage by composing an alternative biographical note:

> Roger Machin's real interests lie outside of medicine and include balling nurses, scoring off ex-wives, getting disgustingly drunk and insulting people whose ideas he has stolen or whose lives he has wrecked. He also enjoys engaging in violent and futile arguments with opponents who are in vulnerable positions. He has woven patients, senior and junior colleagues and taxpayers into a doormat placed on the threshold of his self-advancement. He will be a worthy successor to the late Lord Stool.

A piece for the St Jidgey's Christmas Show? The thought struck Nick that he would not be part of St Jidgey's next Christmas. It was quite probable that he had burned his boats. He sighed again, looked out of the window and rummaged around in his mind for less provincial causes for gloom but came back to his guilt over Felicity. Jidge not that ye be not jidged. He mentally addressed his travelling companion.

"The Home Counties look beautiful in late autumn. But I've told far too many lies to enjoy this view. How about you?" Nurse Anon read on, unaware of his silent soliloquy, thus confirming the notion of the privileged access of the thinker to his thoughts. It was a privilege he would gladly have foregone. "Guilt plays merry hell with one's negative capability don't you find? To be receptive to other than carnal beauty one needs to be inwardly at ease. Otherwise its tranquillity merely provides a surface in which one's sins are reflected. What's the remedy? An enema? A bed bath?"

As if she could hear his thoughts, Nurse Anon folded away her *Nursing Times*, collected her bits and pieces and walked away. The train was slowing down. Time, Nick thought, to find his luggage.

Felicity was waiting, as arranged, by the expanded polystyrene effigy of Britannia in the station buffet. She looked cross. She was also, of course, not Susie.

"I've bought you a present." He handed her his last can of Brewmaster.

"You're late," she said.

"I forgot to wind up my sundial. Give us a kiss."

She consented to be kissed though she did not cooperate sufficiently for him to be able to home in on mucous membrane. His lips brushed the comparatively impersonal epidermis of her forehead and encountered the corrugations appropriate to her crossness. If he had bent down it could have been a lip to lip job but five cans of Brewmaster had undermined dynamic standing balance.

"Why are you so late?" she asked.

"What do you expect me to do? Run ahead of the train?"

"You said you would be on the 3.30."

"I happened to be on the payroll of the NBRI when a citizen of North Brompton fell ill."

"I thought you were off early today."

"Someone had a cardiac arrest in Casualty when I was on my way out. I couldn't ask him to put his decomposition on hold till I got back on Monday."

"But you're not the only doctor in the hospital surely."

He put down his bags and spread out his arms in a gesture of helplessness especially imported from the Mediterranean.

"They looked to me for practical help. I couldn't refuse them. I did try to ring you from New Street."

"And you're drunk as well. You were drunk when we said goodbye."

"Also on railway property. It must be the romance of steam...So I'm late and I'm drunk. Right, that's my best points covered..."

"Thank God you're here," she said.

He kissed her again and this time she returned his embrace. She looked up at him. As their tongues met, he had a mild attack of vertigo. She withdrew and, rubbing her thumb over his palm, as if to exacerbate his consciousness of her and sharpen her own appreciation of the actuality of his presence, looked at him with her dark brown conjugate eyes. Her small hand drew attention to her short stature. Although she had a full mouth and full breasts (which, of course, she drowned far too often in loosely fitting sweaters), these did not compensate for her being utterly other than Susie. And her long brown hair, down almost to the sixth thoracic vertebra when he had last checked, only made her seem, when naked, abbreviated—like the Tenniel Alice. He could not remember when he had desired her without his desire being qualified by his noticing that she was not-fair-haired, not-long-legged, in summary, not-Susie. It was qualified further on this occasion by an outfit that was supposed to look jaunty and/or chic, though in his ill-informed opinion it looked ridiculous.

"Hey, what about my causal net stockings, then?"

"You wait and see," she said awkwardly assuming a posture of sexual mischief.

"To make up for my being late, let's forego your Cordon Noir and eat in that super little restaurant in Greek Street, just by The Ascitic Tap."

In the taxi, and then in the restaurant, she was lovey-dovey and he was lusty-dusty. Affection and appetite share the same ambiguous vocabulary of intimacy, so that she who wished to enter his life and he who wished only to enter her body could use the same signs and interact harmoniously. This state of affairs was maintained when they arrived at Felicity's room in the Nurses' Home. Boozed and weary but still driven by his sub-cortex, he made rapidly advancing love to her, the search for heightened sensation seeming like the sealing of a bond. In passing, he inspected the love bite he had implanted a few weeks earlier on the lower median quadrant of her generous but shortly to be meaningless left breast.

"It's almost gone," she said.

"There's still a tinge of bilirubin. What a perfect clock to measure the days of our mutual absence: the seamless, soundless, tickless healing of a wound inflicted on your body by mine!"

His voice under the blankets addressed not her face but her smooth trunk as he hand-combed her classic triangle of dense, brown hair. He observed the marks left by her knicker elastic—treadmark on an incipient spare tyre—with sadness. The imprint of her vulnerable person on a desirable body that was shortly to become a vulnerable person.

"This last fortnight has seemed like eternity," he heard her say, as she stroked the hair on his vertex.

"Space and time are the staves of the cross upon which we lovers are crucified," he replied taking a nipple into his mouth.

"Nick, why didn't you phone me back the other night?"

"Reasons," he said mumbling wearily, his mouth full of breast.

"What reasons?" The questioning was gentle but persistent.

He emptied his mouth so that he could articulate clearly.

"There was an infinite number of things I might have said and I found it impossible to choose between them. So I came in person. This—my carnal presence—is the sum total of all possible phone calls. After all, a phone call is only a fading zig-zag line drawn across an absence, a geodesic traced on snow-white nothing. While this," he said, suddenly transferring to her right breast, "is my presence."

And he gave her a long, wincing mouth-pinch, a fresh love bite to replace the one fading on the other breast. She took his head in her hands and drew him up.

"I want to look at you and see you looking at me," she said.

There seemed to be anguish, rather than delight, in her face lit by the light creeping under the door from the corridor outside.

He felt a sudden panic of emptiness, loneliness, exclusion and exile that cut through his fatigue, his boozed stupor, his aroused appetites and his entanglement of talk. He was not really present here at all. He was only in flight from absence, absent from absence. If he *were* here, with this woman, it was by a process of double negation: not not-here. He withdrew his gaze and finished imprinting the stigma on her breast.

"Another tickless clock to measure the march of passion to its doom."

"Stop it," Felicity said, squirming with pleasurable discomfort. "You're a devil."

"Last week I saw a spectacular example of the love bites planted by the devil. The devil's pinches or death's love bites planted on an old woman's body by the agents of her own future absence. And yet we call the devil Lucifer—the bearer of *light*."

"Let me see your face again," she said. He complied. "I love you."

"I love you too," he responded, mentioning rather than using the phrase, thinking dazedly to himself that the felicity conditions of the corresponding performative were not such as Felicity could provide.

He aligned himself but not as much happened as either would have liked. Until that moment, Nick had always thought that ejaculation was the sincerest and most spontaneous form of self-expression. And now it had suddenly become an act he could not perform. My God, he was falling apart. Help, however, lay to hand, or to mouth.

"Fellated by Felicity in the fell of night," he murmured enjoying a positively Parisian play of signifiers as the necessary structural alterations were brought about and he was able to operate to their rather separate satisfactions.

So, after the words, the flesh. And then sweet vacancy, quiescence between the end of the flesh and the resumption of words: no absence, no presence, self-mated complete. But after the flesh, the words again: after orgasm, sleep; and after sleep, rows.

And there were plenty of those.

They had a row because Nick, headachy and nauseated, didn't feel like getting out of bed until 1 p.m. on Saturday. "See how time sours Brewmaster to Spewmaster," he said feebly as Felicity scolded him for wanting to sleep away the short, and therefore precious, time they had to spend together. They had a row because Felicity insisted on wearing her new trouser suit and jaunty beret and Nick admitted to a reluctance to being seen in one of the world's great capital cities escorting a master sergeant from Fred Carno's army. They had a row because Nick wanted to buy some perfume and Felicity didn't believe that it was intended for an elderly woman who sported a twenty-four carat Heberden's node on her index finger. They had a row because Felicity wanted to go to a disco on Saturday night and

Nick, still washed out from the week's excesses, expressed a preference for a few pints at The Caput Medusae and early bed. There were other rows on Sunday morning. As row succeeded row, Nick's contributions became less witty, airy and metaphysical and more directly relevant to what seemed to be emerging as their point. By the time they came to the culminating row just before Sunday lunch, he was primed with all the necessary aggression to reply to Felicity's searching questions with the brutal answers she had dreaded. Extracts from this final row are printed below:

> STIMULUS: "You're just using me, aren't you?"
> RESPONSE: "Yes, I *do* use you. What would you prefer me to do? Pay for each item of service?..."
> s: "You never really give a straight answer to a question."
> R: "If I *do* evade the point, I do so only to protect you from the truth."
> s: "You won't even discuss where we're going to. What we are all about."
> R: "Well, we're not heading towards a ring, if that's what you mean. I'm not the marrying kind. And you're quite right, you're not the only girl in my life..."
> s: "I don't understand you. I don't know what you want out of life."
> R: "That makes two of us."
> s: "I can see right through you. You just want sex without responsibility."
> R: "I'm sure you *can* see right through me. No great achievement when I am utterly hollow..."

He felt especially guilty after this row and begged forgiveness as they ate a ploughman's in The Ruptured Varix. Felicity remained sad but, with parting coming nearer, was no longer angry.

"What *is* the matter with you, Nick dearest?" she asked, taking his hand with her antithesis of Susie's.

"I'm in hell," he unexplained briefly, washing a shard of French bread down with the last of his fourth pint. She naturally wanted to know more. He only repeated his assertion, without elaboration.

"Please tell me," she said, her squeezing hand expressing urgency and unwittingly italicising Nick's situation.

"I can't."

"It's that woman, isn't it, the one you bought the perfume for yesterday."

Nick's stagey hollow laughter triggered more tears. He proferred his paper napkin to launder her eyes and nose.

"You can eat it afterwards 'cos it's rice paper."

She smiled through a tear-blasted face.

They arrived at Euston earlier than his train required.

"Time for a coffee."

They went into the buffet where, as so often happened, Felicity turned choice into dilemma. There were several vacant places but each had different advantages and disadvantages.

"Once you understand the basic principle," Nick said, impatiently, "it really doesn't matter where we sit."

"And what is the basic principle?"

"That Life, Felicity dear, is a standing offer of thirty-two varieties of Dayville ice cream to a man dying of hypothermia. Our choice of table is of no consequence, because they all face reality. Sit down there while I get the coffees."

"I'm going to miss you terribly," Felicity said, stirring her coffee.

"Savour this moment, then, while we are still co-present, able to hear and speak to each other. Enjoy the sunlight—the present moment, radiant now…" He was conscious, as he spoke, of the carnassials of absence gnawing at him, blunted only by the beer he had drunk. His being here was merely a condition of being not-there—where Susie was. Here was an elsewhere to which he had been banished.

"What are you going to do on the journey?"

"Study the vista while I get pisseder and pisseder and try to suppress the knowledge that the fields and towns the train is racing through are being inserted between my hands and your breasts.

That British Rail is placing a dozen counties between my dong and your..."

"Are you ever serious?"

"Only if something has gone seriously wrong and I find myself sober."

"When did that last happen?"

"Right now I'm too pissed to remember."

The queue of people with trays waiting to be served brought on an attack of the North Brompton High Street malaise.

"I mustn't start crying again. My face looks sufficiently wrecked already."

"Nonsense," Nick said, noticing a large pimple that had appeared on her forehead.

"My scalp feels itchy. How quickly we seem to have got from Friday when my hair was just washed and bouncy and airy to Sunday when it's all greasy again. It would be so much easier if I knew how long you were going to be up north."

"I don't know what's going to happen..."

"Everybody thinks so highly of you at St Jidgey's."

"*Thought* highly of me."

"I can't understand why you left St Jidgey's when you did. One day I shall understand, I suppose. You might even let me into the secrets of your private life," she added pointedly.

She squeezed his hand harder still to bring him to order. She wanted to part on a moment of closeness not on the flurry of wise-cracks she expected.

They kissed as the train drew in. More precisely, she kissed him, exploring his mouth with her tongue.

"You *will* write?" she appealed. His heavenward gaze signified the redundancy of her question. "Now I'm going because I can't bear to see the train leave the station."

"Nor I the station leave the train. Give my love to our ticket collector and tell him how I cannot resist men in uniform. It's the clash between the formal haberdashery and the natural flesh, between labour and desire..."

"Shut up," she said, tears streaming down her face.

"Take care."

"Another can of Brewmaster, please. It's a monstrous labour when I wash my brain and it grows fouler," he confided to the bar person.

The other customer in the buffet, a large-eared simple soul, further simplified by alcoholic beverages, leant towards Nick.

"Good stuff this," he said, indicating the can he had just emptied. The bar person, who had had rather an excess of the simple soul's random remarks, seized this opportunity to conclude their conversation.

"Why don't you clear those tables for me?" The lad complied, eager to oblige such a personable person. "You seem a bit down in the dumps," she said to Nick. Sympathetic as well as personable.

"Very perceptive of you. Last spring I met a girl who since then has done to my soul what Generals Ludendorff and Haig did to the Belgian landscape."

"Upset you, has she?"

"I am living a posthumous existence. Will you accept a drink from a dead man?"

"Thank you. I'll just take 20p."

Nick poured his Brewmaster into a large plastic cup.

"Yes, she upset me. Since Susie—for that is the young lady's name—I have been exiled from true joy. All pleasures are merest licks of gold paint splashed on a black absence which ashes all meaning."

"Here you are, Miss," said the simple soul.

"Thank you." She was not pleased to see his early return to the bar.

"Here," Nick said to the simple soul, "have a drink on me and listen while I ram my fruitful tidings in your Jodrell Bank ears and pour a pack of matter into thy pink-tipped pinnae. Let your *coeur simple* learn from me that there is never a fair woman has a true face."

"Rubbish," said the bar person. "Who's ordered the Welsh?"

"Mine," said a large, silver-haired man in a Hector Powe suit. "And may I look at the wine list, please?"

"No slander, they steal hearts. And since Susie stole mine I have lost that appetite for life that was born with me. Her absence gnaws through the very roots of delight."

"You must learn to forget her. There isn't a list. There's red and white."

"A bottle of the house red, please."

"Forget her!" Nick said, shouting against the racket of railway points, "You have absolutely no idea what you're saying. To forget her would tantamount to consigning myself to self-oblivion and the spirit-rotting sugary consolations of Monday, Tuesday, Wednesday. To lose the deepest and sharpest sense of myself and become an any-one accumulating anydays staling towards the local authority's flamy solution to the dull conundrum of my life."

"Sorry I spoke. That'll be four pounds twenty-seven pence, please."

"Your intention was kind. Let me explain: whenever I try to lose myself in some external object—let us say an old sunlit wall or the uncovered breasts of a recently qualified nurse—I feel only weariness of mind and body, foredooming any attempt to break out into the great sunlight of presence beyond my great grief at her absence. There is nothing left in me that can take wing…Only insomnia, duty, habit, staleness and, above all, that pathetic bird on a wire called rhetoric."

"Who's next? You ought to see a doctor."

"Don't make me laugh. I *am* a doctor."

"Two toasted sandwiches, a coffee and a tea please."

"Cheese, ham, ham and tomato or ham and cheese? Seriously, doctors can sometimes be quite helpful."

"I laugh because I *am* a doctor."

"I don't believe you," the bar person said, sufficiently interested to press for proof. "Milk and sugar's on the counter there. Help yourself."

Nick produced his banker's card which she inspected.

"But you could be a doctor of anything," the simple soul—using, Nick thought, his entire nerve net in synchronous activity—pointed out. He seemed to have logged back into the conversation.

"Indeed," Nick conceded "of philosophy or car park management."

"There's some glasses over there…Would you mind collecting them for me?" the bar person said to the simple soul, reaffirming his status as superfluous third party. She leant forward over the bar, which was temporarily empty of customers. *Mezza voce* she asked: "Do you know anything about piles?"

"In the north, as you probably know, they are regarded as something of a delicacy. Actually, dear, I never mix business and pleasure. Looking at you is pleasure but discussing your piles is strictly business."

"*I* had to listen to *your* troubles."

"But then, as Patience Strong so tellingly remarked, The Lover's Discourse exists only in outbursts of language which occur at the whim of trivial, of aleatory circumstances. Or is this true also of The Pilebearer's Discourse? Patience Strong does not touch on piles."

The impasse was resolved by the arrival of a middle-aged woman in uniform followed by a division of young children, also in uniform: a Brown Owl and her crack troops.

"Fourteen toasted cheese sandwiches, please."

It was an indirect reminder that, although he was going away from London and hence away from even the remote possibility of Susie, he was also travelling towards Janet.

The rest of the journey was uneventful. The most notable of its non-events was catching sight of Welldorm in time to avoid him. Welldorm's table was almost as freighted with paper as the mahogany desk in the NBRI. Several fat timetables were open in front of him. The idea of Welldorm checking out the passing trains and crossing out those he had seen from his spotter's list lingered in Nick's mind as an activity at once futile and endless. By comparison, the warships in *Heart of Darkness* firing blindly into the jungle were a paradigm of purposive behaviour and Sisyphus' job description enticing. And yet this was what Welldorm lived for; what he cut medical corners to find time to pursue. The saving of lives, the furthering of medical science, international fame, the embraces of women—all were nothing to him, compared with the joy of crossing out, when the 23476298482 passed by, the number 23476298482 in one of his little books. "I saw it. I was there." This was how Welldorm enjoyed being self-present, how he rounded off the sense of the world…

There was a phone message to ring Felicity when he arrived at the NBRI. He decided not to have got the message and to write to her instead, breaking off their relationship. But not tonight. Tonight he would write to Susie. He left Sadie's gift on the kitchen table and went upstairs.

Dearest Aporia,

I walked back from the station this wild end-October evening a castaway on the pier-end of time. Every dead leaf stood proxy for a ruined memory, every wet street a sentence in the labyrinthine text of despair to which you have banished me. Now I long only for the solving oxidation of the council crematorium, for I have become (and my grief incises this thought on the cliff-face of your absence) an empty Page that writing cannot fill…

Nick paused. In the silence between rainy gusts, he could hear McAdam's quadrophonic lamentations. So vivid was the song's morbidity, he could almost see the cerements flapping on a Necropolitan washing line. Here was absolute proof of what juke boxes and Space Invaders merely hinted at—that the eighth cranial nerve, like the heart, has direct access to Hell.

Chapter seven

S adie, you smell gorgeous."

"Thay shouldna dunnit. Arm not one fur kedgin'. Nace week-end?"

"In parts, Sadie. That was a very fetching lament you were play-ing last night, Dr McAdam. Am I right in thinking it was the famous Sexton's Chorus in which they lament a colleague who has accidentally fallen in a freshly dug grave into which he was relieving himself?"

"Dr McAdam 'ad a very nace 'oliday too, with his brother in the hireland of Skye. Dunner thay?" She turned to the newspaper for confirmation.

"I did," McAdam said.

His speech delivered, he left.

"A bit ingrowin' 'airy this moanin'. Side effex are expect. Egg off, Doctor?"

"No I'm just a little bit full," Nick said, not wishing to be offered another.

"Good weekend, Chief?" Sananayake's entrance, smirking and smoking, was an assault of well-being.

"Ask me when I've got over the hangover."

"Or she's a bloody liar or she's a bloody fool," Socrates Poulantzas was saying to Dhar as they both entered. "Christ, Nicholas," Socks said, turning his face, ill-shaven, ill-tempered and ill-starred, towards him. "This place will kill me."

"Fear not, Dr McAdam will comfort you in your last hours. He'll shorten them anyway."

"It was a *mistake*, Socks. Human error," San said. He explained: "Sister Parker, who is covering nights at the moment, wanted a doctor to confirm that a patient on 6A had died. She asked for Dhar and the switchboard put her through to Socks who was off this weekend."

"I suppose you told Sister Parker to phi upsilon kappa omicron phi phi. Really, Socks, I am surprised at an idealist like you laying down spatiotemporal boundaries to your responsibilities."

"Anyway, he refused to come to the ward and so she reported him, thinking he was Dhar."

"I suppose one ill-tempered foreign voice just woken from sleep sounds much like another. Don't worry Socks, I'm sure it'll all be sorted out without recourse to Strasbourg."

Socks was unappeased but the others ignored him as they settled down to the business of separating the edible from the toxic and the raw from the cooked. Dhar was the first to give up. He lit a cigarette and then, after looking furtively at Nick as if to gauge his mood, addressed him.

"I'm afraid," he said, as if embarking on a confession, "we've had a few…"

Nick supplied the word he could not bring himself to utter out loud.

"Deaths? The Good Lord has been unblocking our acute beds?"

"In 6A over the weekend. To speak plainly…"

"Enjoy thy plainness. It nothing ill becomes thee…"

Socks's tannoyed Socratic monologue on injustice made it difficult to hear Dhar but his general theme—Mortality in North Brompton—was clear enough.

"I've only got to turn my back and The Reaper goes berserk, catching them on the upstroke as well as on the down."

"I'm afraid that's not all…"

"What a corpse-intensive start to the week! Like the fifth act of a Jacobean tragedy…"

"Mr Ansell passed away…"

"Ah yes. The navy-blue gentleman with the chronic chest."

"He died last night…"

"Another gentleman falls victim to the Players." Nick added the contents of his plate to Dhar's and, waving away the latter's offer of a cigarette, posed a question. "I hope you didn't torture Mr Ansell with useless heroics."

"When the end was near, Sister Parker insisted that I gave him diamorphine…He just faded away…"

"I'm sure it was a very gentle end with Sister Parker in charge of it, Chief. You must admit, Socks, she's a good nurse," San said.

"Jesus Christ, Nicholas, I came to this country to study micro-neurosurgery, carrying letters of recommendation from the most respected neurosurgeons in my native land. And what am I doing when I get here? Getting screamed at by nurses who want me to certify death."

"So, earth calls and the ploughed fields rise around the beds. Any good news?"

There was none. Indeed, there was more disaster to report.

"Also Mrs Johnson is back…"

"Dr Welldorm's Depressine victim…"

"She took an over…"

This was another word Dhar could not bring himself to say.

"Tried to kill herself?"

"Her husband brought her directly to Casualty."

"Here to the NBRI? He must be after her money. Right, we've got Welldorm over a barrel now. I can't wait to discuss further man-agement with him. A bit of feedback will do him good. Anyway, we'd better get moving, Dr Dhar."

After the ward round, unhindered by Sister Kinmonth who was off ill, Nick was approached in the ward office by a young lady.

"May I talk to you about Mr Simpkin?"

"Please do."

"I'm the speech therapist. You talked to me on the phone about him."

"Ah, Sarah Curry. Pleased to meet you."

The more he looked, the more pleased he was. She was ridiculously beautiful. Tall, with long fair hair, a smooth regular face and blue eyes that sparkled (as also, alas, did the huge diamond on her ring finger) and a figure that even a North Brompton District Health Authority white coat couldn't ruin, she presented an immediate threat to civic order, moral economy and spiritual composure.

"Well, tell us about Mr Simpkin. Dialogue not too crisp, I guess."

"He has a very severe expressive dysphasia but his comprehension is intact at a high level."

"Poor chap."

"May I show you some charts?"

"Please do."

She spread a series of charts on the top of the notes trolley.

"These are Mr Simpkin's scores on comprehension. See, they are consistently high…" She indicated neatly coloured-in columns with the perfectly painted long nail of her perfect long index finger.

Nick looked up and ran full tilt into a full and perfectly lip-sticked mouth, masking and unmasking in its alternately crisp and succulent articulations absolutely snow-white teeth. His attention was divided between the material basis and the symbolic content of her speech as she shaped each sound with the scrupulous care of one trained to talk to the hard of hearing, the hard of understanding and the hard of being. Her mouth wriggled and pouted, became puckered as it closed to pat the bottom of a departing plosive or patulous as it opened to release a vowel. Nick saw worms doing a pre-copulatory dance on the Centre Lawn of The Perfumed Garden. Her speaking mouth, the point of intersection between flesh and word, threatened in all its innocent presence to undermine the basis of Nick's strategy to deal with Susie's absence. It seemed perverse to universalise absence as the ultimate origin and destination of language and even of consciousness, to deny the existence of the unmediated, while his very soul was being fellated by lips whose presence could be denied only at the ruinous metaphysical cost of denying the existence of external reality altogether.

"Poor chap," Nick repeated, actively untrancing. Dhar's cerebral arrest, signalled by the unlit cigarette held to his lips, also melted. "So, I've left some material to help the nursing staff communicate with him. Unfortunately, I haven't got much time to give him individual treatment myself."

She was the only therapist available to cover the needs of all the silenced and the dysphasic, all the speechless and the speech-curdled, of North Brompton.

"Thank you for coming…It would be nice to see more of you. Incidentally, we're having a mess party soon—a week on Friday, in fact—and we'd like to invite you. The presence of someone like yourself might give this frankly experimental occasion a certain amount of credibility."

She blushed and glanced at her ring.

"I'd love to…if my husband is free."

"Very pretty," Dhar said as they walked across the shaven lawns to James House.

"Plainly," Nick responded, glumly scanning the wind-ruined dahlias signalling that autumn was mildewing towards winter. He sifted through the causes of his gloom. A pretty girl with her unavailability broadcast in a diamond as big as the osteoarthritic node on Sadie's finger was not a cheering sight on a Monday morning. But the damp was seeping from deeper down. He had been deeply disturbed by the idea of the one-sided conversation between Mr Simpkin and Mrs Curry. It was a kind of ghastly reverse chat-up—a pretty girl doing all the talking and the man saying nothing other than "But, but, but…", butting his consciousness against the transfixed hesitation of his speech centre. For Mr Simpkin, the world had become an infinitely thick bell jar in which he was sealed, voicelessly butting his head against the buttocks and buttends of silence. His fate was like a more refined version of the chronic asphyxia suffered by the late Mr Ansell.

"He has lost the gift of speech that McAdam squanders and I

abuse. Supposing I were suddenly pruned of all words and became my own opposite—silence. It would seem an apt punishment for my flight into rhetoric."

The thought was insupportable and he decided to cheer himself.

"Dhar, old chap, I'm going to ring Welldorm about Mrs Johnson. And then I'll warn McAdam about the party."

Nick knocked for a second time.

"Come in," said an unexpectedly remote voice.

He entered a large high-ceilinged room with tall sash windows. The middle of the room was occupied by a vast table with ornate legs. It was brilliantly lit by arc lights. Dead centre, on a sheet of bright orange paper, was a slender vase of green-tinted glass into which a perfect rose had been inserted. A sulphuretted smell, like a dilute fart, hung on the air.

"Just put it there, Sadie."

Nick said nothing. I'll wait, he thought; and was reminded of the boyhood thrill of sitting outside a badger's set as dusk fell, waiting for the inhabitant to emerge. There were, at intervals around the room, bowls filled with soaked toilet paper in which flowers of various sorts languished, awaiting a sitting. An expensive camera on a tripod was trained on the Playplant of the Month. Eventually, Nick's curiosity got the better of him and he advanced towards the enormous en suite bedroom. In addition to some rather nice antique movables, there was a huge black plywood object in one corner. A cross between an upended coffin and a toilet tent, it was, Nick realised, McAdam's dark room. The owner emerged from his cabinet blinking at the daylight and, more specifically, at those of its rays deflected from Nick.

"What do you want?" he asked, startled into uttering a whole sentence. The phonological mush, half Tartan, half McMucus he had addressed to Nick hitherto now unfolded into a Lowland Scots accent.

"Dr McAdam, I wanted to talk to you about something."

"I'm developing a picture, it'll spoil."

"We're having a party in James House a week on Friday. To send Dr Dhar off to Scotland. And it happens to be my last day. You are invited, as official post-graduate tutor."

"I don't allow parties in James House."

"Neither do the goldfish in 6A Ward. I'm not asking you to allow. I am simply informing you of a *fait* about to be *accompli* which, glossing the French, means like it or lump it. You can do the flower arranging if you like. If, on the other hand, you wish to be out of earshot, I would suggest taking yourself to the far side of Hadrian's Wall for the weekend."

Nick watched McAdam's face as he spoke. Since the baseline state was so ill-tempered there was little scope for him to look crosser. Besides, pathophysiology and age-related structural changes dominated those features which would be sensitive to, and so expressive of, mood. Perhaps some of his blotches became a little more emphatic. Contrary to Nick's expectation, the latest shaving injury did not bleed afresh in response to rising blood pressure.

"I'm not having it," he said at last, after a long pause in which a damp print in his hand dripped on to the floor.

"You *are* having it. The old order changeth, Monophemus. We have formed a Mess Committee and you are speaking to its President. The party has received the Committee's unanimous support. July 14th 1789 has at last reached the NBRI. *I* have arrived, bearing enlightenment, Babeufism and democracy…"

"I shall speak to Dr Welldorm. Now get out."

"With pleasure, Dr McColleague. But not without observing *en passant* a theft of hospital toilet rolls that has brought Sadie near to an early-ish grave. Anyway, here she is with your lunch. Exit Pseudo-Sadie and enter Real-Psadie. Dr McAdam and I were having a little chat about some toilet rolls. I think Dr McAdam is in trouble."

Nick's bleep went off.

An outside call.

Felicity, crying.

He sat that evening in his room in a fog of guilt. Felicity had rung him again twice during the out-patient clinic. The first time she had been dry-voiced and in control, but the second call had been another amphibious operation. Between these two calls he had been bleeped for a girl who identified herself as 'Margery'. She had heard that Nick was in the area and wasn't it marvellous and a coincidence because she, too, had moved to North Brompton and wouldn't it be nice to meet sometime. Margery's call was rather overshadowed by Felicity's two calls that bracketed it. Nevertheless, it left him puzzled, and he felt a frustration like that of trying to recall a simple word from the tip of his tongue. He invited Margery to the party, mainly as a way of bringing their conversation to a satisfactory closure.

Unable to stand being alone in his room, he went for a walk into North Brompton and found, in the middle of the Housing Action Area, a snug little pub called The Reddened Palm. He drank the reasonable beer at an unreasonable rate. The sharper edges of his conscience and his consciousness blunted, he went to bed.

Alas, rapid metabolism of the alcohol led to rebound insomnia. He woke at 4 A.M. physically and mentally ill. He had been suffering a ghastly dream in which he had lost the power of speech so that the silence between him and McAdam—the sole co-inhabitant of the universe of his dream—could be broken only when the latter chose to speak. He lay in bed for an hour or so, until, unable any more to tolerate being pure duration of sick hours slowed to their component sick seconds, he decided to get up. There then arose the question of what, when up, to do.

One of the most effective, if drastic, cures for the spiritual sin of despair (as prescribed by those wise old soul doctors St Gregory and Enid Blyton) is, he reminded himself, to perform what Brown Owl would call A Good Deed. He therefore wrote Felicity a letter that he hoped would cheer her up without re-establishing his commitment to their relationship.

Dearest Effie,

Put away your starched apron, your Kleenex tissues and your cares. Relax in a Radox bath and read this letter. Soon a smile will spread across your face, uniting ear with ear, salutary and healing mirth will seize the entirety of your perishable parts and the weary, sublunary world will shatter like a broken mirror to an innocent silver rain of joy...

He drew a detailed picture of the NBRI, dwelling upon Sadie and McAdam, Kinmonth and Welldorm, Oscar, San and Dhar, omitting, of course, any reference to Parker or even Lenier, and saying nothing about the great Absence that made the whole scene but a painted vacuum. In short, he told her all the things that, had it not been for his drunkenness, his hangovers, his randiness and their rows, he would have amused her with at the weekend.

As he licked the envelope, he felt marginally better, both spiritually and physically. The letter, like any other good deed, would bring its punishment in due course. It might, after all, raise her hopes. And if it did not, she might, not unreasonably, hate him for cracking jokes for her apparent benefit while leaving her happiness unreprieved on the scaffold. The deed, however, had served his temporary purpose; for he now felt strong enough to howl at the moon—to write to Susie.

Dearest Aporia,

"How blessed are the sleepy ones, for they shall soon drop off." Alas, I am denied even that micro-sleep that is woven in with words; for I have lost the faculty, enjoyed by the sentence-making animal, of disposing of myself in a candy-floss of fugues. I am now so far from sleep as to be in serious danger of needing, and hence inventing, God.

Being rejected by you has made the irremediable metaphysical condition of my existence explicit. And so I am a ballooning lack where words multiply, an echo-chamber of intertextuality chasing a receding horizon of plenitude and self-coincidence. Ignored by you, I send my speech into the unresponsive *scheldeckl* of the sky, even though I have known, since your going unpeeled death and showed it to be as large as life, that discourse is senseless mind-glitter...

"Better but I'm not right yet," Nick thought as, several pages later, he put down his pen.

He stared through his reflection and saw that dawn was breaking over North Brompton. The grey roofs and soot-brown walls of the narrow streets around the Infirmary declared roundly that consciousness was not going to achieve a definitive meaning today or in this place or, probably, any day or in any place. Things would continue nevertheless. They would carry on until he and his kind were wiped out and then they would still continue as if they had never been. The things they would continue in would drag their heels to the same fate. This planet would cool; another would heat up. Life based on carbon would be replaced by life based on silicon and nothing would add up to anything though the entire process would be spelt out in extraordinarily pedantic detail so that when, as now, Oscar bicycled into work round the back of the hospital, he would be served up to Nick's gaze with creases in his trousers and a spinther of Midlands Tuesday dawnlight gleaming on his handlebars. Oscar was even furnished with a fragment of conversation addressed to someone whom Nature, not forgetting for a moment the opacity of brick and the rectilinear propagation of light, kept hidden from Nick.

Oscar pitched his bike on to a heap of coke while he carried on talking to the someone who had a female voice that freshened in through the slightly open window with the dawn air. Of course! Seven thirty. It must be Janet. She was going off night duty. He tore down the sash and leant out, feeling his headache slopping around his cerebral ventricles.

"DISCOBOLUS!" he shouted. She didn't hear. He dialled the switch board. "Could you bleep Night Sister for me?"

Switchboard complied. After a longish pause, she was put through.

"Sister Parker here." She sounded weary.

"Doctor bleeps nurse. Man bites dog!"

"Dr Page!"

"Listen I've written something I'd like you to see. Can we meet?"

During the pause at the other end, Nick realised, with a dismay pulsing in synchrony with the throbs of his headache, that her answer mattered to him quite a lot. He had thought Susie had block-booked all his pain-endings for the rest of his natural life but this was apparently not the case.

"Are you still there?" he asked.

"I'm thinking…"

More silence.

"This must be very boring for the switchboard operator who will certainly be listening in." There was a click as the said employee of North Brompton District Health Authority withdrew. "Alone at last," Nick said. There was yet more silence, given a matte finish by the antiquated telecommunication system. "That's one hell of a caesura, Sister Parker."

"It's difficult," she said at last.

He waited. She kept in touch With sighs intended to communicate her dilemma on-line. Then her bleep went off.

"Now your pregnant silence has been aborted…I thought you were off duty now…"

"Probably an outside call," she said.

"From you know who…And that's the difficulty, I suppose."

"Look. I'll ring you tonight."

Nick put down the phone, suddenly cheerful. A wintry light slanted across his soul. He almost had an appetite for breakfast, though not for Sadie's version of it.

Chapter eight

L ate again," Dr Dhar said mildly.

They were awaiting Dr Welldorm's arrival for his weekly ward round.

"Usual split-century timing. Servicing his bloody private practice in NHS time," Nick said. He glanced through an untidy pile of laboratory results. Since Miss Steele was no longer guaranteed priority access to the case notes to stick the results in at her convenience, she had refused to stick them in at all. "I see Mrs Johnson's electrolytes are back to normal. That was really quite a determined suicide attempt, wasn't it? By the way, I forgot to congratulate you on your initial management. Not that being a good doctor will help you to get your DRCHD. For that you need to be a cabaret artist as well. I hope Scotland will teach you how to perform medicine as well as practise it. It has some famous medical sons, of course. Dr McAdam, for example."

"At least I should be able to study without interruption there. It is so difficult with a young child who has such a surplus of animal spirits."

"She cropped and he ploughed his exams...Ah, here he comes,

looking every inch a Consultant Physician and world expert on
Warrior Class steam engines."

Sister Kinmonth and Miss Steele, who to this moment had
been unavailable, materialised at once. Welldorm's demeanour was
somewhat brisk.

"Morning Sister, Miss Steele, Page, Dhar. I'm afraid it's going
to be a short round this morning. Rather a lot of admin. MEC, BMA,
HMC…"

"Not to speak of BR," Nick murmured, winking at Dhar.

"Thank you for letting me know that Mrs Jackson is back with
us, Page."

"Mrs *Johnson*…"

"I always appreciate it when my junior staff keep me in touch…"
He was looking at the top right hand corner of the room as he spoke
but his manner on this occasion was evasive rather than airy. Nick's
momentary pity for him focused on the schoolboy innocence of his
enthusiasm for steam trains. He did not press home his advantage
and left the *Lancet* article—on Drug-Induced Depression—in his
pocket. "One of the main problems today is communication. Don't
you think so, Sister? People don't know how to communicate in the
way that they used to."

"I've seen changes…" Kinmonth said. When the starting point
is The Golden Age, change must mean decay.

"Well, let's go."

"*You* can push this, Mister," Kinmonth said to Dhar, indicating the notes trolley. "In the old days, of course, you wouldn't have
to ask the junior doctors to do this that kind of thing. It'd have been
automatic, wouldn't it, Dr Welldorm?"

Welldorm did not reply as he had already reached the first
patient—Mrs Johnson. She was in a white gown as she had only
recently stopped vomiting. She was a still little drowsy.

"A little better now, Mrs Jackson?" Welldorm took her hand—
the habitual physicianly tic that neither yielded information to him
nor conveyed sympathy to her. "Dr Page here tells me that you have
been a silly girl but things are going to be all right now…" He moved
two steps away from the bed. "You're getting a headshrinker to see

her, I suppose?" Nick, wincing, confirmed that a psychiatric opinion had been arranged.

They went to the next bed. And on to the next. And the next, and the next. Nick was obliged to give shorter and shorter case histories to keep up with Welldorm, until the patients were being presented simply as labelled exhibits. Welldorm paused only to deliver stale aphorisms and to challenge anything that looked like a major management decision he had not himself authorised. The William Welldorm Formation Dance Team came to a halt by Mr Simpkin.

"Morning," the physician said.

"But...but...but..."

"Mr Simpkin is dysphasic," Nick explained. "And has a right hemiplegia following a cerebrovascular accident."

"What we used to call a stroke," Welldorm replied. "Giving a disease a long name doesn't alter its prognosis, Page. A man is as old as his arteries..."

"But as young as his collateral circulation."

Welldorm stiffened. He did not like Nick's habit of capping his aphorisms with others that brought out their fatuity by being as fatuous.

"Well, it's a problem of disposal, isn't it? I expect you to sort that out, Page. Get the geriatricians to take him over. They like that kind of thing. I don't want a stroke patient blocking an acute bed..."

"Mr Simpkin's comprehension is quite intact," Nick whispered. "He can understand everything we are saying..."

"How do you *know* that if you can't communicate with him?" Welldorm challenged at normal volume.

"Good morning again, Mr Simpkin. Could you kindly lift your left arm for me?" Mr Simpkin complied.

"There may well be an element of reflex response. Could you touch your left ear with your right hand?" There was no response to this. "There you are. I remember my old chief used to demonstrate quite complex behavioural patterns in what were effectively decorticate preparations. But in those days they relied on clinical nous and not CT scans and serum rhubarb."

"Mr Simpson isn't moving his right arm because it's paralysed."

Nick produced Sarah Curry's charts. "This is evidence that comprehension is intact," he said, conscious that he was in a sense playing out last night's nightmare in reverse.

"I take your point, Dr Page. So I don't think we need any more pseudo-science. The man can understand what we are saying. However"—and he beckoned them out of earshot—"it doesn't alter the fact that he is blocking one of my acute beds. Now, Sister, I imagine you want us to get out of your way so that you can start feeding the troops. Are there any other problems, Page, you wish to bring to my attention?"

"No, thank you."

"Who's that woman over there? Looks like another one for our geriatrician colleagues."

"Mrs Rankin. New admission. I haven't had a chance to see her myself yet."

"And the problem?"

"Found on the floor after a fall. The neighbours heard her calling and had to break in. Apparently she had gone off her legs a few days before."

"'Found on the floor.' So much of medicine in the elderly, Dr Dhar, begins in the horizontal position."

"Just like obstetrics," Nick murmured.

"Just stop that, Page, and tell me why she has gone off her legs." Welldorm looked towards the ceiling, his chin supported on his hand, as he awaited an answer. Sister Kinmonth had sought relief in the support provided by the monkey pole. Dhar, who had been leaning on the note trolley, straightened up and moved on to red alert.

"As I said, I haven't had the chance to examine her yet."

"I thought that's what you'd said. Disappointing. When I was RMO at St Neot's I used to examine every patient within an hour of admission. Of course in those days we didn't have time off and clocking in and clocking out and study leave and postgraduate training. Well let's have a look at her...Sister, could you undress her for me? Let the dog see the rabbit," he added by way of non-explanation to Mrs Rankin, who called out as she was undressed.

"Do you notice anything odd about the left leg, Dhar?"

"I thought she had a touch of osteoarthritis. But she is holding it in an odd way, isn't she?"

"Yes she is. And it is *painful*. And shortened and externally rotated."

"She's fractured her femur," Nick concluded, dismayed.

"I think that's rather likely, don't you? Now, let's have a look at her notes." Dhar handed them across to him. "You'll have to learn how to write legibly, Dhar. Case notes are supposed to be the means by which one doctor communicates with another. So that was your diagnosis, was it? 'Osteo-arthritis'. Or 'a touch of osteo-arthritis'. And these are the investigations you are planning, Dhar? Thyroid function tests, auto-immune screen, whatever that is, X-ray of knees and ankles…And a *skull* X-ray. That's a novel way of going about diagnosing a broken leg. Medicine really is going places these days."

"I ordered up the skull X-ray because she was a little confused and I wondered whether she had a…"

"She's not the only one who is confused. I think this lady could be spared some of these investigations now that we have a working *clinical* diagnosis, Sister…This illustrates precisely what I mean about the way medicine is practised nowadays. No clinical nous. Straight to the laboratory without even a passing glance at the patient. The cost to the tax-payer mounts up and all that they get out of it is—I am sorry to have to say this—second-rate patient care…I know examining the patient isn't as exciting as doing a Whole Body Scan but that is what good medicine, even today, still depends on. Medicine, Dr Page, Dr Dhar, still remains a *clinical* science, there's no getting away from it."

Welldorm's triumphal sermon, delivered across Mrs Rankin's bared legs, the one intact, the other broken, continued for an eternity. Welldorm's erstwhile hurry seemed forgotten. Dhar's abashment was signalled by the withdrawal of animation from his face. His eyes seemed as empty of reference as his tiny chin or its double. Nick, his lips sealed tight, smarted.

"So you'd better get this lady to the carpenters as soon as possible. Is that all, Sister?"

"Yes, Dr Welldorm."

Welldorm's triumph was in part hers. It was the triumph of
the Old Order which changeth not. He seemed reluctant to leave
the ward. As he fed the goldfish, he told Dhar that he wished to
be kept informed of Mrs Rankin's progress. "My secretary has my
London numbers."

"Excuse me, Dr Welldorm, before you go. I've got a paper for
you. About Depressine."

"*More* pseudo-science, Page?..." Nick followed him out of
the ward. "I expect you to keep a close eye on our Commonwealth
friends, you know. They're not up to our standard. That's what a
Registrar is for..."

"The paper is about the depressive effect of drugs, including
Depressine. I apologise for the fact that it is rather old but the knowledge has been around for quite some time."

"How *very* kind of you. Perhaps you would be good enough
to leave it with my secretary..." They had reached Welldorm's office.
Welldorm paused with his hand on the doorknob. "Incidentally, Dr
McAdam tells me that you are intending to have a Mess Party."

"Yes. That's right."

"Well I don't think it's on, you know. It isn't in keeping with
the spirit and traditions of the North Brompton Royal Infirmary."

"But it's all been fixed up."

"With drug company sponsorship, so I understand. I don't
approve of promoting drugs by getting people drunk. One's choice
of medication is rather too serious a matter for that kind of thing,
don't you think? If the party goes ahead, I shall have the firm's products banned from the pharmacy."

"Since anything I say now I may regret later, Dr Welldorm, I
shall say nothing."

And, saying nothing, Nick went.

At 10 p.m. there was a meeting of the NBRI Mess Committee. This
was the first such meeting since the hospital had been formed out
of the Brompton and District Test House. Up to that moment, the
Committee had been a mere concept, a coinage of Nick's brain in
the heat of his dispute with McAdam. A few phonings and bleep-

ings had turned the concept into the reality now assembled in the lounge of James House.

"Order, order," Nick said. "Turn the telly off, Dr Chung. Now brothers, we all know what this meeting is about. It's about Rights and Freedoms: the right to self-expression and the freedom to form assemblies..."

"Get on with it, Chief. I've got to go to theatre in half an hour to mend your old lady for you."

"Spare Dr Dhar's blushes, San..."

Nick reported his conversation with Welldorm.

"My proposal is that we continue with the party as planned but that we look elsewhere than Wayne Pharmaceuticals for funding."

Poulantzas arrived. Late.

"Sorry Nicholas. Three times they have called me to an old lady who has fallen out of her cot...And I came to the United Kingdom to study microneurosurgery."

"Each time a different lady or the same lady thrice?" Rai asked, looking for all the world as if he wanted to know.

Poulantzas merely shook his head and threw himself into a chair.

"Well, is the party on or not?" Nick asked.

"Or we shall all get thrown out of the country or no bloody women will turn up..."

"I don't know what you chaps are worried about. You've got nothing left to lose—apart from your chains."

"Divide and Rule," Poulantzas reflected bitterly.

"Unite and Conquer. Come and let's put it to the vote. A show of hands."

Poulantzas' bleep went off.

"Another lady falls out of her cot." He raised his hand as he went out of the room.

San followed his example; Dhar his; Chung his; and, finally, Rai half raised his hand too.

"Passed, nem. con. Now funding. I don't think we'll get anything from the North Brompton District Health Authority or The Medical Research Council. We'll have to dig into our own pockets.

That shouldn't prove any great hardship. Cremation fees should solve the problem. We're all pretty loaded with ash-cash. We could weight contributions according to specialty: £25 each from Drs Poulantzas and Chung in Geriatric Medicine down to £5 from Dr Rai as God doesn't take many patients by their skin or genitalia. As the cull in Surgery is subject to seasonal variation San, we could leave your contribution to your conscience. Gentlemen, let the flames that oxidise the mortal parts of those of our patients who have departed this wretched patch of space-time also ignite the merriment of their immiserated physicians. Let Thanatos' black flames prime Eros' flamingo-pink fires and the Devil's Pinches change to love-bites."

The principle was accepted, though there was a good deal of argument about the actual sums of money. A settlement was eventually reached.

"Now, what about booze?"

There was unanimous agreement that this could be safely left to Nick as he had by far the greatest experience in all aspects of the matter.

"And food?"

San returned from answering his bleep.

"I've got to go, Chief. My anaesthetist has arrived."

"San, I think we could ask Sadie to see to that side of things as no one is going to eat anyway. Could you chat her up, as you are her favourite doctor?"

"My pleasure."

"Glasses we can get from the out-patient dispensary of The Spider Naevus, where I'll buy the booze. Well that's about it, isn't it?"

"Not entirely."

"Dr Rai?"

"Dr Page...who is going to lay on...the women?"

"My dear Rai, we each bring our own woman—or women (according to appetite, capacity and ability to attract). Women are not 'laid on' like booze and sandwiches. You mustn't get carried away: this is still James House, not yet The House of the Rising Sun."

"It is difficult to know how to arrange these things," Rai persisted.

"We are not talking of marriage, only of coitus. We do not have to consult matchmakers, the stars and in-laws to ask a few nurses along to what, in any other context, would seem like a common or garden thrash…Besides, working in the Venereology Clinic, Dr Rai, I should think you are in an especially privileged position. You have had a preview. Moreover, not only do you know who in this town has clap but also, more importantly, who has been successfully treated and may be approached with confidence. You might even be able to issue a few discreet invitations through contact tracers."

"There is a genuine difficulty for those of us from abroad," Chung said in support of Dr Rai.

"Surely there must be a young lady on your wards who, even when her charms are packaged in the charmless livery of the nursing profession, causes quickening of your heart rate. Take your courage in both hands; for only this way will you be able to turn the object of your desire into the substrate of your appetite…"

"I suppose we may invite nurses from other hospitals…I know a Malaysian girl…"

"Let the catchment area of the party be as unbounded as that of desire itself which, as you well know, reaches out beyond the local hours and accidental places of our employment to those far realms where finitude dissolves like falling snow into the seas of eternity. Be warned, however, that since desire is boundless, the girl who is its temporary object will uncover hungers no mere girl could satisfy."

The door opened and Dr McAdam entered the lounge. He grunted with surprise. There was much to be surprised, and to grunt, at: an unusually animated lounge; some kind of meeting; and the television apparently broken or, less likely, switched off. There was a pause while he switched on the television, retired to the far corner of the room and erected *The Tablet*.

"Dr McAdam, we were just talking about entertainment for the party. We have an unfilled vacancy for a stand-up comedian."

The Tablet was hauled down like the flag of a departing colonial power and unveiled a trembling, splotch-faced, thick-jowled, red-necked rage. McAdam raised his finger and, prodding it along the axis connecting his body with Nick's at the far end of the room, spoke:

"I…I'll expose you all!"

He stomped out on his little legs, only to meet, on exit, the re-entrance of Poulantzas returning from yet another bleep summons. The door McAdam flung open struck the ill-starred forehead of his Greek colleague, his brother in Hippocrates, thereby bringing the latter nearer to neurosurgery than at any other time during his stay in the United Kingdom. There was an exchange of non-Hippocratic oaths.

"That, gentlemen, concludes the meeting," Nick said. At which his bleep went off.

It was Sister Parker and the answer was yes.

The rain had eased to a fine mist like the fizz off a freshly poured can of Brewmaster. The pavements, thickly carpeted with soggy leaves, were treacherous. Nick and Janet had linked arms at Nick's insistence, for mutual support. As they walked, he was reading out his poem recounting the impact she had made on him when he had come across her talking to her student nurses about incontinence.

> *A Wet Dream*
> When doctor first saw Sister plain
> the words that she did utter
> related how the human drain
> wet knickers not the gutter…

She interrupted, drawing attention to factual error.

"It was our second not our first meeting when you interrupted my little sermon."

"I had trouble making 'second' scan. Don't be ungrateful. All you contributed was the dull spondee of your christian name."

"It is not quite as bad as some of the things I've received through the post, I suppose."

"Thank you…Look at that sodium light. I told you they look their best at dawn."

"Half-fruit, half-flower," Janet said.

"When we are together, I am almost inclined to believe that there are *two* voices in this world."

They walked on for a while.

"Mr Perkins is away the week after next, presenting a paper on Subarachnoid Haemorrhage at The European Neurosurgical Society in Ghent…"

"Why did you tell me that bit of classified information?"

She smiled and seemed so lovely that he was almost deprived of extensor tone at the knees.

"Make of it what you like."

"Confident that, as yet unconquered, she was still in control of the meanings…" She smiled guardedly but sufficiently widely to bring out the double brackets enclosing her mouth. The uncertainty of her gaze, although it was due only to a slight imbalance in her extra-ocular muscles, seemed to imply a world where everything was woven into a slightly different pattern. He was not in love with her but he was sufficiently aware of the fact that her body was differently animated from his own to want to know how the world appeared when refracted through her consciousness. His curiosity stopped just short of hunger. "You look so lovely, I could almost be deceived into thinking that I am here and this is now…And to think that you can raise such an enigmatic smile after twelve hours on night duty at the NBRI!"

"Your Mrs Rankin survived her operation by the way. Fancy failing to diagnose a fracture, Dr Page."

"To be fair, it was Dhar who missed it. And a fractured neck of femur is easily missed in the very elderly. Dhar's a good doctor."

"Excuses, excuses."

"Galling that it gave that useless physician Welldorm a chance to sermonise his youngers and betters. Just when we needed a bit of credit in the account because of the mess party. Are you going to come, by the way?"

"I'll have to ask my nearest and dearest."

"But he'll be in Ghent. Dearest perhaps still, but no longer nearest."

"He might not approve. Especially if he knows that you're involved."

"Have you told him you have met me?"

"No. Also I'm back on days and won't finish until after nine, assuming I can leave the ward even then. I'll think about it."

"Expertly mixing Yes and No, hope and despair, in precisely the right proportions, she maximised her desirability…"

"That would do nicely framed on a wall, next to 'East, West home's best'."

They had reached North Brompton High Street. Between Marks and Spencers and Woolworths was a newsagent sporting a bubble-gum machine.

"Here, Discobolus, is the shrine to which our steps have been tending." Nick genuflected. Janet did not. "A fine example of the genre." They observed the plastic cube-shaped head mounted on a sturdy red-painted cast-iron leg. Through the transparent cranium one could see different coloured balls approximately the size of a toddler's windpipe. It was rather like looking into a skull full of aphorisms. "Have you got a 2p piece?"

"This is a cheap day out for you isn't it?" She found the coin in her purse.

He inserted the 2p and turned the silver handle until it could go no further. He lifted the little flap over the machine's mouth and there, like a perfectly formed thought or a laid egg, the child of their joint efforts, lay a little round pink ball.

"My favourite colour. But that is not really the point. *This* is the text for my sermon." He pointed to the THANK YOU impressed on the little cover over the machine's mouth. "This deeply moving legend incised on the steel upper lip of this apparently humble machine…"

"Suddenly, I'm feeling I'm rathered knackered, Nick."

"And, who knows, under that figure-erasing anorak, also slightly knockered. Tired and mammopenic but still to me the entirely beautiful…" He took her other hand, looked deep into her eyes and planted a feather-light kiss on her lips. "Will you take coffee with me in a discreet little transport bistro?" She hesitated. "I want to steal only thirty minutes more of the eternity-walled slit of time that Chance has granted you."

She relented. They walked through the Housing Action Area and passed Our Lady of the (Groundless) Assumption. The Wayside Pulpit asserted that "Jesus is The Prince of Peace, Lord of Lords, The Everlasting Father."

"Difficult to see how anyone could hold down all three jobs. Perhaps Lord of Lords is a purely ceremonial office."

"He probably cross-covers The Ancient of Days on the Ancient's days off as well" Janet said a little wearily.

"Perhaps. Anyway, back to today's theme." He invited her to cast her mind back to the laconic discourse of the bubble-gum machine. It had been born polite: the hammer blow that had made its tongue had also made that tongue polite. "Manners makyth machine..." he concluded.

They crossed the High Street and, as if summoned by the needs of the occasion, there bounced towards them from The Modern Shopping Precinct an empty paper bag upon which there was written: "THANK YOU. PLEASE CALL AGAIN".

"A critique," Nick said, "of the concept of sincerity. Like our machine that will say THANK YOU to bona fide customers and vandals alike."

"I once saw THANK YOU done in a vapour trail," Janet said, sounding very tired and huddling into her anorak away from a zephyr revved up to hurricane force by advanced architecture.

"Even Government Property toilet roll is trained to be polite, appending the word PLEASE to the request, printed on every sheet. It all reminds me of those devices Buddhist monks are said to construct to automate prayer. The civilised world, it seems, is knee deep in the output of the secular equivalent of those prayer mills driven by the wind—like poor old God, left by lazy monks to pray to himself."

"What are you getting at, Nick?" Janet asked as he ushered her into the café where THANK YOU PLEASE CALL AGAIN was printed on a notice that, on its other side, declared that the café was CLOSED.

"Simply this, that we must think of talk not as the expression of a subjectivity but as rule-governed moves in a language game. We must see absence where others still cling to the illusion of presence, the Devil's Pinches at the heart of Juvenile Purpura…We must recognise what my howling emptiness tells me: that we are simply not there, or never completely there…We're always on the way to ourselves. And this being the case, the Susie I am missing, the Susie whose absence has emptied my life of meaning, is a figment of my imagination. And my desire, and its frustration and my anguish, are simply figures of speech in the great text that writes itself through us."

"Some of the ideas you have just alluded to were getting stale even when *I* was at University…Besides, if they were true, we wouldn't be here now talking to each other."

"Would you like a bacon and egg sandwich?"

"I'm supposed to be slimming."

"Two coffees please," Nick ordered, catching sight of their faces, distorted, in the Gaggia machine, "and two bacon and egg sandwiches."

"Bang goes my diet."

"I am excited by the mystic alchemy," he said, raising his voice as the machine wet-farted and relieved itself of two old-fashioned expresso coffees, "of transforming an egg and bacon sandwich bought in a dreary transport café in a provincial town into unique and unrepeatable Parkerplasm."

"The trouble is, it turns to Parker-ass rather than Parker-tit."

"If I were an egg and bacon sandwich, I should count myself privileged to become either…" He leant forward across the table, trailing his coat in a slick of coffee. "When I said just now that you make me feel as if there are two voices in the world, I really meant it. That's why would like us to meet again, Janet. And again and again."

"To be honest, I don't know whether we should."

"Whence the uncertainty? Your myocardium or the Great Leviathan of Society?"

"Thank you," she said, taking the coffee and smiling at the proprietor.

"When you smile like that, you look so beautiful you humiliate the rest of the known universe. Your beauty is the lost insight of this bistro, this street, this District Health Authority…"

"It's difficult to believe, when you hear the bullshit, that you're not too bad a doctor. Your Mrs Knight is getting better, by the way."

"Done a Lazarus act, has she?"

"No longer confused and mobilising nicely. Most docs don't take old people like her seriously. They couldn't care a damn."

"Since I have come to appreciate that life is equally senseless at any age, I have also grasped the obvious fact that suffering is equally important at any age."

"So it *is* Hamlet, beneath the clown?"

"What you see before you is Coco-plated Hamlet."

She sighed.

"Time I went to bed."

The return journey through the wet streets seemed, of course, shorter than the outward one. All too soon they were unlinking hands at the final bend of the road before the hospital came into view.

"There it is. North Brompton Royal Infirmary in Light Rain… Makes you wonder whether God shouldn't have taken a second look at The Void, appreciated its positive qualities and left it alone."

"You do sound mis," she said, with what seemed like genuine sympathy.

"Well, I've a feeling I won't see you for at least a fortnight even if you do decide to come to the party…You will come, won't you?"

"Maybe."

"That's all I need to start an effing Wednesday: 'Maybe'. Hope makes a good breakfast but is a poor supper. 'Maybe', like Sadie's cooking, is bad news on any menu."

"I'm sorry but I can't improve on that at the moment. And here our ways part."

Before he could say something, she had gone, leaving behind her the request to PLEASE KEEP CLOSED IN CASE OF FIRE.

As he walked down the broad sloping concourse that was the main thoroughfare of the NBRI, he had an idea related to the party. Suddenly cheered, he went humming to a telephone.

"Dead I may be. But I shall sit bolt upright on the slab."

Chapter nine

People speak of "burying" or "drowning" their sorrows in work. These are striking metaphors; but in practice work consists of separate actions that do not add up either to a solid substance in which sorrow might be interred or to a liquid in which they might be immersed. Nevertheless, Nick thought, you may as well get on with something useful while you are waiting for suffering to fade away or to build up to something definite, like an epileptic fit, a nervous breakdown or a successful suicide attempt. So, now that his anguish over Susie was compounded by a lesser but still unignorable hunger for Janet, he welcomed the fact that his workload at NBRI had got heavier.

By the end of his first month at NBRI, he had begun to impinge on the consciousness of some of the local GPs. The latter were glad to circumvent long waiting lists and the arrogance of junior hospital doctors at the DGH down the road and from time to time referred patients with possibly remediable conditions. These even included patients who might be considered 'teaching material'—who, that is to say, had conditions rare enough to be of interest to doctors as well as to themselves and liable therefore to present themselves in higher medical examinations.

Nick's teaching rounds were well attended. Doctors were drawn from far and wide, from Ward 1A to Ward 32B, attracted by the rumour that there had arrived in their midst if not a Great Teacher at least a little teaching. They came in part out of curiosity as to what this "higher medical training", that they had crossed so many miles of sea and land to savour but had not hitherto tracked down, actually was.

Nick's commitment to teaching was non-altruistic. It provided him with a forum for his wit; and it was flattering to his ego in other ways. By selecting the patients in advance, by appropriate reading before the teaching sessions and by exercising strict control over the discussion of the cases, he was able to create an aura of omniscience.

His preparation of his pupils for the clinical part of the DRCHD was very thorough.

"Don't forget to ask your patient the diagnosis, though be wary of the answers. Patients are a damned sight more reliable than doctors, but they're not infallible."

Nick's general remarks always returned to the theme of The Examiner, that bogeyman who murdered the sleep of so many young doctors of promise. The Examiner, Nick explained, was usually a Senior Physician of some years' standing. He was likely, therefore, to be arrogant, irritable, hard of hearing and somewhat out of touch with recent developments in medicine. The practical management of The Examiner would have to take all of these things into account. In particular, his arrogance would have to be deferred to. Although one should state one's opinions clearly and hold one's ground under questioning, it would be counterproductive to suggest, however indirectly, that the Examiner should climb out of his wine cellar from time to time and consult a medical textbook.

"You must *never*—and I repeat *never*—argue with him. For even where he is *factually* wrong, he is always *existentially* right."

This led Nick one evening to a consideration of The Examiner's Ignorance, which had to be handled tactfully. His Master Class consisted of himself, Chung, Dhar and a couple of Dhar's friends who were clinical assistants at a cottage hospital a few miles away. Rai was also present on this occasion, though his attendance was intermittent as the early evening tutorials tended to clash with *Blue Peter* and *John Craven's News Round.*

"As we get older, we first of all learn more and more about less and less; and then we learn less and less about less and less." This premise was accepted with amusement. "Now your Examiner is quite likely to be a super-specialist of some antiquity. Let us say, a world expert on Obolovsky's disease approaching retirement. He will know fuck all about the common stroke or the even commoner bronchitis. Is that right. Dr Dhar?"

"Plainly—and lamentably—true."

"However, examiners go round, like the police in riot-torn cities, in twos: they have to examine in the presence of other examiners. For this reason the expert on Obolovsky's disease cannot ask every candidate who comes before him about Obolovsky's disease. To do so would betray to his colleague that his knowledge of medicine is as a Swan Vesta match struck in a darkness of inter-galactic dimensions. He is therefore forced to discuss diseases of which he himself has only the faintest recollection. He will consequently be uncertain of the truth or otherwise of your answers. Do not therefore be put off if your examiner does not respond, if he doesn't even tut or nod wisely. His silence is a cloak for his ignorance, not an adverse judgement upon your knowledge."

There was a crash that sent an electric shock through their bodies. Rai, leaning against a large draining-board, had knocked a bed-pan to the floor. They were talking in the sluice because Kinmonth had thrown them out of the ward office and Nick did not believe in standing round a bed while talking of matters not directly related to the patient in it. Nick, who always found himself slightly annoyed by the way in which Rai's main concern at his Master Classes was to find a more comfortable position than the one he was in, dissipated his irritation in humour. He discussed the all-important matter of The Influence of the Time of Day on the Examiner.

"The DRCHD Examiner, like any other organism, exhibits diurnal variations in mood and behaviour. These will have been modified by the fact that most examiners will have grown accustomed to washing down the disappointments that come with advancing years with alcoholic beverages that have the twin virtues of blunting self-hatred and licensing self-pity. Mood and behaviour will therefore correlate closely with predictable patterns of alcohol ingestion. An early morning Examiner may be a rather tetchy animal, especially if he is an-early-morning-after-a-late-night examiner. A mid-morning Examiner will have a rebound euphoria from the matitudinal depression. Immediately before lunch the serum alcohol will be plunging to dangerously low levels. Be careful and, above all, be brief. After lunch a benign stupor may be expected but you must take care not to be lulled into reflecting this in your performance. The Examiner is fighting to keep awake, but you are fighting for your professional life and the happiness of your wife and children. Besides, the old dog, though flushed and humming and smelling like the effluent from a distillery, will still have one neurone cocked for what he thinks is a mistake. Moreover, you never know when the tide of his humours will turn and sobriety set in, bringing in its train bitterness and fatigue which will remain until the evening sherry over which your fate will be decided."

His joke was more private than he had hoped: his audience was exhibiting signs of fatigue. Dhar's second chin was trembling a little as the underbelly of his jaw ballooned in a supressed yawn. Chung's eyes were watering. And Rai's mind-mist had thickened to the point where he was starting to slither down the rungs of the Glasgow Coma Scale.

"We must also consider the *level* as well as the *hue* of the Examiner's consciousness. Elderly, eminent men are easily bored and boredom is the ante-room of sleep. You must not let that happen because one condition of passing is that the Examiner actually remembers you. Your answers must be crisp and, Dr Dhar, *audible*." Dhar regained some turgor at the mention of his name. "Many candidates of potential promise and actual merit have failed to the repeated sound of 'Pardon?' and 'What?' issuing from an Examiner with elderly hands cupped behind ears of precisely the same vintage…Remember you are before the Examiner to *perform* medicine not to practise it: the central and critical events are a cabaret to be rehearsed again and again."

The time devoted to these preliminaries was large in proportion as the number of "teaching" cases was small. There was, of course, no shortage of cases as such; but patients with common conditions such as strokes, chronic bronchitis and cardiac failure were not appropriate material for a higher level medical examination. Nevertheless, with the awakening of GP confidence in the NBRI as a place of healing, "good DRCHD cases" began to arrive along with the rest and with successive tutorials Nick's pupils began to perform with increasing fluency and conviction.

Sometimes it seemed almost too easy.

"Now, Dr Dhar, Mrs Aitken is your short case. Please take a brief history and examine the relevant system."

"Good evening, Mrs Aitken. Could you kindly tell me what has been happening to you."

"Are went to the doctor, say, and 'er 'adn't the foggiest."

"And what were you complaining of?"

"Well, first of all the receptionist was bloody rude. And then the doctor saw me for abate two minutes and gave me a prescription for bleeding valium."

"But what actually brought you to hospital?"

"Marn 'usband borrowed 'is brother's Murris Thighsand…"

"Mrs Aitken, Dr Dhar, would like to know what *symptoms* you were suffering from that brought you to hospital."

"Ar say what thay mean. Are 'ad a silent myocardial infarct followed by pericarditis as suggested by marn ECG. How are my ST segments today Dr Page? He's a very clever doctor marn Dr Page…"

"Thank you Mrs Aitken. I think we ought to move on to the next case…"

"Did are say summat wrong?"

"Not at all, but we've just arranged for you to sit DRCHD in Dr Dhar's place, Mrs Aitken." Nick believed in explaining things to patients but this did occasionally have unexpected consequences. "Really," he added when they were out of earshot "you could trust her to fill in her own death certificate."

Nick's search for teaching cases was wide-ranging and gave him the opportunity to survey the nursing talent in wards he would otherwise have had no excuse for visiting. He could also spread the word about the party. The pursuit of DRCHD cases once took him rather implausibly to the orthopaedic wards where, with Sister Parker temporarily on night duty, Staff Nurse Lenier was in daytime charge.

"Can I help you, Dr Page?"

At third encounter, Lenier looked positively pretty. Remove the ghastly uniform and replace it with something more adhesive to the female form, let down the long black hair so that the gorgeous neck would be exhibited in the private dusk cast by its raven wings, apply a little make up to those generous lips and around those deep brown eyes—and one would be presented with a creole-nuanced challenge to one's moral equilibrium.

"I am beyond help."

"Mrs Illis, the domestic, is making me a coffee. Would you like one as well?"

"Thank you. Beyond cure I may be but not beyond palliation. You look as if you have been exerting yourself. Your brow is moist with saline."

"Bedbathing Mrs Knight."

As she turned to go for the coffee, Nick observed her black-stockinged calves with slight pleasure. Staff Nurse Lenier would be excellent collateral to offset disappointment in case Janet failed to attend the party. When she returned, he began preparing the ground.

"It is now some weeks since I first set eyes upon your pretty, love-bitten neck. The macule of juvenile purpura I observed on that occasion has now almost disappeared and has not been replaced."

She lifted a small chammy leather of coagulated milk off her coffee. Unofficial English roses blossomed in the distribution of her external carotid artery. "None of us can make head or tail of what you say half the time."

"'None of us.' So there is an army of nurse-scholars poring over my table talk?"

"One or two people quite fancy you."

"Reassuring to know. How prettily you vasodilate."

In the brief silence that followed this unanswerable observation, Nick heard their conversation through Janet's ears. His teasing seemed, of course, patronising and his manner fell just short of being sexually harassing. The inner void girded up its loins. He was about about to draw larger, even more depressing, conclusions about himself when the door of the ward office crashed open under the impact of a large nurse animated by panic.

"Staff Nurse can you come quickly? Mrs Knight has fallen out of her chair."

"All hands on deck," Nick said, following Nurse Jones and Staff Nurse Lenier.

As the body ages, muscle bulk decreases and fatty tissue increases; in other words, the engine shrinks within the chassis. There was little chance of Mrs Knight, who seemed good-humoured and calm about her fall, lifting herself. Some lifts are purely nursing procedures. The elevation of Mrs Knight, who weighed between twenty and twenty-five stone net of clothing and accessories, was also an engineering problem.

"We need brute force and ignorance," Nick said. "Someone bleep Dr McAdam."

"Ah just brought Mr Andropov back from x-ray, Staff," Oscar said, popping his head through the curtains.

"Oscar! Bang on cue!"

With Oscar's powerful and skilled assistance, Dr Page and his four nursing colleagues were able to get Mrs Knight back into bed.

There was a pause while everyone repaid the oxygen debt incurred during the procedure. The sound of panting nurses reminded Nick of the real purpose of his visit to 27B.

"And so," he concluded, after an elaborate account of the party, "you are invited, sweet stems of sentience, to attend this unique function…"

"Lively, will it be doctor?" Nurse Jones asked. Her generous proportions suggested that local authority planning permission would be required for any further weight gain.

"Unprecedently so. And if you miss it, you'll have to wait until the year 2005 for the next one…"

"Wee rit?" asked the patient, who had followed the conversation with interest.

"Ah, Mrs Knight. How are you feeling now?"

"Thay must be Doctor Page."

"I am; but contingently, not of necessity. Had I better check there aren't any broken bones?"

"Are knew are'd be infra necksamination."

"I'm afraid you are. My orthopaedic reputation isn't very high at the moment."

No bones appeared to have been broken.

"It's nace to mate you," Mrs Knight said after Nick had completed an unopposed examination. "I wos a bit mithered last tame, Nurse here tells may."

"You were a bit. But you're completely recovered now." The most impressive evidence for this last statement was that the number of pictures of members of the Royal Family on her bedside cupboard had fallen sharply. Nick had observed that the more severely mentally impaired the patient, the more patriotic their choice of knick-knacks. He had even drawn up a scale: one picture, mildly demented; two pictures, moderately demented; three pictures, severely demented; and four pictures, amented. Doubtless the pre-marriage picture of Prince Charles massaging the shoulders of Lady Diana Spencer would one day be a special favourite of the cognitively destitute.

"You know"—and he leant forward to whisper in her ear—"you could do with losing a bit of weight."

"'As ner 'eard? Are zavinner they're babby."

"*My baby*? I deny everything."

"That's what thay're all saying. Now, this party. Wee rit?"

"In the doctors' residence. But I don't think you'll be quite mobile enough to shimmer with your zimmer. But I tell you what, though," he said, working on at least least two levels of motivation. "I'll bring you a Guinness on the big night if you promise not to fall out of anything any more, you old recidivist...You see, there'll be so many fallen ladies on that night, there will no one left to raise you up."

"Thay're an angel!"

"Lucifer, Madame."

"Oscar!" Nick hurried down the concourse.
"Doctor?"
"I need your help. You know about this party?"
"I heard you bin organisin' League o' Nations dance, doctor. Well done!"
"Your congratulations are undeserved. I've cocked it up. I've constructed the trellis but forgotten the roses."
"You've forgotten the music and you think that I, being some kind o' primitive, got rhythm…" He winked at Nick.
"More to the point, being some kind of sophisticate, you got amplifier. Have you got a minute for a word? Excuse us," Nick said to the patient whom Oscar was wheeling up the concourse.
"Make it be quick, doctor. This lady got to be havin' a barium meal."
"You see, the alternatives are not too good. Have you ever tried dancing, necking or balling to a raga? And although Dr Chung has a few records, they sound like tinsel starlings landing on a corrugated iron roof. Chart-busters in the Far East, but not, I think, ice-breakers here in the Mid-West. And Dr McAdam, being opposed on principle to the party is unlikely to offer us the opportunity to dance smooch-ily to his necropolitan love dirges…"
"I will bring my music if I can bring a couple o' friends."
"They're welcome, of course, so long as you promise me that neither you nor they will try to provoke a riot with provocative, not to say illegal, remarks."
Oscar's laughter threatened to accelerate the consequences of chronic underfunding upon the fabric of the NBRI. Nick left him with a sense of having solved one problem and broken the lock on a Pandora's box full of others. For the first time he began to have reservations about the party. It was as if his plan had broken loose from him and threatened to go on the rampage. He stared down the concourse, transfixed with panic. And then an idea recurred to him, this time in the guise of a catalyst of inter-racial harmony. He chased after Oscar again and caught up with him just outside the

x-ray department. On this occasion the laughter that concluded their conversation was bilateral.

Even so, he was still uneasy. He did not know, finally, what powers Welldorm had; what aces he might hold up his sleeve. The party badly needed a pretext to make it respectable.

The pretext materialised a fortnight later when he was summoned urgently from his Susie-less bed to 6A Ward. He raced across the halogen-lit lawn and down the concourse, crushing cockroaches beneath his running feet. There he found Dr Dhar in a very fetching pair of pyjamas bending solicitously over Mr Simpkin, the man with the stroke. Dhar's story was that Mr Simpkin had indicated that he wanted his urine bottle. After he had relieved himself, he had suddenly got out of bed, thus demonstrating his hard-earned mobility skills, and, waving a magnum of urine, had shouted "But...but...but..." and crashed to the floor. The nurse had found him next to the urinal whose contents, despite the non-spill adaptor, were gently lapping round his pyjamaed body. Dhar, crash-called, had discovered him to be pulseless, commenced cardiac massage and had ordered the nurse to crash-bleep Nick.

Nick inserted an endotracheal tube into Mr Simpkin's wind-pipe and a cleaner on night duty was able to work the oxygen bag. Oscar, who often officiated on these occasions, held the patient's arm while Nick inserted a drip cannula. Mrs Johnson, now fully recovered from her overdose, applied the cardiograph leads to the wrists while Dhar attached them to the ankles. In the background there hovered a nervous Senior Nursing Officer. She had also been summoned on the crash bleep, in a spirit of old-fashioned courtesy, but she was out of her depth, haling from an era when all the allotropes of death were equally fatal and cardiac resuscitation was still opposed by the church on theological grounds.

"Ventricular fibrillation," Dhar announced and Oscar, also reading the cardiograph, confirmed this.

"OK," Nick said, "charge up the defibrillator."

This accomplished, Nick told everyone to stand back. He placed the defibrillator paddles on the patient's chest, preparing to deliver the current that, he hoped, would comb the cardiac electricity back to normal. He pressed the button. Nothing happened.

"Supposing we switch the machine on?"

Someone found the on-switch.

"Stand back everyone."

Again nothing happened.

Oscar recommended plugging the machine in, a suggestion that was eagerly snapped up.

"Stand back everyone."

For a third time nothing happened. Nothing, not even switching the machine on at the plug, would induce it to deliver the desired current. Other means of coaxing Mr Simpkin's fibrillating ventricle back to effective contraction were tried but unsuccessfully. Resuscitation was eventually abandoned.

"What a fucking cock up," Nick said. They inspected the machine.

"'Service by 1971' it says here quite plainly," Dhar said.

"Well we've had 1971. It checked out on the morning of 1st January 1972. Servicing is therefore several years overdue. We need another defibrillator while this one is in the wash."

Equipment costs money. The size of the equipment grant allocated to the NBRI could be deduced from its general appearance of unchecked entropy. Revenue and capital, it seemed, had long since deserted this neck of the NHS. A formal request for another defibrillator would not, of course, receive an explicit refusal. That would be far too crude and would court dangerous publicity. Instead it would meet the implicit "No" that is embodied in delay, evasion, obliquity and inaction. This "No" would be underlined by the unavailability or unidentifiability of any person who could make a positive decision or be held responsible for a negative one. Nick envisaged two blizzards of memoranda—one travelling upwards and the other downwards—between the NBRI and higher reaches of the NHS. The whole scenario passed through his mind as he watched Mr Simpkin's absence—clad in a simple white sheet and no longer in North Brompton DHA pyjamas—being wheeled out of the ward by Oscar.

An idea came to him like a bolt of lightning, solving two

problems at once—the minor one of the lack of life-saving equipment at the NBRI; and the major one of making the party respectable. The mess party would double up as a fund-raising exercise. Opposition to it would then raise more issues than even Doctors Welldorm and McAdam would care to get involved in.

Dearest Aporia,

I woke up early this morning, thinking that I had heard a blackbird singing and that Spring had returned. It was only a fucking robin picking over the ashes of the world, the ruins of Autumn. I went for a walk. There was a terrible stillness in North Brompton Victoria Park: the year arrested by grief. She has caught sight of herself in a thousand puddles and, seeing her raddled hair and tits hanging like tripe, her bloated belly and thighs that need ironing, knows that she is no longer beautiful.

Why is your absence more vivid than anyone else's presence? The streets, the corridors, the corners and vistas, the objects and their shadows, all point away from me to your absence. The future leads deeper into it, into nowhere, to diminishing expectation, to death. Time was once the inner openness of space; now it is itself a prison whose sentences are measured out by the slow clepsydra of my grief.

If I cannot get over you, it is because I will not consent to become the absence of your absence. Your face iconically signifies the hope of achieving a perfected self-presence of which my words and daily actions are but the ragged edge. "To those who have looked at the sun, the world seems dark." How should I be satisfied with mere *contentment*, with a lifetime unlit by at least one moment of the ecstasy implicit in your beauty, when I know that Time points to death, that each pulsebeat is a step near heartstop and even Eros' flames char the flesh to Thanatos' fuel?

Think of the price we shall have to pay for having been alive. At best it will cost a quick death and who knows how quick a quick death is? And the price may be higher still: slow death, long pain, disability, bereavement, grief, guilt, humiliation. It hardly matters whether one dies at thirty or eighty: one's meaning does not ripen over the decades towards completeness. The moments do not accumulate to overall sense: the days, the hours, point at random, like cut grass. The weeks are not linked like the succession of words in a story. If meaning is progressive, it is so only towards the point at which meaning is extinguished.

This is how the world looks without you, Susie, when all transcendence reaches only into your transcendent absence.

Better, Nick thought, but I'm not right yet.

Chapter ten

I'm afraid Sister Kinmonth is not in a very good mood this morning," Dr Dhar murmured as he and Nick walked across the smooth shaven lawns towards Nick's last ward round with Welldorm. He had completed almost two months in the NBRI.

"Exhibiting all the old world charm of a slurry tank as usual? What is it this time?"

"Many nurses have been asking for a change of duties so that they can attend the party."

They entered 6A ward.

Nick tried a Welldorm style entry.

"Good morning, Miss Steele. Good morning, Sister."

"What are you going to do about Mrs Rankin? She fell out of bed twice last night."

"I hope she didn't wake the night staff. I shall post Dr Dhar at the foot of her bed tonight to catch her when she falls."

"She was incontinent as well," Kinmonth continued in an accusatory tone of voice.

"Perhaps she's being poisoned with night sedation. That would account both for her unsteadiness when she tries to respond to the call of nature and the lateness of her response. Let's have a look at her treatment card."

"You can't," Miss Steele said promptly. "It's at the pharmacy."

"Don't look so pleased about it." After seven and a half weeks, Miss Steele's heavy dependency for her satisfaction in life upon small or large things going wrong was beginning to irk him. "Incidentally, while we're waiting for Dr Welldorm, perhaps I could interest you two ladies in a party."

"You'd better talk to Dr Welldorm about that. He's not very pleased about it, you know."

"I know he isn't. But I'm surprised that he should be opposed to a fund-raising exercise. Anyway," Nick added, winking at Dhar, "he's going to be worrying about other things this morning."

"Funds for what, for God's sake?" Kinmonth looked genuinely puzzled.

"What *do* you buy a hospital that simply has everything? A defibrillator that works, for a start."

"I don't know why you want to be bothered with all that caper."

"*You* may resent the developments that have occurred in medicine since Vesalius was houseman on 6A ward, Sister. Fortunately your views are not shared by the medical fraternity outside of this blank space in medical consciousness. Nor, may I add, by the Coroner... Morning, Dr Welldorm."

"Morning, Page...Dhar...Sister...Miss Steele...Shall we begin?"

"Your turn to push the case-note trolley, Mister," Kinmonth said to Nick. He complied to prevent the humiliation being transferred to Dhar or an unseemly row breaking out. A row would confirm Welldorm's views about the decline in moral standards among junior doctors and would anyway distract from the main business of the morning—the counter-humiliation of Welldorm.

The first bed they came to was empty.

"Patient been losing weight, Sister?"

Dhar laughed dutifully. Nick, retaining a poker face, explained.

"Mr Smith. He took his own discharge first thing this morning."

The next bed was also empty.

"Another patient on a low calorie diet, Sister?"

Dr Dhar again laughed dutifully. "Mr Simpkin. Right hemiplegia. Motor dysphasia. Pulmonary embolism," Dhar explained.

"Cardiac arrest. Bungled resuscitation. Problem of disposal solved," Nick added.

"Thank you, Page."

"The resuscitation equipment in this hospital does not meet medico-legal requirements."

"Thank you, Page. And who do we have here?"

"Mr Payne," Dhar said.

Profoundly comatose, he was concentrating singlemindedly on deep, even ventilation.

"This is the man we sent to the Russell Brain Neurological Centre. As we suspected, he had sustained a sub-arachnoid haemorrhage."

"And I see that they have cured him. These Centres of Excellence, Sister, are worth every penny they squeeze out of the taxpayers. And next."

"Mrs Rankin."

"Whose fractured femur you gentlemen failed to diagnose." Welldorm perked up on seeing the occasion of his triumph. "And how is Mrs Rankin?" he asked addressing the world at large as he took her hand for vague physicianly purposes.

"Making a splendid recovery from her operation," Dhar said.

"I hope you've both learnt from this experience. We may not have advanced much beyond Vesalius in this backwater, Page, but at least we haven't forgotten what Vesalius knew."

"Indeed, sir," Nick said, leafing through the case notes.

"I suppose you're going to tell me the result of some exotic test."

"No, I'm just looking for your letter, sir. I thought you might like to read it."

"*My* letter?"

"Yes. When Mrs Rankin broke her leg last time. Her GP asked you to see her. She just 'went off her legs' in the same way and you, too, thought she had 'a flare up of her arthritis'. Unfortunately, she was admitted later that day as an orthopaedic emergency to the District General Hospital up the road. Comforting to know that experienced physicians like yourself can make the same kind of mistakes as tyros like Dr Dhar and myself."

"Let me see those notes," he said, discarding Mrs Rankin's hand. There was absolute quiet as Welldorm was slowly hoist with his own petard. Sister Kinmonth seemed as pleased at Welldorm's humiliation as anyone; her alignment with him was not strong enough to overcome the *schadenfreude* that seemed endemic in her office. The rest of the ward round was conducted in an atmosphere of solemnity appropriate to the funeral of a senior doctor's international reputation. At the end of the round, he did not pause to feed the fish and declined Miss Steele's offer of a coffee. "I want to have a word with you, Page, but I haven't got time now. Perhaps we could have sherry in my room this evening as this is your last week here."

"Delighted, Dr Welldorm."

He was received in the same room as before. This served as both office and reception. It was connected with the rest of Welldorm's flat by a rather secret-looking staircase Nick glimpsed as Welldorm closed the door leading to it.

"Good evening, Page. Sherry?"

Gauging the dose—somewhere between the paediatric and the homoeopathic—was a lengthy task. Nick looked about him. He saw, next to an invitation to The Annual Dinner of the Bradshaw Society, a fat volume entitled *A Narrow Gauge Source Book*. Next to this again was a large framed photograph carrying the legend: "The handsome proportions of the 'Teutonic' class compound are well displayed in this picture of an up express on Bushey Trough." Nick had a sudden summarising vision of Welldorm's passion: all those man-hours of missed trains, late trains, cold trains, smelly trains, turned to nostalgia; all those cubic miles of polluted steam condensed to a few drops of rheum in an old physician's eye.

"Your good health," Welldorm said, lifting his own stain-sized sherry to his lips.

"And yours, too," Nick responded with exemplary matching hypocrisy.

"And how have you enjoyed your stay at the North Brompton Royal Infirmary?"

"It has been interesting," Nick replied, taking a middle course between the truthful and the offensive.

"I hope you have learnt something from your experience of working here. We may not be able to teach you anything about serum rhubarb but we can show you something rather more central to patient care—the importance of teamwork. We doctors have been arrogant for far too long. But without a certain amount of humility, Page, and a willingness to listen to, and learn from, others, we shall never benefit from experience. You might make quite a good doctor one day, Page, if you try to be a little more tactful in the way you handle other people and a bit more careful in your daily practice." Nick swallowed a cubic nanometer of sherry. "And I hope you've learnt something about how the other half lives." Nick glanced at The City of Truro roaring into Paddington with all the insightless complacency of a dinosaur asleep to its coming extinction.

"And dies," he said.

"I take your point, Dr Page. This hospital is dying, as you will have realised, from lack of funds. Sit down." Nick complied, settling himself in the same polished leather armchair Maureen had sat in the morning he and Welldorm had first come face to face. Welldorm was in his own rotating chair. "It's the decibel system, Dr Page. He who shouts loudest gets most. I'm too old for medical politics. I came into medicine to help the sick."

"Well there won't be any shortage of decibels on Friday, Dr Welldorm."

Several seconds went by while Welldorm mended his thoughts to the new direction the conversation had taken. He stopped rotating.

"You are intending to continue with this party, despite my explicit instructions to the contrary."

"I am."

"I have forbidden it."

Nick took a deep breath.

"You are faced with a crisis of legitimation, Dr Welldorm. You ought to consult with Miss Steele on how to cope with this. She went through it a little while back. You and she, and Dr McAdam come to that, could form a little self-help group. The feudal era, like the Age of Steam, has passed."

"You have no right to defy me, Dr Page."

"I beg to differ, Dr Welldorm—where so many others have deferred—and will point out that you have no right to feel defied."

Welldorm leant ever so slightly across the desk towards him.

"This will not go unpunished, Page. I shall make sure you will not be employed in this hospital, or this district, again."

"Is that a *punishment*, Dr Welldorm?"

"And you will certainly not get a reference from me."

"Do you think I'd admit to anyone that I'd worked for *you*, *here*? How much weight do you think your name carries? People wouldn't know whether to look you up in the Medical Directory or Bradshaw. So you cannot touch me. But I must admit that I am concerned about our overseas colleagues. As you know, your standing amongst them is like that of the Tay Bridge amongst footplatemen. Because they, unlike me, are vulnerable to your malignity. But don't let that tempt you; for you, too, are vulnerable. Any reprisals against Dhar et al. over what is a pefectly legitimate fund-raising exercise will prompt me to write a letter to the Royal College of Hospital Doctors Committee on Higher Medical Training, outlining the kind of training that has been available at the NBRI since 1950, the amount of paid study leave the junior doctors have had and so on. An urgent visit from the Royal College could follow. A ten-minute discussion, a perhaps rather asymmetrical discussion, with the postgraduate tutor Dr McAdam should be sufficient to to make up their minds. They will almost certainly withdraw their approval from these posts and you won't be able to advertise them. So you will then be left with Dr McAdam to look after your patients. He may have to cut down on photographing flowers, singing in Church, listening to quadrophonic laments and generally playing the whisky-priest manqué and will have to roll up his sleeves and do some medicine. Before this, however, I suggest that you update him on post-Renaissance clinical practice and increase your own personal indemnity against litigation."

Welldorm placed his sherry glass next to The City of Truro. Fixing his eyes on a bunch of plaster grapes he said, in a tone of voice that was neither airy nor weary, neither physicianly nor wise,

"Get out, Page."

And Nick got out, before Welldorm's head of steam exceeded the tensile strength of his boiler.

Half an hour later, Nick had the opportunity to hear the decibel system that Welldorm had referred to in action. He had dinner with Dr and Mrs Dhar. It was a distressing experience because the Dharling howled throughout. Mrs Dhar had clearly gone to a great deal of trouble to prepare a most marvellous meal, which, considering that it had probably been created against the sound of a demented howitzer, was an extraordinary achievement. Eventually, Mrs Dhar disappeared into the tiny bedroom which all three of them shared and the sound of smacks could be heard.

"I suppose, to paraphrase Clausewitz, beating the living daylights is Early Learning conducted by other means."

"She is rather precocious and she is missing her granny," Dhar explained. Nick presumed he was referring to his daughter rather than his wife.

The meal on balance was not a success and Nick was somewhat relieved when at 9.30 his bleep went off.

"Dhar, old fruit," he said, when he returned from the phone. "I've got to collect the glasses and arrange the booze for Friday."

The evening's engagements so far had left him intolerably sober; so, after he had completed his business in the Out Patient dispensary of The Spider Naevus, he decided to have a drink. As he was being served, he caught sight, in the mirror behind a row of optics, of the reflected bodies of Janet Parker and Robert Perkins. His first instinct was to slink off but, seeing the possibility of causing a little mischief, he changed his mind. He was noticed first by Janet and her explicit non-recognition prompted him to address Robert rather than her as he approached their table in the lounge bar.

"*Mr* Perkins!"

"*Dr* Page!"

"Well, our long-term memories seem to be intact. How are you? Just give me the main symptoms and the positive findings."

Robert had half stood up, out of surprise rather than politeness. He indicated a chair.

"Nickel Arse, sit down...Join us...May I introduce you to my...to Janet Parker...Actually, you may know each other as she works in the same hell-hole as yourself."

"How do you do? I've heard of you, of course. But it's nice to actually set eyes."

"I've heard a lot about you from my nursing colleagues," Janet responded, dramatic irony lambent in her cheeks. "One or two of them say that you talk rather a lot."

"He always did," Perkins said. "But then that's what physicians do all day, isn't it? Talk to their patients and hold their hands?"

"Except the ones in coma. Those we send to the surgeons. Thank you, by the way for returning Mr Payne to us in an even deeper coma than the one he was in when we sent him to you. I'm glad he didn't cause you any trouble. Nice man, isn't he? Ready sense of humour when you penetrate beneath the rather reserved exterior."

"I was against operation, myself," Perkins said, becoming serious in his own defence. "But my senior colleagues..."

"The hole you made in his cranium seems to have let out the last of his consciousness. Pity really."

Perkins smiled. "Nick and I were great friends at St Jidgey's... We divided the honours between us."

"Robert won the prize for the year's Most Self-Effacing Student and I won the prize for the Most Tongue-Tied One. We were in such fierce competition that it was lucky Robert chose surgery and I chose to be a physician. The difference, as you know, is that the one injures and the other heals."

Robert was smiling, not at the remark Nick had made but at what he was himself about to say.

"I was asked to see a patient on a general medical ward the other day. It looked like a morgue. There can't have been anyone less than seventy, apart from the staff that is. Well, I thought to myself, what's a physician nowadays? A medically qualified social worker, that's what…"

"Mr Perkins is, as I'm sure you are aware, Miss Parker, prone to characteristic surgical fantasies about saving lives. Of course *nobody* saves lives. We only postpone death—without, I hope, merely protracting it. Surgeons, of course, shorten death, though sometimes at the cost of bringing it forward. But then surgeons mature rather later than physicians. Did you see Roger Machin's got Stool's job?"

"Only a year senior to us, Nick."

"After Alberich, Hagen. Another drink…er Janet, Robert?"

"No thank you. I've got to go back soon. But tell me. What's happened to you? You seem to have moved over from the fast lane to the hard shoulder in a big way. What's it all about?"

Nick outlined in the most general terms the causes of his present condition.

"I've left the rat-race, Robert."

"And so ended up on a diet of warfarin," Robert said, turning to Janet and winking.

"Winking makes you half blind, Mr Perkins," Nick said, feeling irritated. "I've only been out of things for a couple of months."

"You can't live off your past glories, Nick. Dining out for ever on the fact that you passed your eleven plus. I mean when are you going to pull yourself together and get back into a proper job?"

"To be called into a huge sphere and not to be seen to move in't, are holes where eyes should be which pitifully disaster the cheek."

"You can't let it all fall apart just because some brain-damaged scrubber won't let you take her knickers down."

Nick, for once conversationally out-pointed, shrugged his shoulders and changed the topic.

"Tell me about yourself. A two hundred and fifty word abstract will do."

Thus prompted, Robert became a pauseless gargoyle, spilling out past triumphs and future plans. His eyes, which now struck Nick as positively fanatic in the cause of R. Perkins' advancement, stared harder. The aberrant artery bulging on his temple, seeming to stand for the high pressure of the soul within, became more prominent. Nick surveyed with glazing eyes the bow-tie, the dog-tooth check hacking jacket, the silk pocket handkerchief—all unchanged since his student days when his peers, including Nick, had almost universally cultivated a disorderly appearance.

"And so," Robert said, bringing his triumphal case history to the present, "I'm off to Ghent tomorrow to present our first two hundred cases to the European Neurosurgical Society…"

Janet, looking especially lovely in the muted light of the lounge bar of The Spider Naevus, had glanced unhintingly from one to the other as the ball of the conversation had passed back and forth. Time, Nick thought, to include her in the conversation and to do so with a topic that would exclude Perkins.

"You know, you look to me like a discus thrower."

"How clever of you to spot that."

"Used to be a bit of an athlete myself. Javelin. Unfortunately got banned from competition when, with a wild throw, I made a single shish kebab out of four separate umpires."

"That must have been very upsetting."

"It was. But the record still stands, which is some consolation, I suppose…Now, let me guess. I bet you went to university before you took up nursing."

"Right again!"

"So, tell me, what do you think of recent developments in post-Saussurean literary theory? Is Derrida a charlatan? And what about Paul de Man?"

Janet and Nick collaborated in synthesising a conversation about Jacques Derrida and the metaphysics of Presence which had the effect of making Robert feel distinctly *hors de texte* and experience the metaphysics of Absence. Nick was surprised at Janet's cooperation. Perhaps she felt sorry for him: not an entirely comforting thought. He had never before been the object of a woman's pity.

"Darling, I'm afraid we have to go," Perkins said.

"Robert was supposed to be off duty this evening," Janet said.

"I'm not very happy about some of the junior staff I've left in charge of things."

"Well, I'll just nip to the loo. Otherwise I won't feel as if I've had a real night out."

She left the lounge.

"What a remarkable young lady, Robert. Beautiful, intelligent, sweet-natured…"

"We've been going out for nearly a year."

"How did you manage to trick her into squandering herself on you?"

"We met at a Symposium on Urinary Incontinence. I was talking about the neurosurgical aspects and she was covering practical management."

"Typical division of labour. You talk about the spinal cord and she talks about washing knickers. How romantic."

"It *was* rather romantic, actually. Anyway, I was appointed to the Russell Brain and she jacked in her job and got a ward sister's post at the hole where you are currently committing professional suicide."

"Sounds a fairly stable union. Any intention of making it right in the eyes of the police?"

"I haven't really made up my mind yet."

"You ought to snap her up before someone else does. Isn't it about time you got married anyway from the point of view of your curriculum vitae? In a couple of years time you'll be applying for consultant posts. Being single would be a blot on an otherwise impeccable cv."

"I must admit I had thought about it…"

"Seize the time! Look at her! Can you see her remaining yours for long if she's free?"

"You're probably right, Nickel Arse. And you take my advice. Get out of that hole and pull yourself together. We can't have an old Jidgey's man servicing a necrotic workhouse."

Robert's air call bleep went off. As he went in search of a phone, Janet gave Nick a smile that penetrated to and warmed layers of his consciousness that he had quite forgotten existed.

Nick's low spirits on returning to his Susie-less room were

the entirely predictable effects of their antecedent causes. He studied his image in the window and, finding his eyes inevitably looking through it to the undifferentiated darkness housing Susie's absence, he was moved to transfer from the imaginary to the symbolic realm. He wrote to her; at the very least, this would complete his descent to the bottom of the pit.

Dearest Aporia,

Your absence is nothing less than the ungraspability of NOW, made focal; the inescapable flaw in the present tense made itself an experience. I think to myself: "This is NOW; I am HERE" in feeble attempt to italicise my own and the world's presentness. The moment of consciousness, that is, attempts linguistically to reduplicate itself so that it shall become more completely what it is and the moment's bearer wakes up to thisness and can cry THAT I AM.

Recently I have seen proof in a speech therapist's lips that the existent mouth lies at the root of language and all the absences of language. *This* is 0,0,0 point of the egocentric space that tacks language to the world and guarantees that meaning shall stay with reference and reference touch reality. But if the motor of our discourses is the absence of a mouth—my mother's metapsychological lips, your painted ones—if the speaking mouth is foresworn (and is always foresworn, even for those who kiss it), then do we not face a severance of language from reference, of discourse from reality? THIS IS NOW, I AM HERE—these are not the beginning and end of language, only the pistol shots fired at the start of an endless trail of signs.

In your absence, I am your absence. I AM NOT HERE, THIS IS NOT NOW—because I am not lying next to you, my tongue in your mouth, my organs of generation closing in on yours…You have gone, taking with you the last thin film of loveliness able to quilt the bone hard crags of death.

Bored and empty, Nick laid aside his pen. A Necropolitan dirge was soiling the midnight quiet of North Brompton Royal Infirmary, a silence that would otherwise have been broken only by the massed nose-flutes of sleeping patients and night staff and the occasional thud of a tax-payer falling out of bed.

The conversation with Perkins had discomforted Nick most of all because it had taken place in Janet's presence. In his usual tactless way, Perkins had hit the sore spot with stereotactic precision: "Dining out for ever on the fact that you've passed the eleven plus." Susie's absence had licensed behaviour that accorded with a tragic sense of life; but in Robert's presence, made more important by Janet's presence, it was less easy to tolerate the loss of status that must go with it. He dimly appreciated that his letter to Susie might not be wholly addressed to her absence. It was at least half meant to be overheard by another potential presence. Even so, apologias apart, it was obvious that if he stayed in the hard shoulder long enough, he would encounter, when he tried to get out of it, the cold shoulder.

It was time to move back into the fast lane. He had anyway to find a job to go to after he left the NBRI. He therefore abandoned his letter to Susie. He turned to the job adverts in the current *British Medical Journal*. His search was quickly rewarded. He could hardly believe his luck. Tomorrow he would make a political phone call; he might find that he not burned his boats after all.

Part Three

In serene souls there is no wit. Wit
indicates a disturbed equilibrium. It
is the result of a disturbance and at
the same time the means of regaining
balance. Passion possesses the sharpest
wit...The situation of the dissolution
of all relationships, despair or spiritual
death, is the most frightfully witty of all.

—*Novalis*

Chapter eleven

As he walked past the ruined dahlias, Nick felt almost excited. The prospect of tonight's party set one or two long-dormant neurones tingling. But as he entered James House, he was felled by a perfume concentrated almost to disinfectant force. *Absence*! Gripped by crescendo angina, he went into the kitchen, drawn there by the sound of a row.

"Dunner luk at may lark that...Are 'ad henough, Dr McAdam..." Sadie concluded, crookedly pointing at him, in case he did not recognise his own name.

"I'm warning you," McAdam replied, his five foot six inches towering over Sadie's four foot six, "if you have anything more to do with this godless orgy, I'll have you thrown out of this hospital."

"'Godless orgy', Dr McAdam! I hear your appetites, engrossed by decades of denial, breeding hopes that outrace probability."

"And as for you..." McAdam began, turning round to face him.

Nick pushed aside a large plate of sandwiches and sat on the kitchen table.

"As for me, Dr McAdam…"

"You are treading a very dangerous path, young man."

This was only the second time McAdam had spoken long and clearly enough for Nick to hear his accent. This neither palliated his anguish nor appeased his anger. McAdam was no longer an object of amusement, a fascinating freak. He saw him as he must appear from the tilt view of those who could not escape this place. He saw a malignant dwarf, a bully, a parasite, a hypocrite, a killjoy, a destroyer of hope. Some of Nick's anguish decanted itself into spite.

"On the contrary, what I know about you makes me an even greater danger to your happiness than you are to your patients' health. So I put it to you that your best tactic tonight would be to retire to your luxurious apartment and remain there until the party is over."

"Get out of my way," McAdam said, though Nick was not in his way. McAdam's brain's underpractised conversational module simply served him up the nearest it could to a retort, which also had to double for an exit line. He went; and for a moment or two Nick, who took no pleasure in being nasty to people, felt twinges of pity. To be medically incompetent was as ghastly a fate as to be unattractive to women. McAdam was both. But the twinges were chased out by the reflection that pity should be reserved for McAdam's patients and for the junior doctors to whose gloomy lives he added further darkness.

"Now are dunner want thay eating all them snappins before the party, say," Sadie said admonishing him for starting on the sandwiches.

"You look different, Sadie."

"Do thay think are luk nace, Dr Page?"

He got down from the table and, taking her hands in his, inspected her.

She had tarted herself up. Her Afro-pan-scourer hair was curiously flattened and now looked like Shredded Wheat in advanced old age. The cause of this change was a hat which lay on the work surface, next to some sculpted bread. It was an ancient hat, thick with the feathers of exotic birds. An old two-piece suit that may have seen better days, but not much better, clung to her bony body. Her face was mired in make-up. The deep fissures in her forehead had been scrupulously pointed. Peach-coloured powder clogging the pores on her nose led the eye naturally to the slicks of rouge on her cheeks and on to lipstick which, having been applied with Expressionist exuberance, suggested a mouth rather more generous than Sadie's time-thinned one. The long axis of the paint was at approximately twenty degrees to that of the lips, an artless formal echo of her arthritic index finger. She had even put in her false teeth.

"Simply gorgeous."

"Arm glad thay lark it…"

"It's stunning, Sadie. But you've been using the forbidden perfume, you sadist."

"Are thought as it were party nate…" She simpered a little. Nick smiled.

"You wicked, wicked woman." And he lifted her right hand to his lips. It was covered with death's love bites. He kissed it and brushed his mouth against her thickly rendered cheek. "And you've been *drinking*…"

"Are 'ope that's owe rate."

"It's the least you deserve for this *fantastic* spread."

Untidy heaps of sandwiches and the like were piled up on huge dinner plates.

"Are after do marn best…Are thay courting tonate, Dr Page?"

"Bless you, Sadie, you old romantic," he said putting his arm round her shoulder and planting another quick kiss below her zygoma. "Since reliable methods of contraception were discovered, there's no 'courting' any more. There's just copulation and rows."

Sadie looked suddenly uncomfortable.

"Are after watter me 'oss. Arm burstin'."

In her absence, the Absence she had left behind her began to corrode Nick's spirits. Small anxieties magnified themselves. He felt especially uneasy about the rôle McAdam might play in the evening's proceedings. He envisaged regular Malvolio-like appearances eventually bringing physical assault upon him. If McAdam were beaten up, this would put him in the seeming right and Nick, by association, in the criminal wrong. McAdam had somehow to be put out of play. The flushing of the toilet gave him the idea he needed: that hesitant micturition; that interrupted stream. It was an idea so unoriginal and so obvious that a mind so fine as Nick's should never have been violated by it.

"Sadie, I'd like you to do me a favour."

He explained.

"Are dunner lark that. Are thay sure 'er won't find out?"

"Of course he won't. Dr McAdam has never made a correct diagnosis in his life."

Sadie was convinced by this. When she had made McAdam's tea, Nick added 40 mgms of Frusemide BP, a potent diuretic he had obtained from the ward stock. This would keep McAdam occupied all night. Nick's sufferings on the train to North Brompton would be as nothing to McAdam's experience of a six litre diuresis in 10 ml installments.

Sadie ascended unsteadily with the tea. There was a brief exchange with Dr McAdam. She descended a little more unsteadily, alcohol and arthritis acting in concert with guilt to undermine her gait.

"Are dunnit, Doctor Page."

"Don't look so upset, Sadie."

"Are 'ope er'll be owe rate."

"Don't worry Sadie. Here's another gin and tonic. Come, now, let us dance…"

Hand in hand, they entered the lounge. They heard a Sexton's Jig penetrate the pre-party quiet like a damp fog. Nick lifted Sadie's bruised, devil-pinched hand and together they trod the boards.

By 9 P.M., Nick and Drs Sananayake, Rai and Chung were standing in the large empty space of the lounge swigging cans of Brewmaster and trying to amuse each other. This rather desperate scene, though at odds with Nick's hopes, was in conformity with his expectations.

"A trifle XX-openic," he observed to San. The latter agreed but looked strangely complacent, his smoke-wreathed good-natured smirk seeming to be diffused throughout his substantial frame. Tonight he was bursting out of a three-piece suit rather than a white coat.

"Structure seems rather to dominate over event," Nick commented to a gloomy Poulantzas at 21.15.

"Or it will be a bloody shambles. Or no bloody women will come," Poulantzas replied. He was chewing one of Sadie's canapés and drinking some of the wine with a look of mild to moderate disgust.

"More like Domestos than Demestika?" Nick suggested. Poulantzas almost smiled. "I like the fancy dress, by the way."

"Fancy dress, Nicholas?"

"Sorry, my mistake. I thought you were wearing a mask. It's just that I don't recognise your face when it is cleanshaven."

At 21.25, a van ground to a halt outside James House. From it emerged Oscar and two tall, unsmiling companions with dreadlocked hair. Solid state amplification was unloaded. Nick hovered round the van but his offer of help was rejected without ceremony. The process of setting up this equipment was prolonged. It involved a lot of counting up to ten. Ear-splitting fragments of Stockhausen were emitted at intervals.

More males arrived—ambulance drivers, theatre porters, COHSE shop stewards, a cook—prompting Nick, who observed them de-tabbing cans in the kitchen, to remark to Rai upon the XS of XY over XX. Shortly afterwards, some unidentified women arrived in dribs and drabs, and rather drab drabs and dribs they were.

At 21.45 a great wave of amplified sound broke over the party. At the same moment, Dr Chung entered, accompanied by a gorgeous petite Malaysian girl. Nick shouted him a greeting that he himself could not hear and received in reply a response he could not hear either: he had had his first real party conversation. Then Maureen arrived, along with the orthopaedic secretary and the secretary from the GU Medicine clinic. Maureen looked quite attractive, because indistinct, in the rationed light.

She smiled nervously. A tightly fitting short black skirt enhanced her desirability. Although the skirt was ten years out of date, the appetites to which it appealed were not.

"Thank you for coming," Nick lipwrote and busied himself getting drinks for the three girls. They giggled and looked at each other when he did his usual party trick of proving the existence of God while, at the same time, showing the ontological argument to be unsound. This may have been because they could not hear what he was saying.

When he had run out of pleasanteries to shout, he invited Maureen to dance. Poulantzas snapped up the orthopaedic secretary and Rai, who had already made professional contact with her, the secretary from the GU Medicine clinic. They joined the Chungs on the dance floor.

"I had hoped to get Dr Welldorm to open this party," Nick shouted at the ear-ring set like molluscum contagium in the tragus of Maureen's left ear.

"*Really?*" she asked, twisting her head to look at him in astonishment.

"Unfortunately he is in Stockholm receiving the Nobel Prize for Clinical Pharmacology."

"Now I know you are joking. By the way, what have you been saying to him?"

"What prompts your question?"

"Because he rang me up on Thursday morning and asked me not to send off a pile of letters of complaint that he had written about you."

Nick explained. The effort of doing this against the somewhat overstated sorrow of Bob Marley was exhausting and he decided to abandon speech for a while. He embraced Maureen more closely, resting the cupped palm of his left hand against the perfect rondure of her right buttock. He patted her bottom to the rhythm of the music, thus raising tactile experience from sensation to knowledge. Towards the end of the tune, he saw, hesitantly entering the room, something even more stimulating than the black-skirted bottom under his hand. When the music stopped, he excused himself on the grounds that he had to perform hostly duties.

"Margery! *What* a surprise!" he said, kissing her hand.

"The word gets round you know."

He took her coat and inhaled gouts of cheap perfume.

"I'm sorry I was a bit off when you rang me in Out-Patients the other day. I was rather hard pressed..."

"It's been a long time, Nick."

"It has indeed. How long?" he asked.

This was no mere conversational gambit but a genuine request for information. Most of Margery—her political opinions, her taste in music, her position on the Arian heresy, her mother's age, her surname—had slipped Nick's mind. Her breasts, however, voluminous and yet shapely and as always beautifully served up, were as familiar to him as if it had been only an hour ago that he had first unpeeled them and praised them to her face as "brink of bursting beach balls".

"Nearly five years, Nick."

"Let's go into the hall so we can talk."

In the great hall of James House next to the splendid staircase Nick learnt that in the intervening five years Margery had met an ambulance driver and got pregnant by him.

"I got catched as they say around these parts."

The unplanned pregnancy had been followed by the even greater disaster of a hasty marriage. A few months ago Margery and her ambulance driver had finally separated.

"Unfortunately, we keep meeting at parties and he can get quite unpleasant if he sees me talking to someone else."

"How is motherhood?"

"Awful."

She elaborated, giving the impression of a long tunnel of broken nights and shattered days, at the end of which one came out, blinking at the light, chewing valium and talking fluent Mothercare.

As they talked, Nick was able to establish that the rest of Margery had now grown in volumetric proportion to her breasts: still bumpy in the right places, she was now dumpy in the wrong ones. This observation enabled him to recall their relationship without the memory being distorted by revived desire.

They had first met at a party where she had told him her then troubles—minor, it seemed, compared with what was to come—and he had listened with sympathetic interest as one does when one thinks that dipping a toe into someone's unhappy life may lead shortly to dipping something more interesting into her happier-looking body. Magnetised by her breasts and rather uncritical of her brain, he had been drawn into an affair which, apart from sexual intercourse and the stations en route, had been unrelievedly awful. Soon even sexual intercourse palled and he had realised, not for the first time, that the catchment area of the heart is rather less extensive than that of the genitalia. More specifically, he had discovered that breast-fixation does not form the basis of a lasting relationship. The experience had made him fiercely puritanical for forty-eight hours.

"Do you like my hair?"

"Interesting," Nick said.

In her determination to keep up with fashion (a fashion that, unknown to Margery had in London entered the history of fashion), she had dyed her hair with extract of capercaillie and back-combed it. Before him Nick saw the result of putting a briar bush and a multicoloured game bird together into a Kenwood mixer.

"You don't like it," she correctly inferred.

"When it comes to fashion, my dear Margery, I'm a philistine."

"Well what about my dress, then?"

"The boob tube I applaud. The gipsy skirt I have reservations about. In general, I would say that where you dress to kill you scarcely wound but where you partly undress the result spells instant death to all resistance."

"I've thought a lot about you in the five years since our...affair. I couldn't understand a word you were saying half the time but you were fun."

"Really?" Nick's surprise was genuine. Until tonight, most of 'the affair' had belonged to those large areas of his past that the precious gift of repressive amnesia had quite blotted out.

"Mind you, I suspect you valued me for my body rather than my mind."

"You mean I discounted the rumours of the latter's existence?"

"There you are, I was right wasn't I?"

"But why on earth should I be interested in your *mind*? It's probably no more original than that of anyone else here tonight and I cannot, looking around me, see anyone whose mind attracts me one bit. Your claim to distinction lies with your thoracic not your cerebral hemispheres. *They're* what makes you stand out from the crowd."

"Sexist pig."

"That brainstem response proves, rather than undermines, what I am saying. Now listen Margery. Take a look at that chap over there, by the mirror, drinking a glass of wine with such distaste."

"Do you mean that rather ugly-looking Mediterranean?"

"That's Dr Socrates Poulantzas. In his own country he is a neurosurgeon. He has tremendous knowledge and skill...and a marvellous mind. Would you like to meet him?"

"He's got small, piggy eyes."

"Caught you! What's the difference between your not liking people because they've got small eyes and my being attracted to them because they've got big breasts? In both cases, the mind is simply not taken into account."

"Now you're being silly...I admired *you* for your job..."

"Cash and status turns you on? What's more admirable about that? Being attracted by large tits has a charming innocence by comparison. Would you like a drink?"

"Yes please. You can take personal credit for your job..."

"Whereas you can't for your breasts? All right, Socks?"

Poulantzas, who was on the way out of the kitchen as they entered, shook his head.

"I have been called to see an old lady who has fallen out of her cot."

"What a shame. I was just going to introduce you to a young lady who was most interested to learn that you had come to England to study microneurosurgery."

"Or I shall be back soon or I shall go mad."

"Ice and lemon? What were we saying?"

"Thank you. Bodies and things." She giggled.

"Ah, yes. Bodies and things. All right, Chung?"

"Nick, I'd like to take you to meet..."

"I'd love to, in a minute."

Chung left with two glasses of orange squash: the stuff out of which courting, rather than copulation and rows, is made.

"Bodies and things," Margery reminded him.

"My dear Margery, bodies and selves are *both* products of external circumstance. I no more made my own intelligence than you grew your own watermelons."

"You're just arguing," she said, becoming a little peevish.

"Why should your jugs my judgement so deflect / That muddled thoughts at once command respect?"

"There's something wrong with your argument."

"There is and there isn't. But because you are quite unable to put your finger on what it wrong with it, aren't you glad that you are judged by your splendid jugs rather than your dialectic skills?...To be honest"—and Nick usually was honest in this kind of argument, goaded as he was by exasperation—"jugs apart, you would be no more worthy of the attention of the chance-met stranger—as opposed to someone who knows how delightful the inner Margery is—than Maureen, the girl behind you dancing with such little abandon, who has never enjoyed the free gift of admiring attention that you have taken for granted without even questioning. Your boob tube is swollen with the promise of happiness."

"That's quite clever, I suppose, but it's also rude. Do you want to do something with my coat? It's not exactly designer label but I do rather like it and I don't think it would benefit from being stored on the draining-board."

"Marriage has sharpened the ironic edge of your tongue."

"If you met the chap I'd been married to—and you might well do that tonight—you'd understand why."

"Let's get back to your boobs."

"Like old times."

"Your bosom is a signifier to which there corresponds no signified. The paradise to which they so warmly allude is not to be found this side of the grave."

"Is that a compliment or an insult?"

"Thanks for the music, Oscar, it's great." Oscar, who had come into the kitchen for beer for the solid state men waved his hand in acknowledgement. "If my words are rhetoric, your tits are even grosser rhetoric. Their promise cannot even be cashed as sensation—illustrating the general principle that the idea and the reality, the intelligible and the touchable, never coincide. But you could still put them to good use, even validate their rhetoric: show me that you're not a sexist sow and chat up Dr Socrates Poulantzas…He is a lonely, deeply unhappy man and has a fine, unappreciated mind."

Margery was no longer listening. She had a hard expression on her face that he did not recall from his fortnight of nympholepsy five years before. Something behind Nick was distracting her.

"Here comes trouble," she said.

Trouble took the seemingly not-too-troubling form of an off-duty ambulance driver, with a fine regular face, solid build and shortish stature.

"Good evening, doctor," Trouble said, with a slightly menacing emphasis.

"Good evening, driver," Nick replied. "Please excuse me while I do my host bit and distribute petitesse. Nice to see you again, Margery."

It was nearly 11 p.m. and there was still no Janet. Armed with bottles of Guinness for Mrs Knight, Nick slipped into the cool and the quiet outside. As he passed the remains of the dahlias, an xj6, driven at between eight and nine times the recommended 5 mph speed limit, struck a puddle and sent up a sheet of water, part of which collapsed on to Nick's timeless brogues and sensible trousers. Behind the glare of headlights he made out a blonde female arguing with the brunet male behind the wheel. He could not place either of them.

"How is Mrs Knight?"

The part-time nurse, who worked one evening a week consulted with the other, who usually worked on another ward. The name meant nothing to either of them. Since they were attempting to get a rather heavy lady into bed before their coffee break, they were not inclined to institute extensive inquiries.

"*This* is Mrs Knight, the lady you are attending to," Nick pointed out.

"We've only just come on duty."

"Good evening, Mrs Knight."

"Good evening, Dr Page."

"There you are."

"And who are *you?*" one of the auxiliaries challenged.

"It's my Dr Page," Mrs Knight said, smiling at him. "Are knew 'e were coming, so are put me fow staith in."

"Mrs Knight's personal physician," he added, taking her hand and giving it a squeeze.

"Are was up and abite today, Dr Page."

"Then here's your reward, Mrs Knight."

Nick removed the top from the Guinness.

"Thay're an angel to be so good to a lady on burrowed tame."

"Lucifer, madam. The bringer of Light and the Prince of Darkness."

"Cheers, Doctor." Mrs Knight drained the sputum cup filled with Guinness at a single draught and re-filled it.

"Cheers, Mrs Knight." Nick bowed his way out. "Mesdames, demoiselles."

In the nursing station, Nick quizzed a momentarily disengaged nurse about Sister Parker's whereabouts but without success. He was about to leave when one of the auxiliaries rushed in. At her urgent request, he hastened back to the ward.

"She started laughing and laughing after she had finished the first bottle of Guinness," she explained, "and then she went pale and slumped down in her bed and just faded away."

"Like hope in North Brompton," Nick said, feeling for her pulse. No pulse was to be felt. He had no stethoscope and so he laid his ear against her cooling bosom. There was no audible heartbeat. Nick contemplated raising the cardiac arrest team but decided against such a rash act: a few drunks dragged unwillingly from the party and defective resuscitation equipment would have added neither dignity to her death nor duration to her life. "Her time-creditors have foreclosed. She has slipped the noose of space, ladies. She has provided her own, metaphysical, solution to the impending social problems."

"I can't believe it, it was so sudden."

"I do think there is mettle in death, which commits some act upon her, she hath such a celerity in dying."

"It was a very gentle end," one of the part-time nurses com-

mented wistfully. "That's how I'd like to go." And then, more practically: "Could you write something in the notes, doctor?"
"Of course."

31.10.78 11.15 P.M. Called to see. On examination: no pulse; no respiration.
Diagnosis: Dead.

If thou and nature can so gently part,
The stroke of death is as a lover's pinch,
Which hurts and is desired.

"Thank you, doctor."
"Don't mention it. You can share what's left of the second bottle. Guinness, as you can see, is good for you…Good night, sweet ladies."

Nick's spirits, depressed by his Janet-less return from the ward, were momentarily raised on entering James House. Marvin Gaye was singing "I Heard it through the Grapevine", expressing the very essence of the hopes and expectations that the sounds and smells of parties connoted.
"Oscar!" he shouted. "You're a genius!"
Oscar nodded in agreement.
"Coollies seem to be enjoyin' themselves, Doctor."
Nick winced but didn't think it the time or the place to challenge Oscar's choice of descriptors, especially since, in his absence, the party had quantum leapt into partiness. It was louder, thicker, more heavily scented—in short, sexier. A good two thirds of the forty or fifty people in the lounge seemed to be in the grip of some kind of movement disorder. Dr Rai's choreiform agitation was addressed to Maureen, some distance away, who waggled her bottom to goodish effect. Dr Chung's reined-in, Bonsai restlessness was in dialogue with the somnambulistically smooth undulations of his delicious girlfriend. Dr Poulantzas' wild hemi-ballismus—a fragment, perhaps, of

a handkerchief dance—provided a nice contrast to Dr Sananayake's smoochier athetoid evolutions, interrupted as he lunged forward to catch his partner before she fell.

Nick, recognising a medical emergency when he saw one, raced to the spot. Sadie lay back in San's arms as if the two of them were pausing at the extremity of the tango.

"All right Sadie?" Nick shouted.

She opened one eye and began to speak. No sound could be heard above the music. She raised her arthritic forefinger as Nick, gently lifting her legs, brought her to the horizontal. Silenced, but uttering fluent Pointish, the benign gerontocrat, lover of unloved doctors, spoiler of food, comptroller of toilet rolls, trustworthy servant of North Brompton District Health Authority, was carried out of the lounge.

At the top of the stairs, her bearers paused to allow DrMcAdam, trundling with inelegant haste, to cross their path. They laid her in Nick's bed and dimmed the light. She muttered something about her 'fow staith' and San, as a precaution, removed them.

"There's a phone call for you, Nicholas," Poulantzas shouted up. It took Nick sometime to establish, against the music of Beaufort & Richter, that it was Felicity at the other end. The pain of the conversation was mitigated rather than exacerbated by its difficulty. He brought it to an end by implausibly pleading acute medical duties.

"Yes. You're quite right. I *am* at a party. I was called to it because somebody had collapsed."

Felicity slammed down the phone to cut off the flow of his lies.

He wandered disconsolately into the lounge and made out Sarah Curry the Speech Therapist standing with an empty glass in her hand and apparently unattached.

"How nice to see you," he began, with feeble understatement.

She smiled wonderfully and touched her perfect lips with a perfect fingernail.

"I'm very glad to be here," she said gauchely.

It dawned on Nick over the next few minutes that he was in the presence of that most puzzling of all social types: the staggeringly beautiful female who lacks self-confidence and feels, as they say, utterly inadequate.

"So it was *your* XJ6 that nearly brought my life to an end."

"I'm terribly sorry. I'm always telling my husband not to drive so fast."

"I shouldn't have minded dying with the image of beauty in my eyes, though the light was rather poor."

"Did you get wet?"

"Only externally. My appendix and spleen are dry as a bone."

She looked at the floor, where, after a long pause, she found a conversational theme and was able to look up again.

"I like your shoes." Her statement was beautifully lip-written and her lower lip reflected the bright lights of the disco as she spoke.

"They fit well, don't they?" Nick responded; and, warming to the topic, added "And there's exactly the right number of them." After a long pause he added "By the way, I'm afraid Mr Simpkin died the other night. His hemi-death found its other half and so even his silence is now silenced."

"I'm sorry I never managed to get back to see him again. Did he do those exercises I taught him?"

"He died articulating…"

At this moment, Mr Curry, a handsome belligerent brunet, took up position next to his wife.

"So that's where you got to. As predicted I couldn't find anything eatable or drinkable."

"Simon, this is Dr Page, our host."

"Ha d'ye do?" he responded absently. "Isn't it about time we went, darling? I can't see any point hanging round here and I've got an early plane to catch in the morning. I told you this'd be a complete waste of time."

Nick excused himself to spare the lovely but seemingly luckless Sarah Curry further embarassment. Even marriage to a speech therapist was insufficient to cure Mr Curry's speech disturbance. Acute on Chronic Downright Rudeness (ICD Code 3.106) is a very difficult condition to treat.

Battered by the train of unsatisfactory events, he went into the hall and there, her lovely neck redoubled in the great mirror at the end of the hall, was Staff Nurse Lenier. His collateral! As he advanced upon her, he noted how, in the dim light, her glossy raven hair, her tight black sweater, her short black skirt and her black-stockinged legs reinforced the crepuscular charm of her dark skin colouring. All the semi-tones of evening gathered in her physical presence. Her perfect neck was shamelessly uncovered: she had swept up her hair into one large lateral pony tail. Turning to inspect herself in the mirror, she caught sight of his reflection advancing upon hers.

"Staff Nurse Lenier!"

"Dr Page!"

"Would you care to dance The Half Nelson with me?"

She hesitated and looked round the hall.

"Such a delay reminds desire of its roots in suffering."

She coloured.

"Sweet collateral, do not bankrupt my hopes."

She consented to be led into the maelstrom where Smegma, a 'politically hot' group, were bursting tympanic membranes. "This music is dead political," someone dancing in the darkness shouted instructively.

"I'm dead politicised," Nick shouted back.

He took Staff Nurse Lenier into his arms and, in order to be able to shout into her ear, danced cheek to cheek, inhaling her sweet smell. To his surprise, he found that his sensible trousers were hosting a time-less—because at once prehistoric and bang up-to-date—erection.

"How are you?" he bellowed.

"Fine, thank you."

The history taken, he proceeded to physical examination. He summarised the positive physical signs.

"Your neck is as pretty as sin," he said. "It cries out to be bitten by a gentleman of quality."

"I don't believe a word you say." Clearly she hadn't heard a word of it, either.

"No more than I believe your neck," he shouted. "Though perhaps it is unfair to suggest—as I had occasion to remark earlier of an old friend's breasts—that the flesh tells lies. Rather, it is only a tautology, signifying that empty plenitude which is the overall sense of our lives."

"Do you ever stop talking?"

"When my mouth is otherwise occupied. Thus…"

He made as if to kiss her. Staff Nurse Lenier wriggled away in surprise and indignation—a lot of the former and a little of the latter.

"You're dancing with my girlfriend, Doctor."

Nick turned round to confront the speaker. He was slightly below average height but solidly built. Nick noted familiar, rather full, lips and an extremely good-looking face soured by annoyance. Margery's ex, the ambulance driver.

"Wait your turn," Nick said, and resumed dancing.

The ex withdrew, momentarily wallflowered along with Rai, Maureen and a glum-looking Poulantzas.

"Is that lampless brawn your boyfriend?" Nick asked Lenier.

"We have been out together on and off. He's a bit persistent and very possessive."

Margery's ex returned.

"You're dancing with my girlfriend."

"I'm not very impressed by your handling of English pronouns," Nick replied, taking advantage of a welcome breakdown in the musical arrangements to get over a complex point of grammar concerning the way in which the reference of shifters such as "my" and "yours" depends upon who is speaking.

"You're dancing with my girlfriend, doctor."

"That is the third time you have committed that solecism. Of course, your error may be factual rather than grammatical. But those of us who doubt the referential function of language are sometimes uncertain where syntax ends and semantics begins, where meaning gives way to the empirically testable, and where the intra-linguistic opens on to the great wild world of extra-linguistic things."

"You're dancing with my girlfriend, doctor."

"Repetition doesn't always breed quiet menace, you know. Especially when, as on this occasion, it is repetition of error."

"We'll see about that." But the music had started again. In the break, Oscar had reminded those present of the main public event of the evening, scheduled to begin at precisely midnight.

Nick attempted to resume dancing. He was grasped firmly by the shoulder. He excused himself from Lenier and, wondering at his own madness, feeling as if he were in the grip of his own behaviour rather than being its agent, he mimed an invitation to the driver to step outside.

In the comparative quiet of the gravel drive outside James House, they were able to explore their differences of opinion in greater depth.

"You seem excessively eager to engage the alterity of polemics."

"I don't like you dancing with my girlfriend, doctor."

"She isn't, so far as I know, your current girlfriend. I have this on her authority. You do not, so far as I am informed, have exclusive grazing rights."

"I'm telling you, you were dancing with my girl and I don't like it."

"I think we've covered this ground already. Now, if you don't mind, I shall return to the dance floor."

"I don't want you to go just yet, doctor."

"Is that more 'quiet menace' that I hear?"

"I'm warning you, doctor."

Nick didn't need to be told that he was being warned in order to feel warned. His opponent's small but solid body seemed uniformly charged with malignant possibility and he could imagine the first— and probably the only—blow of the fight coming from any part of it. Correspondingly, every part of his own body was on standby to receive the sickening ictus that would separate it from normality and normal unhappiness. He tried to talk himself out of the situation but seemed only to talk himself deeper into it. Out here, in the cold and dark, rhetoric seemed to offer the kind of protection that a paper bag might provide in the hypocentre of a nuclear explosion.

"I can't help observing, driver, that your sentences seem to lack subordinate clauses, illustrating how the knowledge that one is of short stature plays merry hell with the structuring of complex sentences in situations of conflict…"

"I don't like your cocky style, doctor."

"In that case, it looks as if we have got as far as formal discussion will take us. There remains only the silent discourse of the body, since you insist on trying to turn this party into a dress rehearsal of the coming ochlocracy…" Nick took off his jacket and hung it on to the balustrade at the bottom of the steps leading into James House. "But before we resort to violence, I will remind you that I am not only wittier than you but also considerably taller and stronger. You must therefore anticipate defeat in both the isometric and isotonic phases of our engagement. As an experienced ambulance driver, you will be fully aware of the damage even unarmed combat may wreak upon the human body. So if I were you, I should bow out with what little grace your witless frame…Hello, San…"

"All right, Chief?"

"For the moment, yes. But hang about, this little man here may shortly require an orthopaedic surgeon. And you ought to alert Dr Poulantzas. After all, he came to the United Kingdom to study neurosurgery."

"I think he needs an orthopaedic surgeon, anyway," San said, picking him up and carrying him in into James House over his shoulder.

A minute or two passed, while Nick looked at the moon that had risen over the splendid listed building. San, then returned, with his cargo still on his shoulder.

"I asked Staff Nurse Lenier if she wanted him and she said not," he said, walking towards the smooth-shaven lawns. "So it becomes 'a problem of disposal' as your Dr Welldorm would say." San deposited his load among the remaining dahlias. "Bye bye."

"Thank God you came." Nick was shivering. "I might have been killed. Being a physical coward has served me in good stead over the years and I see no reason to change a winning formula now."

"I saw what was happening. That's why I followed you out."

"It was a question of sovereignty and Staff Nurse Lenier's right to self-determination. Actually, I wouldn't have bothered except that

I'm sick of having my id seived through a maze of capillaries. Despair nearly got the better of my cowardice. I was *almost* ready to fight that scorbutic knave. How are things with you?"

"One or two possibilities," San said.

"A harem of faint hopes?"

San laughed.

"Don't despair, Chief. Our luck's got to change."

Contrary to his confident expectation, Lenier was not waiting in the hall to welcome the returned hero. Nor was she in the lounge, as he discovered by scanning innumerable cases of not-Lenier merrymaking in the silvery stroboscopic light. There was a thriving, bustling community of not-Leniers in the kitchen and the staircase proved to be another sub-department of her absence. Nick's search took him upstairs where he noted that someone, kept waiting outside the toilet by McAdam's protracted voiding, had vomited copiously on the landing floor.

Lenier's absence was as nothing to Janet's and Janet's perhaps less important than Susie's; but they all added up. Nick's desolation was enhanced by the sounds and smells, the pre-copulatory promise, of the party detonating below him. Absence hit him like a cannon ball on the chest when he entered his bedroom. Sadie's Brillo pad on the pillow was unbearably not-Susie's-golden-hair. He drew back the eiderdown and checked her pulse and airway. All seemed to be well. There was a tap on the door.

Nick's first thought was that it must be Janet. His second thought was that, precisely on account of his first thought, it would not be Janet. Anyone who imagined that things would happen because he was thinking of them was like the child who goes to London and expects to run into the queen. He did not want to wake Sadie, so he went to the door and eased it open.

"Discobolus?"

"I came to see our patient, Chief. Is she all right?"

"Fine," Nick said, swallowing his disappointment.

"I've also got this message for you."

Nick unfolded the note.

Dear Dr Page
You shit.
YES
NO
MAYBE

Yours
(Sister) J. Parker SRNBA (Hons).

He descended the stairs, leaden-hearted.

The hall was now in semi-darkness, lit only by light spilt from the kitchen. One or two males made love against females sandwiched between them and the astonished walls of James House. The unfortunate Dr Rai leant against the wall staring at the unfortunate Maureen. No lovemaking there; and no conversation, either. What is there for A to say, if A wants only to screw B and B wants only to go home? The lounge door opened and an ear-murdering bolus of music escaped.

"Where you been, doctor?"

Nick looked at his watch. It was ten to twelve. He followed Oscar into the lounge and threaded his way in darkness through dancing, scented, sweating and inebriated employees of the North Brompton District Health Authority. Oscar cut off the flow of music in mid-stream.

"Ladies and Gentlemen, Dr Nicholas Page."

Introduced, Nick began.

"Ladies, Gentlemen and Ambulance drivers…"

He spoke, in spite of, or perhaps because of, interruptions for nearly ten minutes, to an increasingly resentful audience. His themes—medicine and mortality, love and death—were of no interest to anyone, but he uttered them none the less, determined to bring to their climax the motifs that had increasingly had him in their grip since his sorrow had begun.

"As you must all know, the North Brompton Royal Infirmary

is shortly to be expunged from the annals of medical science and from the debit account of the DHSS. Starved of funds, this hospital is already dying along with its patients; the very anoxia that darkens the lives of our bronchitic charges also afflicts the gas cylinders in the corridors. We are, in short, moving from crisis to necrosis..."

Nick hesitated before continuing. The scene in the dimly lit lounge was not encouraging. The expectancy that had been aroused by Oscar's announcement was already dissipated and most of the audience—drunk, restless, randy, frustrated—were regarding his speech simply as the unexplained hold up that it was. Margery's Ex was licking mighty Nurse Jones' neck and she was pushing him away without conviction. Maureen seemed to be shrinking away inside the body that was pressed involuntarily against Rai's. Oscar and his two friends were bent over the broken strap of a skateboard.

"Our work is dedicated to the fight against those fleshly ills that shorten, darken or narrow life. But have you ever considered, ye auxiliaries and porters, ye domestics and administrators, how strange it is that only in human beings is matter explicitly aware of its own mutability and raises it to the status of an opponent—to wit death—to be fought? I would put it to you that you should become giddy at the fact that human consciousness can encompass the idea of its own its finitude and oppose it with an instrument as complex as the National Health Service. Imagine a badger writing a thesis on meline TB! Or a cockroach idealistically choosing a career in which she will nurse other cockroaches!"

"What are you on about, you fucking burk?" Margery's Ex called out from the increasingly restless darkness.

"I understand your resentment at the sumptuous polysemy of my discourse; for in such a place as this the shimmering dialectic of philosophy is as ectopic as a leopard's fart in a drawing room. However..."

"God save us!" his interlocutor shouted. There were murmurs of agreement, mainly from guests he did not recognise. San, who was quite near to him and looking rather pleased, winked at him and raised a can of lager. He was enjoying his role of minder.

"...we are committed..." Nick continued, feeling his despair intensify as he heard his own raised voice, "We are committed, we health workers, to expanding the light and pushing back death. And yet, is there one amongst us who has not at times longed to be shot of consciousness and to be liberated from those very Tuesdays to which we have restored our grateful patients? A longing that leads us to *seek out* rather than *shun* the darkness and to search for those exits from the world where what we hear is not the trumpet but the crumpet, or indeed the strumpet, sound, even though we have to bruise ourselves or others to pass through them? Only this evening I had occasion to recall that

> The stroke of death is as a lover's pinch
> Which hurts and is desired…

Yes, and a lover's pinch is as a stroke of death."

Margery's Ex mouth-farted against Nurse Jones' neck. There was an outbreak of laughter.

Nick's anguish turned to anger. He *was* going to be heard.

"That's the most intelligent noise you have emitted all evening." This retort was loudly cheered by San, who banged his lager can on a table. Margery's Ex, sensing that he might be due for another episode of ambulatory or even trajectory orthopaedic surgery relapsed into a sullen silence. Nick continued.

"Now where was I? Ah, yes. Love and death and the ambivalence that runs through our lives. You all know how certain modes of death may provoke curiosity as well as terror, a curiosity that reaches for the darkness signified in another's flesh just as fiercely as on other occasions it reaches out to the light of clear understanding. And from this inescapable ambivalence stems the paradoxes on whose slopes our lives, and in particular occasions like this night's joyful gathering, are pitched: whoever brings light, differentiates; and so separates; and so brings darkness. To live is to long to know the Other; but the price of all knowledge of the Other is becoming the Other; our longings, ultimately, point to our release from ourselves; to death…"

"Christ, man…" The problem of the broken skateboard strap seemed to have been solved.

"Oscar, do not overdetermine my speech with your allusions. Humankind can only bear so much intertextuality...What I am asking you, ladies and gentlemen, guests and gatecrashers, employees of the North Brompton District Health Authority and their friends, is to consider how love-bites and the devil's pinches, juvenile and senile purpura—bruised exits for those who are intoxicated by absence or who have drunk deep of the bitter sea of separation in our over-enisled lives—wear each other's colours. And to consider, too, how a crumbling hospital that is a danger to its patients is a perfect metaphor for that ambivalence. Nothwithstanding which, ladies and gentlemen, we must takes sides, back Eros against Thanatos and raise two fingers to La Mort and our cold step-mother the Department of Health. For we, the living, are in the end implicitly and existentially on the side of life. Consider this very party, fuelled by ash cash. Thus do the flames of our dead patients redden the cheeks of the living, and ignite their desires, surprised by hope and opportunity. (Consider, likewise, how my wit is fired by pain.)"

"It's past midnight, doctor."

"I know. But take heart, land is in sight. Our fight against the mandarins of the DHSS and our political masters is of course as hopeless as our fight against death. And (bringing these two themes together), we must recognise that, while there is an infinite need for health care, there are finite resources available to service that need. No generation can hope to secure a permanent tenure on time. Even those of us who have been privileged enough to live on the leeward side of History must concede that we all, inescapably, live on the windward side of Time. Nevertheless, we must cling to our melioristic vision and fight on. Which brings me to the point of my speech..."

"And about bloody time, too," someone, unidentified said.

"A response that had a probability approximating unity. Even so, your interjection, whoever you are, is not entirely without interest; for you speak as if the sidereal could be joined to the haematological and the downward passage of everything could be clocked by lovebites...

"This was not, however, the purpose of your oral footnote. Rather, you wished to express impatience at the delay I am imposing on your path towards the climax of coitus. But, although my discourse is futile, it may be less deluded than the saccharine zeros you have all bellowed into each other's ears against the message-corrupting asemy of Oscar's music, if only because *my* utterances explicitly avow their own rhetorical status…Be that as it may, I would ask you to be generous in your sponsorship of our gallant competitors as they skateboard for your delight. Put your tragic sense behind you and remember that death, though an irremovable metaphysical category, can be temporarily bought off with hard cash. The money you subscribe to our cause may permit another citizen's heart to beat another beat, though bringing him or her not one whit closer to immortality or his or her life nearer to the absolute closure of total sense…"

Having finally come to his point, he wound up his speech.

"So, ladies and gentlemen, friends and ambulance drivers, follow me to that spectacular piste which runs through our crumbling hospital and cheer on our doctors and friends as they embark on the Great Skateboard Marathon up and down the concourse and harness the myth of Sisyphus (that final critique of our busy days) to the modest utilitarian end of paying for a new defibrillator, in order that even in the NBRI, death may rejoice under the new name of 'Cardiac Arrest' and (who knows?) become slightly less fatal…"

There were boos and ironic cheers. He and Oscar led out the two teams and the crowd in the lounge unwound to a ragged file in the now cool, now November, night. At the top of the concourse, on a starting line chalked between wards 1A and 1B, were six skateboards, three each for Dr Sananayake's and Oscar's teams. The former consisted of its captain and Drs Poulantzas and Chung.

"Or I am bloody pissed or I am bloody mad," said Poulantzas, who looked both.

"*Suivez la piste*, you madman," Nick exhorted.

And they were off, each lap of each body sponsored to an average of a one pound sterling, into the twilight of 10B, 15A and beyond.

Nick turned away and his gaze ran full-tilt into Janet's.

Chapter twelve

Discobolus!"

"You shit."

"Meaning?" he asked, as they walked away from the concourse.

"When I eventually managed to get to your bloody party, having left the ward late and changed out of my uniform at high speed,
you were already busy kissing Staff Nurse Lenier."

"I'd assumed you weren't going to turn up."

They walked out into the cold November night. She was wearing paint-snug jeans and a pretty white blouse. By the light spilt
from James House, he registered the soft peach bloom of her face
and longed to hold her hands and kiss her.

"I left the party and didn't intend to come back. I felt humili-
ated. *My* Staff Nurse as well!"

"Please don't be angry." He took her hand in order to communicate his genuine anguish; but also in order to take her hand. It
was warm and beautiful. She withdrew it.

"Not so fast, Page." Even by the dim light, he could see that she was not merely pretending to be cross. To make things worse, he inhaled a familiar scent.

"Janet! *You're* wearing that bloody perfume now. First Sadie and now you. What are you women trying to do to me?"

"Don't flatter yourself. Nobody's trying to do anything to you. You're just an innocent bystander caught in the cross-fire." She turned to look at him, her crossness softening into a smile. "You looked desperate during your speech."

"I was desperate, Janet. Please forget about Lenier. That bird was just a magpie twice removed."

"And I suppose I'm a magpie once removed?"

"Only inasmuch as you have been removed by one R. Perkins."

"I should really tell you to piss off."

"The second, unvoiced, 's' in piss proleptically signifying the absence—mine—that you seem to desire."

Relenting further, she shook her head.

"No. Uniquely amongst the members of the audience, I liked your speech very much. It may have saved you."

"I was serenading your absence."

This time his attempt to take her hand was successful. They paused on the lawn littered with dahlia petals. Caressing her palm with his thumb, he invited her to admire the banded rustication, ratcheted eaves and coupled pilasters of James House.

"Look at that perfect moon," she said. The moon, full as on the night he came to the NBRI, was clad in a lingerie of cloud and surrounded by a ring of phosporescent vapour.

"It looks surprised at us."

"Or at what you've done to this place," she suggested.

James House was a blaze of light. A few who had not wished to watch the skateboarding had continued dancing. The music from Oscar's amplifiers threatened to shake the moon out of its orbit.

"When I came here less than eight weeks ago, this place was in total darkness and the only sound was McAdam turning over the pages of *The Tablet*. Now look at it! It restores my sense of original sin."

"Don't go on. It's cold."

"Before we go in, let me show you something." He led her round to the open front door of James House. In a pool of dead leaves by the step, he found what he was looking for: the lion knocker, still grinning fatuously.

"I pulled that off, trying to get in the day I arrived."

"Let's dance. It'll warm us up."

As they entered the lounge, the music changed to something slower and less deafening. In Oscar's absence, Rai was disc-jockeying. He smirked at Nick before re-clamping himself to a helpless and unhappy Maureen. Margery, with the centrifuged ptarmigan in her hair, was dancing resentfully with her Ex. The latter looked at Nick with loathing, at Janet with hard interest and at Nick with renewed loathing.

"Dr and Mrs Dhar!" Nick exclaimed. "Welcome to the party."

"Sorry we are so late," Dhar said, "but we have only just managed to get Bulbul to…"

He smiled; and he and Mrs Dhar glided away, two swans on a glass-calm lake, the image of serenity.

Nick and Janet drifted round the floor. Invisible, silenced, and engaged in stereotyped activity, she eluded his mental grasp. He resented this, as he did the way in which the clichés of the dance floor made him into a poor copy of any dancing male. The record came to an end and Margery's Ex, pushing Rai aside, chose more pandemonium. Margery must have told him she had a headache.

"The loudspeaker loudspake and the people called it music," Nick bellowed.

"You're a lousy dancer," Janet replied.

"At four I was county standard at Ring a Ring o' Roses. More recently, I have preferred to dance across semantic rather than Euclidean space."

"I can't hear a word you're saying."

"Then we must go. I'm not going to struggle to converse against the din of music that does not even have the virtue of being primitive."

She acquiesced. They collected a bottle from the kitchen, where they were surprised to catch a haggard-looking McAdam picking over the ruins of the food and drink. They went up to Nick's room. It was still heavily scented with Absence, though Janet's wearing it had taken away much of its power to hurt. Sadie was still asleep.

"Three's a crowd even when the third is in coma," Nick said.

He carried Sadie like a babe in arms to another room. The first door Janet opened revealed an interesting situation in which one employee of the North Brompton District Health Authority was warmly hilted in the uniformed, but off duty, body of another. Nick recognised the mighty Nurse Jones, but not the gentleman of quantity dovetailing with her. Janet closed the door hastily. They found Sadie a home in the next room, where clothes rather than bodies were piled on the bed. They switched on a side-light, removed the coats, tucked Sadie snugly in and, after Nick had given her a kiss, closed the door.

"Well, bullshitter, bullshit on," she challenged, stuck, Nick suspected, for something to say, when he had poured them both a glass of rotgut. She was sitting in his desk chair, he on the bed.

"Am I forgiven? Or will that have to wait until amnesia, that holds no grudges, wipes me out?"

"You are forgiven—just."

"Sealed with a kiss?"

"Sealed with a full stop…When I saw you kissing Lenier, I thought 'I bet that's the first time he's stopped talking since I last saw him, the perfidious bullshitter'."

"I hate the word 'bullshit'. That was what she used to say when I said something she couldn't understand. And she seemed so pleased with herself, as if she had made a brilliant diagnosis or seen right through me. In fact, I only had to say 'Good morning' a bit quickly and I'd lost her."

"You're referring to Susie, I suppose."

"Indeed."

"If she was so empty, why did you spend so much time trying to talk to her?"

"She was beautiful, wasn't she? And, almost uniquely among the women I have fancied, she didn't want me. She should, in the ordinary run of things, have been a walkover. So I became obsessed with her. And this was made worse of course by the fact that she played with me—blew hot and cold as they would say. When she eventually told me to sod off, I was left with the choice between playing with myself and playing with language. I chose language and, as you can see, I have nearly disappeared into words."

"So your style is Wounded Love?"

"Please don't reduce me to a text to be assigned to a genre."

"'Romanticism is an insufficient response to our metaphysical condition. Wavering between a tragic recognition of, and angry rebellion at, human limitation, it is simply inadequate to the true mystery of life.' I got my First in Finals for talking like that. And when I think about it, I thank God I nowadays lecture on incontinence."

"I thought I'd done my share of Eng. Lit. for the night, deconstructing the fight talk of an ambulance driver who wanted to give me a dental clearance."

"'Irony also is insufficient. For the deepest response to life is not anger at its ultimate senselessness but astonishment that it should make any sense at all.' That's the kind of crap you have to talk to get a First. That's how the shit who sacked me at university earned his living. He impressed me enormously when I was a student." She laid down her glass of wine. "You seem suddenly very solemn."

"I long to speak, just for once, without a nano-smirk of irony. And to find silence…and perhaps sleep."

They listened to the customary party sounds: someone vomiting and either gasping for air or sobbing between heaves; glass or a glass being smashed in the usual capital-intensive way of human celebrations; a scream followed by swearing; and the music pursuing its senseless goose-stepping gaiety with merciless inattention to those whom it was supposed to be making gay…

The skateboarding party seemed to be returning, prompting Nick to turn the stout North Brompton lock in the door, a precaution that was not a moment too soon as shortly afterwards the handle rattled angrily.

"Come and sit next to me," he said.

"No thanks, I'm quite comfortable here. And I don't think the cause of my comfort would be advanced by you groping me."

"So you will remain safely enclosed in the extra-uterine contraceptive device of my desk-chair."

"Shut up. So this girl was beautiful. What of it?"

"Beauty is, as all the popsongs say, the ontological counterweight to death…Not that I'm entirely against death. It unblocks the acute medical beds. And who would want Sister Kinmonth to live forever? Even so, one does need a film of loveliness to quilt its bone-hard crags."

"But could you imagine—if she really was as thick as you said she was—*living* with her? *Marrying* her?"

"Of course, marriage wasn't in my mind at all, notwithstanding her body seemed to contain a message addressed especially to me—even if the message was 'Lay off!' I'm not too sure if I believe in marriage anyway. Only crazy idealists believe that happiness lies in the coincidence between the body you copulate with, the body you converse with and the body you go shopping with…I suppose you *are* such an idealist. Like the police, you believe in married love."

"I believe in love, anyway. And also that presence, as well as absence, can make the heart grow fonder."

"You're going to marry Robert, aren't you?"

"He did propose to me on Wednesday night. In The Spider Naevus, after he came back from answering his bleep."

"I thought he might."

"Why?" she asked, startled.

"You think that none but your sheets are privy to your wishes?" He paused before he asked his next question, appalled at the abrupt change in his heart rate. "Did you accept?"

"What do you think?"

"I really don't know. But let me tell you one thing: Robert will use his affection where it is. He will *marry* but his occasion…"

"That is a very serious insinuation." She did not sound as angry as her words or as she should have done. Nick breathed an inward sigh of relief.

"All's fair in love and rhetoric," he said. "So you and Robert…?"

"I really don't know."

"But you've just told me you believe in married love," Nick persisted.

"Not necessarily married…but in the idea of someone special, unique, irreplaceable."

"Ah the idea of the unique someone who picks us out of the crowd and so confers uniqueness upon ourselves, confirming what we knew all along that we are the centre of the universe and will live forever! Someone who will quash the rumour of our own generality, our expendibility. Someone who will deny the truth that, in the eyes of nature we are but a disposable soma, mere husk of the immortal genome, and in the eyes of society a substitutable atom of a thousand crowds…I know all about the myth of love…" He stood up, activated by the energy of his own rhetoric. He opened the drawer where his letters to Susie were stored. He unfastened the old catheter (French Gauge 8; whistle-tip with staggered eyes) that tied the bundle together. "Read this lot while I go for a pee."

He returned five minutes later.

"Well?"

"You have bloody awful handwriting. Even so, I can decipher enough to to see that you're in no position to mock romantic love. We learn from your correspondence that this girl has 'unpeeled death'!"

"She was beautiful."

"So you said but that doesn't explain everything. But what about her mind? And her personality? And her beliefs?"

"Mind and personality are only constructs. In her case they don't happen to have been constructed…But so what? As for her beliefs—how could they matter when her tits and her face and her legs are a thousand times more interesting than the most brilliantly argued ideas and a million times more subversive of the established order and quotidian reality than the most inflammatory of radical opinions."

"She's a fantasy object who appeals to the latent wanker in you. What does she look like anyway?"

"Open the drawer next to you."

Janet took out Susie's photograph and studied carefully.

"Beautiful, I suppose, in a stereotyped way. But with that stupid smile on her face she looks positively gormless—or hypogormic, anyway."

She replaced the photograph. Nick defended his infatuation.

"'We desire that which we see other men desire.' The object of desire will necessarily conform to the stereotype of desirability. How otherwise would we recognise ourselves in the pursuit of the desirable?"

"What about the uniqueness factor? She hardly looks *non-substitutable* to me. If you want someone on account of her blonde hair and blue eyes, you will by definition want everyone else who is similarly endowed. So this Susie is just one of a series of Susie-look-alikes, one of thousands of females who, during the span of your sexual life, will instantaneously turn you on. In short, she is totally replacable. And she would become so as soon as she stopped refusing you."

"It's you, not me, who believes in the myth of the unique object of love. I believe *everyone* is totally replaceable."

"You're confusing desire with appetite," she said.

"But so does my body. Unlike the average Agony Aunt, it doesn't make these distinctions. The body doesn't lust after the other's unique self. The latter is not actually on display and cannot be touched. Besides, it would be no more respectable in your eyes if it did; for the self is, as I had occasion to say at an earlier meeting, only an effect of language and therefore as general as the body. More general, in fact; since the body at least has the accidents of presence and opaque particularity while whatever is intelligible is purely general. Even so, having said all this, I think you're wasted on Robert."

"Don't be patronising."

"I'm only trying to say that he would not appreciate a true philosopher like you. Where you are, Janet, there is no dissociation of sensibility: your thoughts are French kisses of the mind. As my logic destroys your argument, my soul is beginning to yield to it. Tell me, what makes a person irreplaceable, worth dying for?"

"No one is *instantaneously* irreplaceable," Janet said. "People become truly irreplaceable to one another only when the unique outline of one life intermeshes with the unique outline of another.

Lust at first sight, yes. But love takes a little longer—it grows out of the relationship lust may or may not inspire. Desire is appetite's intuition of the possibility of love."

"So true love is *a posteriori*, arising out of experience, not *a priori*, triggered by the conformity of a leg or tit to some archetypal pre-conceived or socially marketed ideal...?"

"Possibly. Of course the idea that love is *a posteriori* is good news for girls like me with fat bottoms...So I may be biased."

"What a fantastic job Brown Owl did on you. She saw that, with your soul being packaged for your journey through space-time in such a delicious body, you were especially at risk. How you and she must have argued round the camp-fire about the integration of the erotic with the civic and the ways of reconciling the urge for the total satisfaction of the moment with being a useful citizen contributing to the slow processes by which the collective solves its problems of scarcity and stability! Well, I don't give two hoots for Brown Owl because she has overlooked at least two important facts."

"And these are?"

"First, since we are all doomed to die, the idea of non-tragic love is self-contradictory. And, secondly, there is a flaw in consciousness so that it does not seem to have a fully developed present tense."

He was conscious as he spoke that neither of them was smiling inwardly any more. It was almost as if they were determined, jointly, to get to the bottom of things. He realised that she, too, had once been where he was now, though doubtless her anguish had been less flamboyant than his, less dissipated in words. This was a discovery as profound, exciting and disturbing as the revelation of his early twenties that some women enjoyed sex almost as much as some men. For all that her white teeth were slightly stained with red wine, she looked perfectly beautiful as she settled her glass down on his desk, next to the letters she had been reading, and looked up at him.

"In that case, I can't see that unhappy love is much worse than everything else in life," she pointed out.

"Better, I would say. Unhappy love which makes explicit what I am anyway—i.e. (a) doomed and (b) never quite here—at least *localises* despair. Now if this were true, then the consolations you hint at would be an even greater threat to my equilibrium than my Great Grief...Janet, I am at my pit's end."

"Perhaps you have at last touched the bottom of the abyss."

"As Brown Owl said when the guy-rope broke."

"Don't be boring." This was not to deflate him—they had left their adversarial positions some time back—but to prevent him from throwing away what had they had so far achieved.

"It could be that I'm afraid of being argued out of my despair. I might start hoping again...I might find happiness...and truth. Lose the sour and sterile bliss of rhetoric, where even a fart is a kind of citation."

"Stop it!"

"It's this perfume that you and Sadie have splashed around the room. How shall I sleep in this bed tonight, now that it has been turned into a sty of connotation? I feel almost sick with fear."

For the first time he heard pathos, unironic sincerity, in his voice.

Janet, too, must have heard it because she got out of her chair and walked across to him. She looked down at him for a second and then sat down on the bed.

"After the history-taking, there follows the physical examination," she said; and took his hand by the wrist and recorded his pulse. "For someone supposedly in an emotional turmoil, your heart's not beating very fast."

"Unhappy love and metaphysical despair are inotropic rather than chronotropic: the heart beats not faster but more thickly."

Still holding his hand, she looked into his eyes.

"How you talk!"

"I flee, my beautiful, long-limbed Discobolus, into words as into sleep, weaving sentences into a rug of stupor to insulate my consciousness against naked self-consciousness..."

"You're not really a philosopher. Just a very angry man trying to destroy himself as an indirect act of revenge upon her."

"You've been reading too many textbooks of Orthopaedic Nursing. But you have convinced me of what I already knew about Susie...Her beauty is only an enchanting but empty sign. There is no difference, even at the level of sensation, never mind at the level of knowledge or understanding, between her body and that of a thousand other women. When the knicks are down and Nick is up, ejaculating into one body is pretty much the same as ejaculating into another, if it's bodies rather than people we are talking of. The special secret that the pretty girl's body seems to hint at is merely the secret of when and how and with whom she will share that secret. It's the tautology of the flesh again—the sign that signifies only itself. And Eros itself is one great lie, promising to round off the sense of the world. Only death—the big sleep, not the little one—can do that and extinguish the howling gaps between what we are and what we want and what we know and what we should like to understand. I suspect that sexuality merely displaces desire from its true, its undefined, its undefinable object…Traps an infinite wish in a finite object…" There was a scream and then the sound of more glass being broken and a male voice shouting, "Sock him, Socks! Kick his nuts!" The stale freneticism of the music continued unmodified. "Always where the pursuit of happiness is most intense, there unhappiness will find its acutest manifestations," Nick observed rather vacantly.

He was the site of several astonishments all dawning at once. The shouts from without had given him the opportunity to measure the distance they had travelled—first in parallel with and then towards one another—over the last few minutes. And he was astonished, also, at this woman, whose beauty seemed to have proved no impediment to the acquisition and expression of an intelligence that outran his own. Finally, he was amazed at how theoretical his anguish over Susie had become and how small a shadow she now cast over his spirits. It was almost as if she had, all along, been the emotional equivalent of a thought experiment that had simply got out of control.

"Oughtn't you, as host, be looking into what's going on?" Janet asked, not letting go of his hand.

"Let the whole fucking place burn…" he said, adding—to disguise his delight in the abatement of the customary anguish—a small extension to a long-running motif: "Since the erotic fever and fervour of this party has been primed by the crematorium, since my wit is fired by pain and fanned by the freezing wind of her absence, since

Phoebus tans with amorous pinches and The Prince of Darkness is the sun, since discourse grows into and out of silence and absence, let this night's hot pursuit of life and pleasure end in ruination and destruction..."

"I half-believe you are half-serious."

"I half-believe I am."

She leant closer to him, smelling of Absence and her cheeks at their most beautiful in the shadows of a room lit only by an acentric desk lamp. For the first time since Susie had ushered in The Ice Age, he was possessed by intense sexual desire, a delicious terror in which brilliant hope and fierce longing were in perfect equilibrium. She smiled at him in a way that melted many things (none of them resistance) and had the opposite effect on one other.

"Your pupils are quite dilated," she observed, looking into his blue eyes with her brown ones.

"Beauty is mydriatic. So is awe..." And he purse-strung his mouth in a parody of surprise. "I am leaving the cardboard landscape of rhetoric. I am now fully three-dimensional."

"I *had* noticed..." She scrutinised him. "You're quite good-looking, aren't you?" And she suddenly kissed him with such a total concentration of carnality that he was overwhelmed as well as astonished. Her soft lips were followed by her even softer tongue. He drew back for a moment, breathing, and beating, fast; but he said nothing, as if his language had been skewered on the silence of her tongue. The scent of Absence was sweet again, as it had been in the spring: it signified presence. She kissed him once more and his tongue probed her mouth, and felt its discourses fellated by her silence. Like two forearms in an Indian wrestling match, their bodies tilted one way and then the other. At length they sank on to the pillows marked NORTH BROMPTON DISTRICT HEALTH AUTHORITY. They kissed with renewed vigour.

"Anthony kissed away kingdoms but together we have kissed away something greater: the vast nothingness that Susie uncovered...She is dying, Brompton, dying...Listen, I can hear her burial chant."

McAdam was pitching one of his interment galliards against

the quieter but still insistent thud of the music trudging on below. They kissed yet again. He unbuttoned her blouse and uncovered her breast buds.

"You're not wearing a bra."

"Scarcely, as you can see, a pressing need. Are you disappointed?"

"Not at all. For asp-like in a generous pair / May lurk the stuff of nightiemare."

A sudden image of Margery's excessively generous, excessively available, but meaningless, udders, made this sincere. He kissed her thorax thoroughly and admired the smoothness of her skin. He was careful to leave no mark.

"No tactless asp I," he said, "to place macules of juvenile purpura where they would become speaking mouths and tell tales."

He extended the scope of his explorations.

"No," she said, seizing his hand as it moved downwards over her abdominal wall.

"Reserved for Robert?"

"That was vulgar…Maybe."

"Christ, that word again."

He smiled at her. Her tenderly smiling face was fathomless, signifying all that was absent from his life, all that his various aches ached for. And yet, at the same time, it was more than that: its meaning was here, not elsewhere.

Unexpectedly, she fastened on his neck and kissed him with such force that he cried out with pain.

"The biter bit," he said.

But her undivided sexual attention melted further speech. It was as if, for these moments, she knew no world outside of their immediate co-presence. With her warm, long-fingered hands, she dexterously uncovered the warm tumour inside his sensible trousers and, springing it from the little-ease of his underwear, observed it carefully before switching off the bedroom light. Nick was glad of this; for the heavier aspects of lovemaking do not slot easily into the popular conception of love. The instrument involved is too explicit, its terms of reference too simple, its degrees of freedom too few, to be the plausible agent of the culminating events of something as complex as the relationship between two human beings—or not in broad lamplight, anyway.

Her lips touched him where he most hoped they would.

"Real Presence piercing the absences of language with its indisputable hereness, its haecceitas…" But his sentence dissolved in the deliciousness of her tongue slowly tracking back and forth. He felt her mouth softly ensleeve him. "A girl who sucks seed like this is sure to succeed…" He began; but again his voice discontinued into his pleasure as he was engulfed in a wordless awareness whose outer layers were a glimpse of her smooth blouseless back widening towards her hips, the outline of her head inclined over him and a breast bud…Without withdrawing from within her mouth, he moved so that he could reciprocate the pleasure she was giving him. This time there was no veto and she assisted his unsheathing her hips and thighs. His tongue entered what had once been Aporia, the unpassable path, and encountered the sharp taste of an indisputably extra-linguistic reality beyond the Page. The flesh routed the word.

He closed his eyes and entered the inner core of sensation, an absolute closeness of touch. He passed through to the inmost place where it was only himself; and he was plenitude; and peace and sleep and silence could be found.

"After the words, the flesh," he murmured sleepily after he had come. "And after the flesh the sleep."

"Ssh," she said wiping her mouth with a mixture of tenderness and fastidiousness that made him hug her more tightly.

"See how the nurse sucks him to sleep…"

"Ssh," she repeated, laying her head on his chest.

"This is now. I am here. I am happy. Thank you."

At the heart of his gratitude was the certainty he now felt that his mind had found the bottom of itself and so could now rise. All the tiredness of the months of pain and talk and insomnia gathered itself together, recognised its true nature, and deftly put him asleep.

"When you wake up," she said softly, "I shall be gone."

Closure

And when I woke up, you were.

It was still dark as, partially clothed and mainly on top of the blankets, I came to. I did not have a headache and there was no racket from downstairs. I sat up quickly, enjoying a well-being I could hardly credit. I then moved gingerly into the standing position. This made me neither sick nor giddy; and so I was encouraged to take a few steps, to relieve my bursting bladder in the wash-basin and draw back the curtains. In the pre-dawn darkness, I could just make out a few sodium-lit clouds and for once they were not wetting the town below them. I did not look through my reflection to Susie's absence but focused on my own image looking back at me. I saw a blue-eyed, rather handsome face. To judge by its pleased expression, it quite liked what I saw.

"I am here," I told my reflection, "and it is good."

I had work to do. My plan, formed almost as soon as I had woken, was to work outwards from the centre. The latter was now occupied by my reinstated or re-centred self: 0,0,0,0 was the present location of my present body. I washed, brushed my teeth, dressed, made my bed, tidied my room and packed my bags. On the desk was your note:

You won't ever forget me will you, Dr Page?
Your Discobolus

I wrote briefly to Welldorm, promising him a cheque for the North Brompton Defibrillator Fund. I thanked him for an instructive stay at the NBRI. I wrote to San, wishing him non-specific well. A third, more pedagogic, note assured Dr Dhar that if he played his cards right the Royal College would be delighted to welcome him as a member.

You had put your note on top of Susie's photograph; the latter I tore up into small pieces that I let fall into the waste paper basket. I kept my letters to her, tied up into a bundle with the ancient catheter, as being of autobiographical interest, biopsy specimens of my soul.

In search of Sadie, I went into the room where we had carried her the night before. There was revealed to my startled gaze the bodies of one junior Orthopaedic surgeon and one Staff Nurse from 27B ward enjoying a rapt and panting antisyzygy. The former adversaries were reaching that supreme moment of co-operation—he, the invader, being welcomed by she, the invaded—between man and woman. San's heroic disposal of Driver Anon had clearly been rewarded. I had never seen San's buttocks before and this was my first glimpse of the upper reaches of Staff Nurse Lenier's widely abducted thighs. In my present state of contented satiety, I found each as meaningful as the other. I withdrew, having first made sure that the hyperventilating lovers had not simply tossed Sadie on to the floor in their haste towards coition.

Creaking open the door of the adjacent room, I made out two slumbering forms, one of whom woke up.

"Kalemera, Socks."

"Kalemera, Nicholas," Poulantzas groaned, hoarsely. He sat up and focused on the generous dollop of not-Mrs-Poulantzas sleeping next to him. He looked distinctly overdrawn on the sperm bank. "Or I was bloody pissed last night. Or I was mad."

A quick glance confirmed that Sadie was not there, either. I said goodbye to Socks—quietly so as not to wake up his open-mouthed and snoring companion whom I identified from her hair to be Margery.

"Unite and conquer," I said, by way of farewell.

Socks, staring at the mass of stuporose womanhood next to him, dissented.

"Divide and rule," he replied mournfully.

In the next room, I found Dr Chung, asleep in his own bed and alone. My cautious entry woke him. He passed at once from coma to respectfulness without any intervening stages of confusion or querulousness. Even his shiny auto-Brylcreemed hair had woken kempt.

"Good morning, Dr Page." He donned his thick glasses to de-ish the world, sprang out of bed and assumed a neat, though dragon-infested, dressing gown.

He was unable to throw any light on Sadie's whereabouts. He did, however, impart information of almost equal importance. The Sponsored Skateboarding had been a great success. Oscar's team had won easily. They had shown breathtaking skill in the wheelchair and zimmer slalom and had notched up no less than 250 laps in the allotted half hour. Dr Sananayake's team, plagued by acute drunkenness and chronic unfitness, had managed only 58. The contest had ended in good humour and inter-racial good will was now back at the pre-1960 levels. No structural damage had been inflicted upon the NBRI though one wheelchair was unlikely to see useful service again. Complaints had been received from night nurses on 1A, 2B, 5B, 6A, 8A etc. wards and from a couple of out-patients who were still awaiting ambulances to take them home from clinic appointments. These had been diplomatically handled by Dr Dhar, who had been summoned from the dance floor for this purpose. A blanket provision of night sedation for both patients and staff largely resolved the problem before it looked like surfacing in official complaints.

The contest had had an unexpected coda when Dr Rai, following Dhar from the dance floor and desperate to shine before Maureen, had undertaken a solo journey down the piste. After a slow and wobbly start he had gathered speed to a fast and wobbly finish, burst through the fire doors at the end of the concourse, sped across the yard and landed with a sickening impact on a heap of coke in an out-house. His most serious injury was a fractured clavicle inflicted by the handlebars of Oscar's stationary bicycle. Maureen was the only unattached person sober enough to drive him to the District General Hospital down the road. A perfect end to her perfect evening.

"If everyone pays what they have pledged, we should make nearly one hundred pounds," Chung said.

"That we means we can be confident of at least a fiver, anyway."

We located Sadie underneath an upturned sofa. I surmised what had happened. Successive copulating couples—to whom she clearly presented a serious problem of disposal—had passed her on from one room to the next until the supply of rooms had run out. She had then been laid out on the downstairs sofa. A tide of jubilation or a fight had upturned the sofa and she, oblivious of all outside of the contents of her coma, had remained thereunder.

"Moanin', Dr Page," she said as Chung and I rolled back the sofa and revealed her to the daylight.

"Morning, Sadie. Are you well?"

The reply did not relate directly to the question.

"Do thay know anything abite them tilet rolls, Dr Page?"

"I'm afraid I don't, Sadie."

"Are 'ope it weren't thay what put them nasty dirty things down the tilet last nate?"

She was still in those borderlands of consciousness where the deepest anxieties and prehistoric terrors reign unopposed by current realities.

"Still pissed," Chung demotically hissed. "And there is extensive bruising."

She had a huge mark on her bony forearm and an impressive periorbital shiner. It would seem, I thought angrily, that at some stage during the night the problem of disposal had been dealt with rather peremptorily. Bruises apart, however, she did not look much worse for wear. I suggested that she might be approached as a DRCHD Grey Case.

"She needs careful observation," Chung said.

I concurred.

"And what else?"

"TLC?"

"You mean Tender Loving Care. You mustn't use abbreviations Dr Chung. You'll antagonise the examiner. Now, what about the social factors? Do we know anything about her home circumstances?"

We did not. Neither of us had any idea where or under what conditions she lived or with whom, if anyone, she co-habited. For all we knew, her existence was intermittent, beginning each day with the serving of vulcanised rubber eggs and complaints about toilet rolls and ending each evening with burnt fish fingers and more complaints about toilet rolls.

The obvious solution was to tuck her into my vacated bed and for the junior medical staff to keep her under observation for a twenty-four-hour period. As my last act of authority before leaving the NBRI I drew up a duty rota. We carried her upstairs and slotted her slumbrous, still fragrant body between the sheets. I left an envelope by the bedside table containing my thanks and a sum of money which modesty forbids me to specify. We then began the clean up.

During the search for Sadie, I had had an opportunity to assess the damage to James House. Though widespread, it was superficial and mostly reversible. Dr Chung kindly agreed to perform the elementary gastro-enterological procedures in the lavatory. Sadie's food, for the most part thrown around instead of eaten, was spread in a thin layer over the kitchen, hall and staircase. Dirty and/or broken glasses were to be found in various likely and unlikely locations. A thick paste of footmarks, food, spilt drinks, cigarette ash, menses and semen coated the kitchen floor. Furniture was soiled, stained or simply upturned. A spew-and-fag-and-ullage fragrance hung on the air. Powered by a dynamo of well-being that almost audibly hummed within me, I fell upon chaos with all the forces of order I could muster.

The lounge presented the severest challenge. Here all the

destructive tendencies of a party had been most completely expressed. Dancing, lovemaking, arguing, eating, vomiting, drinking and smoking had here left their characteristic stains. Through a broken window I saw that it was now a clear, bright, cold morning: the first morning of winter, bare-leaved, glinting with frost, blue-skied, with pigeons wheeling round in casually brilliant platoons.

I sang as I worked.

It was several minutes before I noticed an erect copy of *The Tablet*.

"Dr McAdam! The very topmost cream of this new-minted morning to you."

The Tablet shook like a summer aspen. I worked on, developing a progressively narrower definition of McAdam's territory. I refrained from flicking a duster over the man, his chair or his newspaper.

"Well," I said, addressing him from behind, "this seems as good a time as any to say goodbye. I think it's been a learning experience for both of us, don't you? I know we haven't seen eye to eye over some things but that doesn't detract from the value of our discussions, far into the night, about recent advances in medical treatment, new approaches to postgraduate education, the future of the National Health Service and the different strategies for health care delivery. I am only sorry that we have had to break things off at such an exciting stage…"

The Tablet was hauled down and McAdam turned round, his rubrous, simian face charged with a rage that lay far beyond the scope of its owner's under-exercised powers of public articulation. He almost growled and for a moment I feared that he would leap up and bite my throat. Like Sadie, he did not look too bio-degraded by the night's experiences—though the initial state did not allow much room for deterioration: he could have undergone burial and exhumation with little adverse cosmetic effect. I stepped back a little to allow him to stomp out.

"Bye bye, Monophemus."

Dr Chung came in with three letters for me that he had found scattered amongst the litter in the hall. All had London postmarks.

The least interesting looking one proved to be from Professor Fibrin. I read it while Chung made coffee.

> Dear Nicholas,
>
> Thank you for ringing the other day. My secretary passed on the message.
>
> Yes, I am sure you should go ahead and apply for the Senior Registrar post in Haematology at St Jidgey's and I shall be glad to act as your referee. I should be able to persuade the other members of the committee to support your application. Certainly you are—the recent lapse apart—a very strong candidate; so if you don't say something frivolous or irrelevant at the interview, things should go in your favour.
>
> Looking forward to seeing you at the interview. Don't let me down: I've given you a splendid reference.
>
> With best wishes
>
> Professor John Fibrin MD FRCP FRCPath
> Professor of Clinical Haematology
> St Jidgey's Teaching Hospital

I decided to save the other two letters for the journey. Putting some of my new-found optimism to good purpose, I wrote a Get Well Card to Rai which Chung undertook to deliver. In it I enclosed a short poem which I venture to reproduce here:

Paradise
In Paradise, the girls are free—
they're there, sweet Rai, for you and me.
We won't need money, looks or charms
to be made welcome in their arms;
We'll say 'Hello!' and they'll say 'Yes!'
and wrap us in their willingness.

Now my advice is: Don't go mad
and wolf down all you've never had;

responding to the first who's pleasant's
the way to early detumescence.
Don't shoot your bolt right by The Gate—
it might be best, you'll find, to wait.

For when we've had our instant thrill,
there's still Eternity to kill.

I hadn't written to Socks and, not wishing to fuel that ill-starred neurosurgeon's paranoia, I penned him the following brief moralising squib that I thought might harmonise with his sour morning-after regrets:

Microbes and Morality
The poet says "*La chair est triste*"—
as Socks will vow who scores when pissed
with girls at parties hot for sex
and wakes up next to clinging wrecks,
his headaches cradled in the arms
of persons now devoid of charms.

The moral code that aims to right us
protects us from the urethritis.
Be like subscribers to the *Lancet*
who're really not prepared to chance it;
aware what gathers in the crannies
of polyvalent pricks and fannies,

That places where its heaven inside
quite likely harbour hell beside
(the clap that comes in sixteen grades
from Candida to full-blown AIDS),
they advocate the family life
and sex confined to man and wife.

And if you think I tell a lie

just check the facts with Dr Rai
who knows that those who work in clinics
view love and sex with eyes of cynics;
for all the ways of being close
are means to propagate a dose.

The choice (to simplify the picture)
is moral or urethral stricture.

After that, I drained my coffee cup, wished Dr Chung a very
good day and a long life, picked up my bags and walked out of a
James House restored to the tidy and somnolent condition in which
I had found it. I paid Oscar for his contribution to the festivities
and bad him farewell.

"Well done, doctor."

Our handshake was the warmer for Oscar's refraining for once
from remarks that would make me wince.

I walked to the station whistling my own setting of *"Per saltire vert"*
and *"Or foun fer de Moline..."* My route took in some of our old
favourites, including the Library and The Housing Action Area
and Our Lady of the (Unfounded) Assumption. In The Modern
Shopping Precinct I resisted the temptation to buy souvenirs such as
a North Brompton District Health Authority loving spoon, a table
mat depicting one of the citizens in traditional dress (shirt and tie,
trousers, socks and shoes) or miniature porcelain mugs depicting the
Employment Centre. I did buy a key purported to have been made
by local craftsmen.

In the station buffet, I studied the light on a scrap of cello-
phane torn from a cigarette packet and observed the tiny, precise
shadows cast by sugar grains on the formica table top. I watched the
steam unpacking from my coffee and compared it with the smoke
unfolding from the cigarette held in the tremulous hands of the old
man opposite me. Illuminated from the side by the radiant winter
morning, the complex currents and counter-currents of smoke and
steam—the skewed varicose, the cross-roll, the zig zag—formed the

escapment of a soft clock measuring the forward movement of now-unfrozen time.

The man went away and I inspected the empty packet of Players he left behind him. On it, England's Hero, flanked by sail and steam, surveyed the sea, a life-belt framing the trusty bearded mush he had loaned, perhaps unwittingly, to pushing fags from hoarding boards…I thought of England's Smoker, Mr Ansell, whose ultimately peaceful end you officiated over; Mr Ansell, flanked by sputum pots, fastened to his bed by chest disease, his lips navy blue. The life belt would have been of little use to him, as he drowned on land, in seas of open space, his lungs losing their grip on the foul North Brompton air.

I took a deep and delighted breath. Time, life had their uses. The train drew in, casting a sharp shadow incised out of the sunlight on the platform. The brilliance slanting through the gap between the train and the station roof caught passengers as they alighted and boarded. Faces were suddenly sun-struck and as suddenly returned to the shade. The short fair hair of a punk-haired girl was transformed to radiant fuzz outlining her skull vault.

I boarded the train.

"This is North Brompton…this is North Brompton…" the station informed the train already quickening out of it.

"That *was* North Brompton," I replied to the station, now withdrawing from around the train.

Out of habit I sat opposite to an attractive female—the girl with spiky blonde hair. She had pierced ears and nose and piercing blue eyes. I did not, however, attempt to engage her in conversation. When she asked me the time, my reply was severely factual. She was wearing a Sony Walkman which to the unpierced ears unprivy to the headphones emitted a sound like that of cutlery being shaken rhythmically in a drawer. My trip to the Buffet quenched a thirst of normal magnitude. It was, in short, a journey void of theatre; for I had no need to escape from a felt nothingness into an audience of strangers.

I opened the remainder of my mail. The first letter was from Felicity, informing me that she was coming to the NBRI because she 'had to have it out' with me 'once and for all'. It was too late to stop her coming north: she would be already on her way. We might bump into one another at New Street Station. That the second letter was not from Susie did not greatly disappoint me—dazzling proof of the completeness of my recovery. It was from Miranda, one of the co-signatories of the letter that had accompanied the Black Forest Gâteau I had received on my first working day at the NBRI. She had heard, she wrote, on the grapevine, that is from Prof's secretary, that I was hoping to return to St Jidgey's soon. Was it really *true*? If so, *super*.

"It's either a feast or a famine," I thought. I looked across the crisp fields to a greenhouse whose glass windows were polythened by frost. Just now the famine seemed to be over. It was *my* absence now, that filled or emptied other people's lives, rather than theirs that emptied mine.

"What time do you think this train is getting in?" the punkess asked me, removing her earphones in preparation for my answer.

"I'm not sure," I said, failing to be drawn. My days of casual and promiscuous use of tongues were behind me.

A mist of sleep crept over my consciousness. The ghost of your tongue began to move around my mouth. I decided to write to you. I wrote rapidly, pausing only while the train passed over points.

Dearest Discobolus,

1. For a wedding present, if you become Mrs Perkins, I shall send you a cloud specially flown in from North Brompton. Nevertheless, I would remind you that the contents of a urine bottle are only a cloudlet brought down to earth.

2. Supposing you decide not to become Mrs Perkins, I shall still send you a souvenir from North Brompton: a key that unlocks nothing.

3. In either instance, I should like to thank you for saving my life, you subtle-tongued magician.

4. Let me know which present I have to send you.

Yours till the sun's snuffed out.

(Dr) Nicholas Page MB ChB DRCHD (UK)

I still had a sense of unfinished business. Susie had to be signed off. I began my farewell in New Street, where I did not see Felicity, though I did make a phone call, arranging to be met on arrival at the capital. I finished the last line of my letter to Susie as the train drew in at Euston.

My Dear Aporia,

The Unpassable Path By-Passed
O empty-headed blue-eyed girl
with gorgeous golden hair,
I knew, but could not feel till now,
what emptiness you were.
You set my stupid heart on fire,
my ventricles were charred
and when my hopes were oxidised,
I took it very hard.

Last night I found my peace again
in Sister Parker's arms
and sleep returned and freed me from
your over-rated charms.
The ECG they took today
shows healing on the trace
and I can't wipe, moronic nymph,
the smile from off my face.

This supersedes all previous communication.

There, on the other side of the ticket barrier, and eclipsing the great hall of Euston Station, was Miranda. looking lovelier than I had remembered her seeming before.

"You look pleased to see me. Or are you just pleased with yourself?" she asked as we walked out of the station into the perfect winter day. She carried one of my bags so that we could walk hand in hand.

"A bit of both. Or, rather, a lot of the first and a bit of the second." We paused next to a pillar box in the sunlight while I decided not to post either letter. "I have just got over a great illness. I have been in hell. But here I am back again, and it seems like heaven."

"I am sorry to hear that. What was hell like?"

"Rather wordy."

"You haven't got much of a tan."

"I'm just a little charred, that's all."

She squeezed my hand. "It was a woman, wasn't it?"

"Perhaps. Or perhaps she was just the occasion. Sometimes," I said, having to shout against the traffic, "the self suddenly presents as a cliff-face over which you want to throw yourself, just to see what it is like...Still, that's all over now...Where shall we eat?"

"What about that little place at the back of St Jidgey's that we all used to go to before you started neglecting us."

"Before poisoned hours had bound me up from mine own knowledge."

"Professor Fibrin was quite worried about you. He's glad you're going for the Senior Reg. job...Even Susie seems *most* interested that you may be back again. She's been looking rather mournful recently. She had a dreadful bust-up with the moron who used to bring her to work in a Porsche...And also with the other one, Keith someone or other. I shouldn't be telling you this, really."

"When fate smiles at last, it is always too late: her teeth have gone black. At thirty I can buy all the Dinky toys I could not afford when I was seven; and of course I no longer want them."

"So it *was* Susie. And it's all over...?"

"A love affair, as the poet says, leaves either a shrine or a scar. In my case, a scar is forming. Can't you hear the fibroblasts gathering? Yes, it most decidedly is all over. Henceforth, I'm going to be one of those perverts who like women for their minds..."

"I would be surprised if you had been idle up North. In fact my spies tell me..."

"Say no more:

Read not my blemishes in the world's report
I have not kept my square, but that to come

227

Shall all be done by the rule…"

"That is not what I would call a straight answer, Dr Page," she said, squeezing my hand and fixing me with her crystal gaze.

"I don't suppose it is. I'm going to have to lern arfer toke rate. My wit shall aestivate until beauty, bearing its promise of completed sense, again rejects me and again unsheathes my wit with suffering."

"Tell me more."

"That's all there is to it. Now *I* want to hear *you* talk. I shall unnerve you by listening."

And I did, in smiling silence.

This morning I received two letters, both postmarked North Brompton. The first read as follows

Dear Dr Page,

It is my very great pleasure to inform you that I have now satisfied the examiners for qualification of the Diploma of the Royal College of Hospital Doctors. To speak plainly, I am DRCHD!

I cannot tell you how much I feel indebted to you for this quite undeserved success…

Plainly we are now going to return as soon as possible. We have already booked our passage. Bulbul is counting the days before she will see her grandma. Mrs Dhar is thanking God on an almost daily basis…I tell her it is not God we should thank…

Yours most sincerely
Vijay Dhar DRCHD (UK)

And the second letter was, of course, yours, bearing even better news. Well, here is my reply.

Dearest Janet,

1. I attended the interview; I bullshat; I was appointed; and now I am Senior Registrar in Haematology at St Jidgey's. I

can now resume my work on senile purpura. And, who knows, on the juvenile variety as well.

2. I am of course delighted that you will not require the cloud flown in from North Brompton. I really wouldn't worry too much over Robert: I am sure he will soon be able to find someone else to complete his CV.

3. Don't just write to me my discus thrower, my discourse thrower. Rather, come to me, bearing your triple gift of presence, meaning and truth.

4. With all my love...

(Dr) Nicholas Page MB ChB DRCHD (UK)

So ends my tale. Or is this where another tale begins, dovetailing with yours, proving that in your end is my beginning, in your aperture my closure?

About the Author

Raymond Tallis

Professor Raymond Tallis has been Professor of Geriatric Medicine at the University of Manchester since 1987 and is a Consultant in Health Care of Older People at Salford Royal Hospitals Trust.

He is a leading figure in British gerontology and has been awarded many prizes and visiting professorships. His major research interests are in stroke, epilepsy and neurological rehabilitation and he was elected Fellow of the Academy of Medical Sciences in acknowledgement of this work.

He has published fiction, poetry and many books in the fields of the philosophy of mind, philosophical anthropology, literary theory, and cultural criticism. He was awarded Doctor of Letters (Hon Causa) from the University of Hull in 1997 and LittD at the University of Manchester 2002.

In 2004 *Prospect Magazine* identified him as one of Britain's top 100 public intellectuals.

Absence is his first published novel.

The fonts used in this book are from the Garamond family

The Toby Press publishes fine writing,
available at leading bookstores everywhere. For more
information, please visit www.tobypress.com